Negotiations with God

by R. W. Sowrider

6.8 Books

While in part based on actual historical events and figures, this book is, for legal purposes, a work of fiction. Any resemblance to actual persons, living or dead, is purely coincidental. With respect to the Gods, however, it's a totally different story. All divine characters herein are based on actual supernatural beings. Fortunately for the author, though, they don't have the balls to appear in court and sue him for libel. Pussies.

First Edition: December 7, 2018

ISBN: 9781731108791

PRAISE FOR NEGOTIATIONS WITH GOD

"The force and energy of this book could power a tricycle." – Brick Ricker, *Literary Muscle Magazine*

"A transcendental work of lyrical beauty and emotional heft, this stunning achievement dares to satisfy us in a way that stories of an earlier age used to. Which is to say, missionary style." – Ralph Johnstone, *AARP*

"Sowrider reveals the terrible beauty of human nature and divine influence with the skill and precision of a six-year-old on Ritalin." – Walter Willingsby, *The Philadelphia Pedophiler*

"Although this novel is not about vampires, all the while I was reading I couldn't stop thinking about vampires." – Harold, *Goodreads* member

"A triumph ... but not like one of them winning-the-*Escape-From-Alcatraz*-Triathlon triumphs ... more like a walking-up-a-flight-of-stairs-without-getting-winded triumph. – Wendy Seargrass, *The New York Times*

"A bounteous miracle that transforms the way you experience life; everything becomes freshly energized and of vivid importance; infused with humanity, vitality, and pathos. I'm assuming of course that you begin each chapter with a chilled glass of Red Bull and mescaline." – Scott Dillinger, *Reader's Digest*

"This book will without a doubt be taught in universities someday. Not so much the four-year kind, but more likely the two-year kind. In particular, the two-year kind where they teach you how to change car transmissions yet for some reason have an English requirement." – Zen Whitesmith, *Barely Legal Review*

"Could Bill Walton be the worst announcer ever? Guy is a fucking clown." – *Big Steve's Boston Sports Blog*

ACKNOWLEDGMENTS

Tim Ferriss is annoying.

Scott Maltby is the 2000-2050 edition of *Grays Sports Almanac*.

While cheeky and irreverent, Ben Franklin's essay entitled *Fart Proudly* is not his best work.

Randee is that being so stalkingly attractive that you gun down a music legend just to impress her.

Lick My Arse, a symphony by Mozart, is good but not great.

Pat Aguirre is the program you upload to your brain that lets you instantly know Kung Fu.

Religion is man-made.

Anselm Bensch-Schaus is the Spearmint Rhino stripper who did everything in the Champagne Room gratis.

Dick pics do not work nearly as well as I thought they would.

M.F. is that rare one-night stand you don't instantly regret.

Passing out early and pissing yourself sucks.

DEDICATION

This book is for you. Everything I've ever done has been for you.

Well, I guess not everything. I mean, I've done a lot of stuff for money. And a lot of that money has been for Big Macs, Exotic Berry wine coolers, and strippers. But other than that stuff, pretty much everything I've ever done has been for you.

I guess it probably goes without saying, but just in case, I'm not talking about any of the delinquent stuff that I've done. Like when I drunkenly charged the field in the 4th inning of an exhibition game at Yankee Stadium ... or when I switched out the Baby Jesus doll in our church's nativity scene with a Funshine Care Bear doll ... or when I tried to take a dump on the hood of a taxi cab in Tokyo. That stuff definitely was not for you. Just the good stuff.

Just the good stuff has always been for you.

"Success is not final. Failure is not fatal. It is the courage to continue that counts."

- Winston Churchill

I'm not gonna lie to you people, I got that quote by watching the movie, The Darkest Hour. They displayed it right before the end roll credits. The movie itself was meh, but the quote is damn good. I just hope that it somehow ties into this story or I'm gonna look pret-ty stupid.

VERIXION

"Is the abomination finally awake?" a gruff voice sounded as Rowen regained consciousness and began to take in his surroundings.

He was lying on a silk carpet but was unable to see it as a cloud of cool mist hovered over the entire floor, flowing gently through the room.

The walls, while he couldn't quite make them out, seemed to be made of gold and decorated with silver sculptures, busts, and reliefs. And the ceiling seemed to sparkle with diamond chandeliers.

"Sit up!" the voice boomed as Rowen felt a sudden sharp pain in his left calf, as if a venomous snake had just sunk its fangs into his flesh. But no sooner did he begin writhing in agony than did the pain disappear.

Confused, Rowen slowly adjusted his body so that he knelt in the direction of the voice.

As he lifted his head toward the voice, he couldn't help but wince and shield his eyes from the radiating light.

"Look at me, you vile creature!"

As the voice roared, Rowen heard a loud crack as if someone had slammed a fist down hard upon a table.

Rowen again endeavored to look up and this time was able to see an ornate table at chest height. Behind the table sat the owner of the voice. Rowen struggled to adjust to the blinding light, but he saw what appeared to be the muscular, hairy torso of a man with the head of a great crocodile.

From behind this being's head, the glaring light beamed in a circular pattern.

"Have you nothing to say, you filthy louse?" the being thundered.

Stunned and wincing, Rowen struggled for a reply. "Who are you?"

"I am Delemor, you half-witted piece of rotten

garbage."

"… Where am I?"

"You are in my chamber. In Verixion."

"Verixion?"

"Know you nothing, you ignorant pile of horse dung?"

"…"

"You are in Verixion. You can think of it as a lower level of Heaven where we can look back at your life on Earth and decide whether you will be advancing to Empyrean. And by 'we,' I mean 'I.'"

"Empyrean?"

"Yes. Empyrean, you braindead cow's fart. The highest Heaven. The goal of your existence. What you've unwittingly been fighting for entrance into. So tell me, vile creature, what do you think of your effort?"

"My effort?"

"Yes, your effort, you scurvy dog. What do you make of your life?"

"What life?"

Delemor's jaw dropped in shock. "Your ignorance never ceases to amaze. The life you just lived, you skid mark. Do you not recall? Perhaps this will jog your feeble memory. Arr, matey, is it treasure ye seek?!" Delemor wailed in a deep, sarcastic voice.

Suddenly, images from the life Rowen had just lived fluttered through his mind. *Treasure … an earthquake … Sera!*

"Oh my God, Sera!" Rowen shrieked. "What happened to Sera? Is she okay?"

"She's dead," Delemor replied, flatly. "Like you."

Rowen's entire body slumped as he fell into a stupor.

"Oh, don't be so melodramatic. She's dead. You're dead. Everybody's dead. It's not that big a deal. More important is what comes next. So tell me what you think of your life?"

Rowen remained fixated on Sera. His heart ached, but if she was in the same situation as he was, perhaps it wasn't all that bad.

2

Delemor roared again. "I said tell me what you think of your life!"

Rowen was flustered. "Ummm … I don't know. It was pretty good, I guess. I think I lived a pretty decent life."

"So you think you deserve to ascend to Empyrean?"

"Ummm … Is Sera there?"

"Don't worry about Sera. We're discussing you!"

"Well then … ummm … I guess I think I do. I did my best to be a good and loyal son, mate, and lover."

Delemor burst out laughing. "Oh, that's cute. A good and loyal son, mate, and lover. Absolutely adorable. Access to Empyrean granted."

"Really?" Rowen replied, timidly.

"No. Not really. Access denied! You know why?"

More images of Rowen's life flashed through his mind. "Was it the pirating? All the fighting, stealing, and killing?"

"Wrong again, you braindead maggot. It was that stupid pink shirt you wore all the time. The loose-fitting blouse with the lace-up front and ruffled sleeves."

Rowen couldn't believe his ears. "But those were made with the finest silk from China."

"You're only digging yourself a deeper grave. It's like you were trying to make me hate you. And I *really* wanted to like you because you engaged in some very entertaining endeavors."

"Well, can't we focus on those?" Rowen pleaded.

"No. In fact, there were some other atrocities that you committed. Like the way you convinced your captain to change his trademark flag. It took a lot of the fun out of it."

"You can't be serious. His flag was too ridiculous for words."

"And your sword-fighting style left a lot to be desired. Just block, block, stab. Block, block, stab. Quite boring, really."

"I was fighting for my life in the most effective way possible."

"No, no. You were boring me to tears is what you were doing. Long, drawn-out action-packed fights are where it's at. I want to hear swords clanging as you duel with your enemy on your pirate ship's railing. I want to see you swing recklessly on the boom from one side of the ship to the other. And I want to see the surprise and awe in your enemy's eyes as you stab your dagger into the main sail, zip down it from the crow's nest to the deck, and then stab that dagger deep into his chest. Have you no sense of showmanship?!"

"But nobody fought like that."

"Didn't they?" Delemor replied, giving Rowen a condescending you-know-they-did-so-just-admit-it look.

"No, sir. No one fought like that."

"Well, that's not the point. The point is, your shiny, fluffy pink shirt was an outrageous offense! I mean, really?! A pirate dressed in pink?! Really?!!!"

"I honestly don't know what to say … I'm sorry you didn't like my shirt."

"Well, no worries, you retarded little scamp. I'll give you another chance. We'll discuss soon, but first you need to wash. With that stink you've got all over you, I'm having a hard time not vomiting."

A door opened behind Rowen and a cool breeze blew in over the cloud of mist.

Delemor pointed outside. "The bathing facilities are just on the bank there."

Rowen stood up slowly, still unsure of exactly where he was and what was happening, and staggered outside.

He found the showering facilities a few paces down a stone path on the edge of a body of water. A flowing mist filled the air making it difficult to take in the surroundings, but the water seemed to be vast, like a lake, yet flowing in different directions, or swirling, or maybe both.

Sitting down on one of three stools, Rowen pushed a lever and warm water began gushing out of a detachable showerhead.

On a counter below the mirror were three transparent bottles of shimmering, viscous liquid. One crimson, one chocolate, and one cream-colored.

"Use the cream-colored one!" Delemor shouted from his chamber.

"What is it?" Rowen called back tentatively.

"It's for you to wash with. It's unicorn urine."

"What?!" Rowen shrieked.

"It's shampoo, buddy, okay? It's just shampoo."

As Rowen massaged the shampoo into his scalp and rubbed it all over his body, he felt a tingling that started at the surface of his skin and slowly worked its way to the core of his being.

When he had finally rinsed it all off, he found himself basking in a glow of warmth, levity, and luminance.

"Care for a drink?" A sultry voice inquired, bringing him back to his senses.

Holding a pearl goblet filled with a golden beverage was the most beautiful creature Rowen had ever laid eyes on. He was overcome by her flowing blond hair, emerald eyes, teardrop beauty mark, button nose, naughty smile, caramel skin, and voluptuous breasts.

She was the epitome of Rowen's ideal woman even though he had never known it. It was as if someone had stolen into his subconscious to design her.

"Here you go," she said, handing him the drink. "Enjoy!"

He remained dumbfounded as he watched her saunter out of view, slowly disappearing into the mist.

Not surprisingly, the drink was the most delicious thing that had ever passed his lips. As he savored each sip, in an effort to grasp his surroundings, he did his best to peer through the mist.

In the water, there appeared to be a few resplendent beings who, much like Delemor, seemed to be emitting rays of bright light. Further, there seemed to be iridescent orbs floating here and there as well as islands of various sizes.

On the shore, next to the showering facility, Rowen noticed a perfectly manicured miniature evergreen tree. Branching out from its thin, zigzag trunk were seven branches, each with a dense cluster of pine needles at the end. The clusters formed a staggered pyramid with the largest ones at the bottom and the smallest one on top.

Eyes seemed to peer back at Rowen from atop the lowest cluster. As he took a closer look, he realized that the eyes were patterns on the wings of a moth, which promptly took flight out over the water and headed in the direction of one of the luminous beings.

"Have you rid yourself of that odious stink yet, you filthy dung beetle?" Delemor roared from his chamber.

"Yes, sir," Rowen replied, bolting upright.

"Then bring your filthy pig carcass back in here."

Rowen dutifully returned to the chamber and sat obediently on his heels across from Delemor. The light radiating from the divine creature was almost unbearable.

"So," Delemor began slowly. "What can I do for you so that you live the right life?"

"Ummmmm…"

"What kind of person would you like to be?"

Rowen's brow creased as he considered what kind of life he would like to lead. What kind of person he would have to be to earn entrance into Empyrean.

"Well, I think I would like to be pure of heart," he ventured.

"Oh, very interesting," Delemor replied, almost gleefully.

"And faithful."

"Indeed."

"And … and I would like to be a leader."

"Oh. Perhaps you'd like to deliver your people?"

"Well, I wouldn't go that far. But if I could lead others

to be pure of heart and faithful too, I think that would be wonderful."

"Done, done, and done. It looks like you've caught me on a day where I'm particularly generous to wretched abominations.

"And what of your appearance, boy? What would you like to look like? Based on your first requests, I suppose you'd like to be tall, dark, and handsome?" Delemor leaned over the table such that Rowen and he were cheek to cheek. Or cheek to side snout as it were. "Perhaps with eyes as blue as mine?"

For the first time, Rowen was able to catch a clear glimpse of Delemor. Albeit only an eye. A frightful, reptilian eye with a long black slit surrounded by sparkling sapphire blue. Further, welling in the corner of the eye was what looked like a diamond tear.

Rowen was taken aback by the divine being's proximity and could only manage an answer once Delemor sat back in his throne. "Well, I suppose that physical appearance isn't everything … but if being tall, dark, and handsome isn't too much to ask …"

Delemor clapped his hands together gleefully. "Oh, no. Not at all. I live to give. And for the finishing touch on our statue of David, how about a beauty mark?"

"A beauty mark?"

"Indeed. A distinguished mark for a distinguished human being. Perhaps it will help spread your name among your followers and beyond."

"What kind of beauty mark? … Where?"

"Right above your lovely smile."

"That has a nice ring to it."

"Indeed it does. Sometimes, I am nothing if not charity incarnate. One can only hope," Delemor continued, switching to an eerily sinister tone, "that you'll be able to do the same, hmmm?"

Rowen felt a shiver run down his spine.

7

"Meng Po!" Delemor shouted abruptly. "Let's have that drink!"

Before Rowen could grasp the situation, a sweet old lady with a hunchback was at his side holding what appeared to be a cup of tea. She wore coke-bottle glasses which were framed by salt-and-pepper curls dangling out from underneath her lily-white bonnet. "Here you go, sugar," she said with a pleasant smile.

"What's this?" Rowen asked as he received the drink.

"The negotiations are over!" Delemor barked. "No more questions from you. Drink and be gone!"

Rowen took a quick glance at the bubbly beverage. It was a thick olive green with silver flakes floating in it and had a pungent aroma which made him gag.

As Rowen dutifully downed the bitter concoction, Meng Po leaned in close. "Don't be takin' no candy from strangers!" she said, unnecessarily loud. "Unless you wanna be eatin' needles and razor blades."

"I'm sorry?" Rowen replied as Meng Po cackled mysteriously.

"I said drink and be gone!" Delemor shouted.

"What do you mean?" Rowen whispered to Meng Po as she helped him to his feet.

But before he could receive an answer, he found himself stumbling around as his field of vision warped violently and his memory went haywire.

Then everything went black altogether.

CLOYES, FRANCE

EARLY 13TH CENTURY AD

News of Rowen's miracle spread like wildfire. Upon hearing the news, people of all ages and social status were drawn to his home like moths to a flame.

"I didn't even know he was sick," Rowen said to his parents when asked about the incident. "I just thought he was really ugly."

The truth of it is that Dionysus—God of Mischief, the Drink, and One-Night Stands—had been responsible for everything. The opportunity for mischief arose when Rowen had been accosted by an unruly homeless man.

"And I'll be having one of these sheeps for dinner," the unruly homeless man had said.

"Over my dead body," the 11-year-old Rowen bravely countered before striking the man on the crown of his head with his wooden staff.

At the precise moment of impact, Dionysus struck too, knocking the leprosy clean out of him.

"What's leprosy?" Rowen asked his parents as they sought the truth of the incident.

"Hansen's Disease," his mother replied as his father paced back and forth, nervously drinking his nightly ale.

While Rowen felt that for the first time in his short life he had acted truly nobly in the face of grave danger, his father was clearly irritated by the gathering crowd outside. Rowen was forced to defend himself lest he be unjustly punished. "All I know," he pleaded, "is that a man with a gross, retarded, scaly face and nubby hands was trying to steal one of our sheep."

"And so you cracked his head with your staff?!" his

father replied, incredulously. "Darlin'," his father said, turning to Rowen's mother. "I find it hard to believe that the boy has enough strength to even lift that staff over his head, let alone hit someone so hard that he knocked the leprosy out of him."

"Oh no," Rowen's mother replied, incredulous in her own right that Rowen's father would say or even think such a thing. "No, no. He's a very macho boy! And so handsome with his golden locks and bright blue eyes."

"Well, being girl handsome ain't never helped him plough the field."

"He's a shepherd boy; and he does a great job at it."

"All I did was hit him with my staff to protect our sheep," young Rowen implored. "That's it. Nothing else."

"Well, you try telling that to the mob!" his father roared back.

Desperately wanting to be a good son, Rowen complied. But try as you might, reasoning with a mob is like reasoning with a drunk toddler. Completely useless.

"I merely struck the sinner with my staff," Rowen called out from his doorstep.

"And with that blow, I was cured!" the unruly homeless man called out. "I used to have scales like a lizard on my face," he continued. "And my limbs, when whacked with force, would fall straight out of their sockets until this boy … nay, this Angel of God, cured me."

"Hoorah for the Angel of God!" the people cried.

Until now, Rowen had desperately wanted the mob to leave so that his father would calm down and they could return to normalcy. But something stirred deep within him when the people shouted, "Angel of God."

He had spent his first 11 years as an average shepherd boy. But those three words changed everything.

Sure, he had spent countless hours hoping that he had been touched, praying that he was no mere sheepherder, and fantasizing that he was destined for greatness. But he had always known that those were just pipe dreams.

Until now.

There were people calling for him. There was a movement.

"Look at his face," a hysterical woman called out. "On the face of the angel is the mark of the Messiah. An extraordinary beauty mark above his upper lip!"

And now there was proof.

He had been chosen, and he would not let his people down.

Even more so than the birthmark, what Rowen really had going for him was that he was born to a pair of poor, pious serfs. They hadn't the means to give him an education, so the only one he had received was from the front pew of the church on Sundays.

As he tended to his sheep (i.e., stared off into space as they grazed, baaa'ed, and pooped), he had a habit of replaying each week's sermon over and over in his head.

And over and over and over and over.

He knew the story of Christ better than the priest.

He knew the hymns better than the choir.

And he knew the history of past Crusades better than any of the religious warriors who had actually participated in them.

He knew that some of the Crusaders had sought to right the wrongs committed by the swarthy heathen who had stolen the Holy Land that is Jerusalem.

And he knew that others had simply sought a piece of land and a pocket full of gold.

The former had failed while the latter were failures.

For as long as he could remember, Rowen had dreamed of taking the Holy Land back from the infidels.

And now, with the people at his doorstep calling him the Angel of God, he had a feeling that his chance had come. And much like his hero, King Richard, Rowen would happily give up everything to lead the most noble and honorable quest mankind had ever known.

There was just one problem. All he had done was hit some creep in the head with his staff. The people wanted miracles.

"My son is blind," a middle-aged woman called from the crowd. "Please, could you cure him? Please?!"

"My father is paralyzed," a young girl cried in a sweet yet desperate voice. "He cannot walk. We need a miracle. Please, could you help? Please?!"

"I have like ten people coming over tonight," a young gentleman shouted. "And there's nothing to drink but a cask of water. Please, could you hook a brother up and turn it into wine?! Please?!!!"

Rowen was overwhelmed with pleas for help. Could he hit the blind son with his staff and cure him? Whack the paralyzed father in the legs and make him walk? Reggie Jackson a cask of water to turn it into wine?

Perhaps he could. But more likely, he would just wind up battering a bunch of cripples who had it bad enough as it was. He needed time.

"Good people," he shouted. "I understand your pain. Today has been an incredible day filled with the mercy of our Lord. Tomorrow, too, we will bask in the glow of His glory as He continues to bless us. But the day is gone and we must all make our way home to break bread with our family and give thanks to God for his love and protection. Tomorrow, we will meet again. Good night, sweet people."

With this short yet heartfelt speech, the people were satisfied and peaceably began to make their way home.

All except for the young gentleman in urgent need of wine who let his peace be known. "You suck! ... Fraud!"

When Rowen returned inside, his kindly mother burst into tears as she threw her arms around him.

"You done good, son," his father said, patting him on the back.

Rowen's heart overflowed with joy as this was perhaps

the first time he had ever received a bit of praise from his old man.

"But correct me if I'm wrong," his father continued. "Did I hear someone say that the proof you're a Messenger of God is that booger mole you've got under your nose?!"

***

The following day, Rowen decided that he would cure that poor woman's blind son.

He had spent most of the night tossing and turning, wracking his brain as to how he might be able to perform another miracle, and what he came up with was … nothing.

Which he found to be the perfect solution. *He* had not cured the leper. *God* had cured the leper.

Likewise, *he* would not cure the blind boy, *God* would.

All he had to do was believe. Which, after all, is what he was best at. Believing in God and in His miracles.

So he would do his best to cure the blind boy and if God had it in His plans for him to do so, the boy would be cured.

Further, he would be taking the second step on his quest to reclaim the Holy Land from the heathen scum currently in possession of it.

When Rowen arrived at the home of the middle-aged woman, she threw herself at his feet. "Oh, thank God you've come!"

"Please, stand up," Rowen replied, helping her to her feet.

"He's inside," she said, pushing him through the entrance. "Please, please, *please* cure him of his blindness."

Upon entering the living area, Rowen immediately spotted a young man hunched over a table. Even from behind, it was clear to Rowen that this poor fellow was depressed. That his happiness had been sapped by his disability.

Rowen took a wide stance behind the young man, raised his hands in the air, and shook his whole body as he looked to the heavens.

Then, without warning, he slapped the young man on the side of his head. "Begone, cursed demon!"

"Owwwwww. What the fuck, man?!" the young fellow cried as he turned around wincing in pain.

Rowen's face lit up when the young man locked eyes with him. "You can see!" Rowen cried.

"Of course I can see, you twerp. My little brother's the blind one, not me."

Rowen's euphoria quickly deflated into embarrassment as his face turned beet red.

"He's over there by the hearth," the young fellow continued, pointing to the other side of the room.

As Rowen slinked around the table, another wave of shame washed over him. "I see that you can read, too," he said, noticing the open book on the table in front of the young man. "Good for you, sir."

On the other side of the table, Rowen finally spotted the boy. He was twirling his fingers timidly on the floor by the hearth.

"Hello," Rowen said, gently.

The boy lifted his head and Rowen saw clouds in his eyes. This time, he was hit with a wave of compassion. He wanted nothing more in the world than help this poor boy see.

"I'm going to try to help you," Rowen continued as he placed his hand on the boy's head.

At the precise moment he did so, Dionysus struck, knocking the boy's blindness right out of him.

Rowen felt a jolt of lighting in his hand and the boy screamed as he collapsed to the floor, covering his face.

"What did you do to my baby?!" the middle-aged woman shrieked. "Are you okay?" she cried frantically, rocking her son in her arms. "Are you okay?"

But the boy was quiet.

He slowly lifted his hands from his face and looked up at his mother and at Rowen, his round green eyes sparkling.

"I can see," he gasped.

"It's a miracle!" the middle-aged woman yelled. "A miracle!"

***

The next day, a little weary from being paraded around town and again touted as the Angel of God, Rowen decided that he would cure the paralyzed father of the girl with the sweet yet desperate voice.

If God would grant this miracle, Rowen's destiny would be sealed, because it would be his third miracle in three days. When a pair of three's line up like that, no further proof is required. You're clearly dealing with a prophet.

The stage would be set for Rowen to lead a Crusade to reclaim the Holy Land from the vile swine currently inhabiting it.

Much to his surprise, he found the home of the paralyzed father to in fact be a castle, and the paralyzed father to be Lord Chevalier.

Equally surprising, upon meeting Lord Chevalier's daughter, Sera, he felt as if half of his heart had been torn from his chest while the other half exploded.

Sera, just one year older than Rowen, was an absolute vision. She had delicate skin, long shiny brown hair pulled back in a lustrous braid, and glowing green eyes. Further, she was wrapped in a flowing, honey-colored dress with intricate lily embroidering along the sleeves.

While Rowen didn't realize it at the time, she too experienced the feeling of having half of her heart ripped out of her chest while the other half burst.

The reason for this was that at the precise moment their eyes locked, Aphrodite—Goddess of Beauty, Horndog

Love, and Shitty Dramas—had ripped half of their respective hearts out and fused them with their counterparts.

Not surprisingly, the resulting feeling is that of a hydrogen bomb going off in one's chest.

Their silence was broken when Sera recalled the task at hand. "Please," she entreated softly. "Please cure my father."

"If it is God's will," Rowen replied, his heart aching at the sight of her sorrowful yet sparkling emerald eyes. "Then it will be my honor."

Rowen followed as she led him through the castle's entrance hall, saloon, and library, and into the smoking room. Seated on an ornately carved oak throne, gazing despondently out of the window, was a man who appeared to be Sera's father.

Rowen approached. "Are you Lord Chevalier?"

"I am, young man."

"You are unable to walk, right?"

"That is correct, my dear boy. My legs are lame."

Rowen turned to Sera. "This is definitely the guy, right?"

"Yes."

Rowen turned back to her father. "Get up and walk," he said confidently.

Lord Chevalier eyed his daughter.

"This is the boy who has performed two miracles already," she said with a nod.

"Get up and walk," Rowen repeated, lifting his arms in the air.

Lord Chevalier's eyes widened with hope—the one sin remaining in Pandora's box—as he leaned forward on the throne, pushed off the armrests, and did his damnedest to support his weight with his legs.

"Father!" Sera cried as he fell to the floor with a great thud.

"What is the meaning of this!" Lord Chevalier barked as

16

he shot eye daggers at Rowen, who looked as if he'd peed his pants. "Do you mock me, boy?!"

Sera turned to Rowen, her eyes more desperate than ever. "Rowen, we need a miracle. Please!"

"I'm sorry," Rowen said. "I think the sun was in my eyes … or something. Or maybe I need to be touching the afflicted for the miracle to occur."

Feeling fainthearted, Rowen timidly approached Lord Chevalier and leaned over his crumpled body. Trying to regain his confidence, he locked eyes with Sera and they nodded determinedly. "Be gone, demon!" he called out as he smacked Lord Chevalier on the rump.

"I'm not constipated, son, I'm paralyzed."

"Father!"

"Sera," Lord Chevalier said, sternly. "If you and your little friend here are done terrorizing your poor crippled father, then please help me back into my chair so I can get back to watching clouds float by."

"Oh, father," Sera exclaimed. "I'm so sorry. This was not meant to be a prank. As I said, he's already performed two miracles. He cured a leper and a blind boy. They call him the Angel of God. I just … I just don't understand."

"Just help me up already."

As Sera grabbed one of her father's arms, Rowen did likewise. "Let me help," he said.

At the precise moment that Rowen grabbed Lord Chevalier's arm, Dionysus, who had been laughing his ass off since Rowen had had the balls to command a paralyzed man to "get up and walk," flew into action and knocked the paralysis clean out of the lord's body.

Sera felt the blow too and staggered backward in shock.

Slowly, Lord Chevalier put both hands on the floor shoulder length apart, drew his knees to his chest, pressed both feet to the ground, and stood.

"It's a miracle!" Sera cried.

Lord Chevalier was standing. *"Putain de merde!"* he

shouted. "A miracle!"

In an instant, the three of them were rejoicing in the middle of the room, tears streaming down their faces as they held hands and danced around in a circle.

***

Before long, all of France had heard of the Angel of God and they flocked to him for a multitude of reasons.

Some, in hope of a miracle. Others, wishing to hear him speak. And still others, just to catch a glimpse of the golden-haired boy bearing the mark of the Messiah.

Most curiously though, were the many children who came to inform Rowen of the miracles that they had performed.

"When I touched a dead bird, it returned to life and flew away before my very eyes," a starry-eyed young scamp explained to Rowen and Sera as they were enjoying a picnic after Rowen had given a sermon on the importance of hope and faith.

Rowen and Sera had taken to spending time together every day since the Lord Chevalier miracle, and her family often prepared lavish feasts for the two to enjoy.

It was clear to both of them that they were in love, but neither broached the subject. They were young, pure, and devoted to God, and they intended to stay that way for as long as possible.

Further, Rowen instinctively understood that innocence and purity would play pivotal roles in the coming Crusade.

"You are a special boy," Rowen replied to the starry-eyed scamp. "You are most welcome into my band of disciples."

"Do you really think he performed such a miracle?" Sera whispered to Rowen as the scamp merrily took his leave.

"Surely, the Lord's wonders know no bounds," Rowen replied. "But in this case, it is more likely that the bird was just sleeping or something."

"I thought so, too," Sera said, smiling first at Rowen, then at a very serious-looking young boy approaching them.

Rowen greeted the boy with a wave. "Hello, friend."

"Hello, Messiah," the boy replied, furrowing his brow, puffing out his chest, and plunging into his tale. "My friend Didier and I were at play and my friend Didier rolled some dice and covered them up before I could see what they were. Didier then says to me, 'Guess what I rolled?' And I said, 'Hmmmm,' while I was thinking. Then Didier said, 'You'll never get it.' So I said, '11.' Didier couldn't believe it and he said, 'You're right!' Then I said, 'It's a miracle!'" A wide smile broke over his face as awaited Rowen's acknowledgement. "Isn't that an amazing miracle?!"

"Indeed, that is amazing," Rowen replied. "It's more of a good guess in a game of chance than a miracle per se, but nonetheless, I welcome you as an esteemed disciple."

"Indeed," the boy repeated, clenching his fist and teeth in triumph. "A miracle of miracles."

No sooner did the dice-guessing boy leave than did another youngster approach.

"Messiah," he said, kneeling in front of them. "You will never believe the miracle that I experienced."

"Go on, my friend."

"Just this very Sunday, I was on a hill just like this one, and I put my hands on the ground and the heavens and earth flipped upside and whizzed and whirred and I realized that I was levitating. And then in the blink of an eye, the heavens and earth flipped upside down again and *bang*, I was back on my feet. Have you ever heard of such a wondrous miracle?!"

"Oh, you sweet thing," Sera said, patting the boy on the head. "That's what we call a cartwheel. You did yourself a cartwheel."

As Sera's words washed over him, he stared off into space with a look of self-awe. "A miraculous cartwheel."

"Just a cartwheel, my friend," Rowen said. "But nonetheless, I am very impressed."

"Does this mean I get to be in your group of miracle-workers?"

"Yes, my friend. I would be happy to have you as a disciple."

"Woo-hoo!" the cartwheel boy shouted as he joyfully sprinted down the hill. But as he reached the halfway point, he stopped suddenly, looked back to make sure that Rowen and Sera were watching, then head-planted himself into the ground in an epically failed cartwheel.

"Why does everyone think they need to perform a miracle to be one of your followers?"

"Not sure."

"It's so weird."

"Yeah, but whether they've performed a miracle or not, the important thing is their belief. Belief in God. Belief in miracles. And belief in God's will."

***

Once the number of Rowen's disciples outnumbered his entire town's population, he knew that the time was at hand.

So on the third Sunday of the third month, he gave a sermon on the hill that would change the fate of the world.

"Peace be to you," he began, raising his hands high in the air.

"And also with you!" his followers replied.

"I have wonderful news.

"Jesus Christ, our Lord and Savior, has spoken.

"He said, 'Restore the Holy Land to its rightful inhabitants.'

"He said that only *we* can do it.

"The Father and Son grow weary of the heathen occupying Jerusalem; those foul creatures who continue to commit atrocities against the true believers.

"For too long, the wicked have oppressed with tyrannical violence our religious brethren in that hallowed land.

"On a daily basis, the unclean unleash dogs on our people.

"They use our fathers as slaves, our siblings as punching bags, and our mothers as pelvic punching bags.

"No longer can we sit idly by, watching in silence.

"The time has come to put an end to the persecution and rape.

"For the sake of the one true faith, for the sake of the world, and even for the sake of those ignorant barbarians, this war must end.

"And we, my faithful followers, are the ones to do it.

"We are the only ones who can.

"Many of our predecessors heard of the atrocities committed in the Holy Land and some of them made gallant attempts to stop it.

"King Richard, in the name of God, gave up everything he had to try to right the wrongs committed against the true believers. Unfortunately, the power of evil was too strong and he failed in his quest.

"It is no secret why. While he was righteous and just, his followers were flawed.

"Three times thereafter, our fellow Christians took up the cause and failed.

"They know not why. But I know. All of us here know.

"They lacked faith, resolution, and purity of heart. Some even sought personal gain.

"It is a common thing among adults. In their youth, when faced with grave injustice, their hearts burn to remedy the iniquity. But as they age, the fire retards and rather than thinking of others, they become selfish cretins, caring only about food to eat, a roof to sleep under, and a wife to beat their children with.

21

"I do not blame them. Such is nature. And if their heart turns cold, surely they will be defeated. Surely, they will fall prey to the wicked heathen whose destructive desire knows no bounds. Who continue to commit their atrocities in the Holy Land to this very day.

"'Who can win?' some may ask. 'Who can possibly oust an army of hell-sent demons?' 'Whose hearts are pure enough to defeat the infidels once and for all?'

"Why the answer is simple. And everyone here knows it.

"It is *us!*

"Like King Richard, I pledge to give up everything and devote my life to this noble cause. I ask that you do the same.

"They will disparage us as mere children, but it is precisely us mere children who can succeed.

"Jesus Christ has told me so.

"It is because we are faithful, and we are pure, and we are innocent.

"Only the innocent can defeat the wicked.

"This may come as a surprise to some, but there is something even more surprising: Unlike our predecessors, we need not bear arms.

"They thought that spilling blood was a necessity.

"But that was their downfall.

"Jesus Christ did not preach murder.

"He preached mercy and forgiveness.

"Those shall be our arms. We shall march with faith, purity, and innocence and retake the Holy Land with mercy and forgiveness.

"Nary a drop of blood will be spilt. For it is God's will as told to me by Jesus Christ our Lord and Savior.

"We will begin our Crusade when the new moon rises.

"Some will tell us not to go. We will ignore them.

"There is nothing for us here, but there is the glory of God there.

"Here, there is brackish water, unleavened bread, and

only our hands to do cartwheels with. There, the rivers flow with milk and honey, the fields teem with fresh baguettes, and the streets are filled with wooden hoops and sticks.

"Yes, my friends. When the land of milk and honey is ours, we shall, with bellies full, roll those hoops with those sticks. We shall race them up and down the streets while giggling so hard that we fall over in pain.

"We depart at the new moon. First, we will march to the capital where King Philip will provide us with provisions, transport, and an escort to Jerusalem. I will see you all again soon, my friends.

"Praise be to God!"

"Praise be to God!" the crowd roared back, bursting into applause and tears of joy.

***

When Rowen informed his parents of the news, his mother greeted him with a long, impassioned embrace.

"We're gonna miss you, my sweet boy."

"I'm gonna miss you too, Mother."

"I'm so proud of you. I always knew you were special."

"Thank you, Mother. I have trouble believing it myself, but it is God's will, and I'm blessed to be His servant."

"We believe in you, honey. And we know that you will help to spread good in this world. Don't we, Papa?"

"Quit smothering the boy, you're gonna make him go soft."

"But you believe in him, Papa, don't you?"

"Yes, yes," Rowen's father said, uncomfortable with all the emotion rippling through the room. "I believe in the boy. I mean, I believe in his passion. His ability to give a coherent speech on the other hand ..."

Rowen's mother shot him a how-dare-you-question-the-Son-of-God's-surrogate's-speech-giving-skills look. "What do you mean, Papa? His speech was magnificent. Did you not see how fervent his followers became? They cannot wait to march."

"Yeah, sure," Rowen's father replied, defensively. "He stirred them up good. But what was with the King Richard stuff? I hope you weren't being serious there, Row. You were like, 'Just like King Richard, I'm going to give up everything I have for this just cause.'"

"That's right," Rowen replied, defiantly.

"You don't have anything to give up! King Richard had a kingdom and castles. He had riches and court wenches. You're just an 11-year-old with absolutely nothing worth anything. Hell, it's been your lifelong dream to move out of this dump."

Rowen's mother, despite being his biggest supporter, couldn't help but giggle. "Plus," she chimed in. "Like two seconds after he said he'd give up everything for the cause, he said there wasn't even anything here for him."

"Mind yourself, Woman!" Rowen replied, vexed.

But his father couldn't help but let out a derisive snort-laugh. "I'm sorry, Row, I think you're a heck of leader, I do. All I'm saying is that you're lousy at not contradicting yourself and looking like a boob. But I'm sure the Crusade thing will go fine."

***

When Sera informed her father of the news, he greeted her with a warm hug, then led her through the entrance hall and armory hall, up the east stairwell, through the parlor and dressing room, and into the corner library before withdrawing from the room by himself and locking the door.

"This is your new home until the day after the next new moon."

"But Father," Sera protested in desperation. "You cannot do this. You know that I must go with Rowen. You know that it is God's will."

"Well, if that's what God wants," Sera's father replied as he bolted the door with a great thud. "Then I'm sure He'll come down and open this door up for you."

***

Sera awoke the next morning to find her father standing stone-faced above her with a breakfast tray. "I am very sorry, my little cabbage, but I forbid you to ever see that boy again." He paused for a beat before unleashing a ridiculously cheerful smile. "But on the bright side, here's some pomegranate, onion soup, and bread pudding."

"But Father …"

"I know what you're going to say. You wanted apple sauce, but I'm afraid apples just aren't in season!"

"Father, please …"

"I'm sorry, my sweet. I'm afraid that that's the end of the discussion. I hope you'll be in a better mood when I see you tomorrow. Your mother will bring you lunch and dinner. Do be a good girl and don't give her any trouble."

***

Sera had much better luck with her mother in the sense that she was at least able to get a sentence out. "Mother, I *must* go. I feel it in my heart. I must go with Rowen."

"My dear sweet child," her mother replied, gently stroking her soft hair. "I understand what you're feeling. But you must remember that you are young, and sometimes your emotions get the better of you. Sometimes you feel like something is the most important thing in the entire universe, but then a year or two later you've forgotten all about it. You have a crush on a boy. I did too when I was your age. But when you get older you'll see that that's all it was. A crush. Someday, you'll meet the right man for you, and this man will give you the life that you deserve, not tear you away from your family to go on some outlandish fool's errand that can only end in disaster."

"No, Mother, it's not that. I mean, I like Rowen, but it's not about that. God has shown us that we must go. The miracles that Rowen performed are proof. He will lead us on a Crusade and the righteous will again inhabit the Holy Land as God intends."

"Sweet Sera. Even if I agreed with you, there is no changing your father's mind. He loves you too much to allow you to go on such a dangerous escapade. You can see that, right? He's doing this because he loves you. If something were to happen to you he would go mad with grief and regret. You must understand that."

"But what about the miracle? Rowen cured Father of his paralysis. Surely, Father cannot dispute that. Surely, Father cannot doubt that Rowen has been touched. God will protect us. You need not worry."

"Oh, I don't know, darling."

"Yes, you do. And you must convince Father as well. *Please*, Mother. Convince him."

***

The subsequent days ticked by in almost exactly the same fashion. Sera's father refused to allow her to finish a sentence while Sera continued to beg her mother to change her father's mind.

The only thing that changed was the food that she ate and the utterly unnecessary reason her father gave for not giving her what he thought she wanted.

"I know what you're going to say. You wanted crust-less herb quiche, but I'm afraid that all the herb quiche I could find had crust!"

On the fateful morning that the Crusade was to begin, Sera remained silent until her father finished his needless explanation and marched toward the door. "I love him, Father."

His body stiffened as if he had been stabbed in the back. Slowly, he turned around. "I thought you discussed this with Mother," he said sternly. "I thought you understood that it's just a schoolgirl crush."

"It is not. I love him. And with each passing day I've spent locked in this room, my love for him has only grown stronger."

"Your feelings have only appeared to grow stronger because I have forbidden you to ever see him again. It is a mirage. You will see."

"I care not for forbidden love!" Sera roared back. "I care only for Jesus. And for His faithful servant. And I will follow them both. Do *not* forget who cured your disability! Our Lord and Savior Jesus Christ through the living prophet, Rowen. They will deliver us the Holy Land. And I will be there to witness, and God willing, to help."

Sera's father fell to his knees, weeping. He could no longer fight it. For it was God's will.

Well, to be more precise, it was Dionysus' will.

***

By the time the Children Crusaders arrived at the capital, they were an army.

Each time they marched through a town, mobs of enthusiastic youngsters full of faith, purpose, and freshly performed miracles, joined their ever-growing ranks.

"Your Majesty," Rowen called out on the entrance steps of the royal palace, making sure that all in attendance could hear. "I present you with a letter from Jesus Christ, our Lord and Savior."

It had taken quite a while for the king to emerge from his palace, but that he did at all was a testament to the movement.

Rowen and Sera gazed at each other with hopeful eyes as King Philip II read the letter.

The journey thus far had been trying, but many kind souls had selflessly offered their assistance throughout, so they were in good spirits. While their mutual feelings had continued to blossom, until now they had not even so much as held hands, knowing that their campaign hinged on their virtue and chastity.

As Rowen clasped Sera's hand for the first time, the moment was ruined by the king's disparaging laughter.

"*Putain de merde!*" he cried, incredulously. "Jesus has anointed you, a girly-faced boy whose nads have not yet dropped, as his prophet?"

"Yes, your majesty. You must have heard of the miracles."

"And he wants you to march to Jerusalem to drive out the heathen?"

"Yes. Where others have failed, we shall succeed."

"And he further wants me to provide you with, and I quote, 'transport, escort, and provisions including daily rations of meat pies, sweet crepes, and cheese waffles'?"

"If the meat pies are an issue, we can be flexible."

"Get out of here, you little turd. *Tout suite!*"

"But …"

"Begone! Now! You have given me a great laugh, which I thank you for, but I can no longer stand the sight of you. You are making my stomach upset and if I am caused to vomit you will swing from the gallows. Vamoose!"

King Philip II looked up at the throngs of believers outside the palace gates who were staring at him in shock. "Scram, children!" he cried. "Go back to your homes. Back to your parents. This boy is no prophet. He's just a delusional toddler with a mole on his face that looks like a booger. It is a sign, alright. A sign that he will be executed after his face makes me puke."

NEGOTIATIONS WITH GOD

***

The journey to Marseilles, on the Gulf de Lyon, was much more arduous.

While Rowen's followers had not been discouraged by their harsh treatment at the royal palace, no longer did their numbers grow. Further, villagers along the way offered them little to no help.

Yet somehow they arrived at the port as faithful as ever.

Until, that is, they were faced with a vast blue sea that for all intents and purposes was a dead end.

"What shall we do?" Sera asked.

"Fear not, kind Sera," Rowen replied. "God will shepherd us through. Just like He did for Moses and his flock of fugitives on the banks of the Red Sea, so too will He part these impenetrable waters for us now."

At the precise moment that Rowen pompously lifted his arms toward the Mediterranean, Dionysus—administrator of mischief—did absolutely nothing.

The wind blew.

The seagulls cried.

And that was it.

Sera looked at Rowen with concern.

Rowen nodded his head resolutely and strengthened his grip on his staff. "It will be a *miracle*!"

At the precise moment that Rowen shouted 'miracle,' Dionysus snort-laughed.

…

"A *MIRACLE*!"

…

"Ummmm, Rowen," Sera said, timidly. "I'm not really seeing a miracle here."

Rowen felt as if he had been kicked in the gut.

"Greetings, good children," a man called out from behind them. He was big-boned and had a bulbous nose, lively eyes, and scraggly mullet. His shifty smile also revealed a distinct lack of premolars. "It appears you are in need of some assistance."

"Why yes, kind fellow," Rowen replied, flashing Sera a smile. "We could indeed use a helping hand." While the sea had not been parted, perhaps God had other means in mind.

"My name is Francois," the stranger said, bowing his head. "But I am known as the Lion of Lyon."

Rowen gasped. "Clearly, it is a sign from God," he whispered to Sera. "First, Richard the Lionheart, then Rowen the Lionheart, now the Lion of Lyon."

"Who calls you Rowen the Lionheart?" Sera whispered back. "Are we calling you Rowen the Lionheart now?"

After shushing Sera, Rowen turned back to the Lion of Lyon. "It is a great pleasure to meet you. I am Rowen."

"You need not introduce yourself, good child. I, of course, have heard of the Angel of God. It is an honor to make your acquaintance."

"The honor is mine, Lion of Lyon."

"I have heard that you are on a Crusade to the Holy Land, and it just so happens that an acquaintance of mine, a wholly trustworthy fellow, has at his dispense an idle fleet of seven ships. It would be my pleasure to ask my acquaintance, a generous Christian like yourself, to provide safe transport for you and your followers. I, of course, would be happy to bear the expenses and to escort you during the voyage."

"That is wonderful news, kind sir. We would be ever so grateful and our Lord and Savior will surely bestow upon you infinite blessings for your generosity."

Sera cupped her hand over Rowen's ear. "May I have a word?"

"Excuse us, Lion of Lyon. I need to have a quick aside with my companion."

"But of course, young Rowen. Be my guest."

"Rowen," Sera said sternly, once they were out of

earshot of Francois. "Are you sure we can trust this man? He looks quite suspicious and his offer is beyond belief."

"Have faith, my dear. He is a Christian just like us. And no doubt, he is a gift from God."

"How can we trust him?"

"Faith, my dear. It is what we do best. Believe in God and His will will be done. Do you not remember how God aided the Crusaders in the last siege?"

Sera looked blankly at Rowen.

"After three long years of battle, the army was poised to strike Jerusalem," Rowen explained. "But in their way were 50-foot walls that were 10-feet thick. An insurmountable obstacle.

"In order to scale them, they needed ladders and siege towers, but of course, they had nothing. And of course, the heathen had leveled all trees in the area.

"But the Crusaders scavenged the terrain for wood, and as God would have it, they uncovered a hidden hole in the ground that contained enough ready-made logs to produce the necessary ladders and siege towers.

"God had given them a gift. Just like He is giving *us* a gift now."

Sera furrowed her brow. "Rowen, that's a lovely story and I don't mean to question it, but if it was God who had lent them a hand, don't you think He would have already assembled everything? I mean, yeah, it's great to find ready-made logs and all, but there's still a lot of work left to be done. And I can't imagine it's easy when you're a sitting duck. I mean c'mon, You're God, it's not all that hard to finish the job, is it?"

"What are you getting at, my dove?"

"I'm just saying that if the logs were a gift from God, perhaps they would have already been in the form of ladders and siege towers. And if this gentleman were a gift from God, perhaps he wouldn't look like a homeless pedophile."

"Faith, my dear," Rowen replied with a condescending God-works-in-mysterious-ways look. "God works in mysterious ways."

"Well, if you truly believe it in your heart, I will trust you."

"God is great!"

***

"Land, my boy," Francois said, pointing from their ship's deck to the Port of Alexandria in Egypt. "We're just about there."

Sea gulls had come out to greet them and as they swirled above, their calls mixed with the sound of waves crashing against the hull and wind thrashing against the sails.

As it was a clear, sunny day, Rowen had no trouble spotting the coast. "Praise be to God!"

"I'm so pleased to have been able to guide you all this way," Francois said, placing a fleshy hand upon Rowen's bony fingers.

"I delight in your delight," Rowen replied.

"When I was a boy your age," Francois said, squeezing Rowen's fingers. "I spent every night wondering where my next meal would come from."

"That sounds horrible," Rowen replied, compassionately.

"It was. I thought for sure that even if God existed, He'd forgotten about me."

"God would never forget one of his faithful servants. He has a plan. Although we may not know it, there's a reason for everything."

"I couldn't agree more. I certainly didn't know it, until I saw you and your invaluable followers. You are a gift from God."

"I appreciate your kind words, but I am nothing more than a servant of His will."

Francois flashed a depraved smile. "And I am nothing more than a servant of opportunity. By simply delivering you to the land of milk and money, I'll never spend another night hungry again."

"God helps those who help themselves."

Francois shifted his fleshy grip to Rowen's wrist. "I couldn't have said it any better."

"I know that He will take care of you for all that you have done," Rowen replied, patting Francois' hand amiably, but eager for him to remove it as it was causing him considerable pain.

"Yes," Francois replied, licking his lips as the ship began to dock. "God, and a few wealthy slavers."

Rowen, smiling in confusion, glanced at Francois whose eyes sparkled with greed and madness.

"There's nothing so tasty as a free meal," Francois continued. "Thanks to you and your multitude of mommy-less followers, it's free meals for me for life."

"I'm sorry?" Rowen asked.

"And even though you have a disgusting booger mole on your face, those golden locks and blue eyes will fetch me a pretty penny."

"I do not follow," Rowen replied, trying to free himself from Francois' grip.

Francois jerked him back to the railing. "Just look in front of you, boy. Open your eyes. All you'll ever need to know is right in front of you."

Rowen lifted his head to the shore. Just off the docks, there was a dusty square where groups of forlorn men, women, and children stood in chains.

"Come now, boy," Francois snarled, tugging Rowen toward the exit ramp.

"What's going on?!" Sera cried as she dashed toward them from the cabin upon detecting Rowen's distress.

"We've arrived at the promised land," Francois said mockingly as he seized Sera by the wrist as well.

While being forced to disembark, Rowen spotted all the sinister-looking men in flowing robes and fine turbans. They were inspecting the helpless captives and bartering amongst themselves with great zeal.

"Do be good little Angels of God and do what these men tell you," Francois hissed as he led Rowen and Sera into the market where they were put into shackles.

Within hours, Rowen and his remaining followers – two of the seven boats had shipwrecked along the way – were sold into slavery.

Within a month, Rowen died from malnutrition and unrelenting beatings.

***

"Come to the light," a reverberating voice sounded once Rowen had breathed his last breath and his soul slipped away from his French 11-year-old body.

With muddled consciousness, Rowen went gently into the bright white light.

"Have a seat," the voice said soothingly as Rowen neared the source of the light.

As if by gravitation, Rowen found himself straddling what felt like a horse. "What's happening?"

"Your life is over. I'm taking you back to Verixion."

"Who … who are you?"

"Al-Barghest, at your service. Consider me your chauffeur."

"What's the deal with this light?"

"Like a moth to the flame, the human soul is drawn to light … that is to say, to divine truth."

The source of the light was the tip of the divine being's long tail which was currently dangling in Rowen's face, in effect blinding him.

"Also, would you have answered my call having seen this?!" she asked, dimming the light to reveal her form.

"Holy shit," Rowen gasped, feeling at once frightened and nauseous.

Al-Barghest, despite having the graceful body of a winged horse with a fluffy pink tail, was not much to look at from the neck up. The distinguishing features of her fully rotatable wolf-head were her pig nose, mole rat teeth, and naked sphynx cat ears.

As Rowen gagged vehemently, she rotated her head forward, let out a maniacal laugh, and galloped off for Verixion.

The last thing that Rowen remembered was a crashing sound as if the universe were ripping.

VERIXION II

"I'm so honored that you're back, young Angel of God," a sarcastic voice sounded as Rowen slowly regained consciousness. His eyes were once again flooded with bright light, so it was difficult to make out the surroundings, but the mist flowing around him seemed very familiar.

Then it clicked. *Verixion. Delemor.*

Rowen reflexively adjusted his body so that he was sitting on his heels deferentially.

"What happened?" he asked feebly as his eyes slowly adjusted to the light and Delemor's intimidating figure began to take shape on the opposite side of the table.

"You died."

"I'm so confused," Rowen said meekly as images from his past life fluttered through his head. "One minute we were being taken to the Holy Land, the next minute I was a slave."

"Yeah, life's like that."

"But why?"

"That guy. The one that told you he was gonna escort you to Jerusalem. He made a boat-load of money selling you and your army of followers to slave traders. A pretty shrewd move, financially."

"What happened to Sera?"

"Oh, my young cabbage-cabbage, you do *not* want to know. It's about a thousand times worse than the most dreadful scenario you could possibly dream up. You realize that you were in Egypt, right?"

"But why? Why did that have to happen? Especially to Sera. She was a loving, faithful follower of Jesus Christ and God the Father. No one believed more than she did."

"Yeah, I'm sure Yahweh really appreciated that."

"So then how did that happen? Wasn't everyone on our side?"

36

"Everyone on your side?!" Delemor let out an incredulous laugh. "Do you have any idea how boring it would be if we all took the same side?!"

"But we were taught to have faith in the one true God."

"Yeah, isn't that funny?" Delemor chuckled. "It seems like everyone's taught that. And they all think theirs is the correct one. Talk about hubris. To think that you're so special that only the God that you believe in is the 'one true God.' Re-*dick*-ulous! But it makes for good watching."

Rowen's mind was swimming in confusion.

"So aside from being sold into slavery and being beaten to death, how was it?" Delemor asked. "How would you grade yourself?"

Rowen continued staring off into space trying desperately to make sense of what had happened during his life and what Delemor was saying to him now.

"Answer me, you testicle-less surrender monkey!" Delemor roared as Rowen felt a pain of outrageous proportion in his thigh.

"Eeeeeeeep!" he screamed, partially due to the intense pain, but more partially due to the sight of the jet-black cobra with its neck fanned out who had sunk its venomous fangs deep into his leg.

"Oh My God, I'm Gonna Die!!!!!!" Rowen shrieked.

Delemor once again burst out laughing as the snake released its bite from Rowen's thigh, spit on it, and slithered back under the table.

The instant the snake retracted its fangs, the pain coursing through Rowen's entire being vanished.

"Oh my God, what was that?" Rowen asked, panting.

"I guess you could call that my tail. If you'd like to avoid visits, I suggest you answer my questions in an expeditious manner."

"I'm very sorry. What was the question again?"

"How would you grade yourself? How do you think you did?"

Rowen furrowed his brow while reflecting on his life. "I think I did pretty good. I did my best as a son and shepherd, and then once I was touched by God, I did my best to lead a Holy Crusade."

Delemor burst out laughing again. "I still can't believe you thought you had anything to do with those 'miracles.' You should have seen your face. 'Get up and walk!' you said. The guy was paralyzed!!!"

As Delemor laughed so hard it seemed like he would suffocate, Rowen heard a loud thud on the table, then a rolling sound coming toward him, and then another thud as an object fell directly next to him.

"What … what is this?" Rowen asked cautiously once Delemor's laughter had subsided.

"You can keep it, my *chou-chou de pute.*"

Rowen eyed the crystallized, fist-sized orb in wonder.

"Well, I'll tell you what," Delemor said. "Your innocence … nay, your *ignorance* provided a few moments of entertainment, so I'll give you a little credit there."

"So I did good?" Rowen said, swelling with hope. "Do I get to go to Empyrean? I'm sure Sera's there and I'm aching to see her again."

"Absolutely not," Delemor replied, seemingly offended. "I admit you had a couple things going for you, but you're nowhere near passing the test. Not a chance."

Rowen's heart sunk. He felt as if the life had yet again been knocked out of his body.

"But you've earned another try," Delemor said as the door to his chamber swung open and a cool mist wafted in. "Wash that disgusting stink off and we can chat again."

Rowen slumped out of the room, sparkling orb in hand, and staggered down the stone path to the bathing facilities.

After setting the orb on the counter beneath the mirror, he considered the three bottles full of shimmering liquid.

"Use the crimson-colored one!" Delemor shouted from his chamber.

"May I ask what it is?" Rowen replied, suspiciously.

"Goat blood."

Rowen gasped.

"It's just soap, buddy. Just soap."

As Rowen washed his body with the raspberry-scented shampoo and basked in the transcendent tingling, he noticed a pinky-sized tiger staring wide-eyed at him from atop the second lowest pine cluster of the miniature evergreen tree. It had a fluffy black and orange-striped coat and was beaming at him.

"Hey, guy," Rowen said cheerfully, stretching a hand toward it.

The tiger playfully jumped into his palm and began licking the base of his thumb. As Rowen brought his hand back toward him to get a closer look at the adorable creature, its eyes flashed and it leapt at Rowen's family jewels, managing to sink its teeth into one of his testicles.

A searing pain shot through his body and he reflexively clapped his hands on the creature as if trying to crush a mosquito.

The little tiger let out a piercing yelp as it fell to the ground where it promptly shot Rowen a dude,-what-the-fuck?! look and scampered off.

"Care for a drink?" a sultry voice inquired.

Rowen turned to again see the gorgeous vision from last time. He couldn't help but admire her voluptuous breasts.

"Was that a miniature tiger?" he asked, reaching for the intoxicating beverage.

"Yup. Cute little devil, isn't he?"

"Not really."

"I see you've got one of Delemor's tears," she said, indicating the sparkling orb with a slight nod of the head.

"One of Delemor's tears?" Rowen repeated.

"Yeah. Isn't it gorgeous?"

"It's like a huge diamond," Rowen said.

"Care for a dip?" the Goddess asked, turning her

attention to the mysterious, misty body of water.

Rowen polished off his drink. "Sure."

The soothingly warm water contrasted nicely with the cool air.

"May I ask your name?" Rowen said as they floated along a current heading toward a luminous being who seemed to be gesticulating by himself on an island for one.

"Aphrodite," she said, flashing a seductive smile.

"It's a pleasure to meet you."

"The pleasure is all mine."

As they floated closer to the being, Rowen couldn't help but feel in awe of the light radiating from behind it in concentric circles.

"You talkin' to me?" it said menacingly, pointing at a reflection of itself in what appeared to be a floating mirror. "Who the fuck do you think you're talkin' to?!"

"Who's that?" Rowen whispered to Aphrodite.

"That's Yahweh—God of Wrath, Salvation, and Inferiority Complexes Of Preposterous Proportion."

"Yahweh?!" Rowen repeated, trying desperately to align the recollection of God he had from his past life with the being that he was now looking at.

"His name means, 'I am what I am.' It's the appellative equivalent of the expression, 'It is what it is,'" Aphrodite explained, raising her voice so that Yahweh could hear. "So yeah, he's kind of a douche."

At the sound of Aphrodite's voice, Yahweh spun his head in their direction while giving a swift kick to what appeared to be a pair of winged bunnies sprawled out at his feet. They immediately snapped to attention. "Holy! Holy! Holy is Yahweh! His glory fills the whole world!"

While short in stature and quite hairy, Yahweh's body was ripped with muscles and he had a presence about him that was at once awe-inspiring and confoundingly pathetic.

"It is a great honor to meet you, my Father," Rowen said, bowing.

Yahweh flashed a self-satisfied smile.

"As I'm sure You know," Rowen continued. "I dedicated my life to You and Jesus."

"Who?"

"Jesus. Your son born to the Virgin Mary who preached about You and died for the sins of mankind."

"Oh yeah, Jesus. Good dude, that Jesus. He really helped spread the word about Me, which I like."

A moth fluttered close to Yahweh's ear and he squashed it with a clap of his mighty hands. "Pesky gnats. They never stop bothering me."

Aphrodite giggled.

"So what can I do for you ... ummm ..."

"Rowen, my Father. My name is Rowen."

"Right. So what can I do for you, Owen?"

"I um ... I uh ... I guess I don't really have any questions for You, I was just kinda floating in that water and it brought me here."

"Why is there so much injustice in the world?" a voice sounded from behind, and suddenly Rowen realized that he was not the only mortal present.

"How dare you question Me!" Yahweh snapped. "You want some of this?! You want a piece?! I will smite the living shit outta you!"

Rowen turned to get a look at the object of Yahweh's fury and was surprised to find that it was none other than the wicked Francois.

"I'm very sorry," Francois said to Yahweh, slinking back into the current.

"Me too," Rowen said, bowing his head. He wasn't quite sure why he was apologizing, but he felt somewhat disillusioned and the urge to flee was overwhelming. Further, he felt an almost gravitational pull toward Francois, so he waded into the current behind him.

Once they had drifted away from the island, Francois turned to Rowen with a this-is-more-awkward-than-the-time-I-was-hitting-on-a-girl-at-a-bar-and-for-some-reason-said-to-her-that-you-never-know-if-you-might-kill-someone-someday look. "I'm really sorry about the selling you into slavery bit."

Rowen nodded in acknowledgement and waited for Francois to continue.

"I knew it was wrong, and yet I couldn't help myself. Could you find it in your heart to forgive me?"

An awkward silence hung over the two as Rowen thought back on the experience and searched deep within his soul. Surprisingly, he found little resentment. And what little there was, was not for his own suffering, but for the unimaginable suffering that Sera must have gone through.

Rowen gave Francois a half-smile. "Yeah. I forgive you. I'm not really sure why, but I feel almost no animosity toward you."

"Oh, that's wonderful," Francois replied, extending a hand. "You're a really good person. I hope we get to meet again under better circumstances. Like in Empyrean."

"Okay, enough fraternizing," Delemor boomed as the two were shaking hands. "Get back in here and let's get down to business."

The current took Rowen back to the bank in front of Delemor's chamber and he clambered up the stone path, into the room, and once again sat deferentially on his heels across the table from the resplendent Delemor, seated high on his throne.

"So," Delemor began slowly, stroking his long, reptilian jaw. "What can I do for you so that you live the right life?"

Rowen was at a loss, uncertain of how to begin.

"Let's again start by looking back at your last life," Delemor continued. "What did you find unsatisfactory?"

"Well, I guess it was cut rather short."

"There we go. So you'd like to make it to adulthood. I'm in a generous mood today, I can grant you that."

"On the plus side, I really enjoyed being a leader.

Perhaps I could be a king?"

"Denied," Delemor said, flatly. "That would be taking advantage of me, now wouldn't it? But I tell you what. How about I make you one of the most powerful men in all the land?"

"That would be great."

"And how about the ladies?"

"If Sera's not already in Empyrean, could I be with her again?" Rowen requested, timidly.

Delemor's tail hissed from beneath the table. "No talk of Sera. She's not up for negotiation. Not now, not ever."

"I apologize."

"But I could arrange for you to be surrounded with the most beautiful women in all the land. Is that something you'd be interested in?"

"Well ... would they like me?"

"Of course. I already told you I'd make you one of the most powerful men in all the land."

"Then that would be wonderful, I think," Rowen said, warming up to the idea of this next life.

"Then it shall be done, my little cabbage-cabbage. However, I cannot guarantee that your fire will burn as hot as theirs?"

"What do you mean? I'll be surrounded by beautiful women, right?"

"Right."

"And they'll like me, right?"

"Right."

"Then there will be no problem," Rowen replied, now relishing the thought. "While I renounced all wicked desire in my last life, if I'm to understand that it is okay to lay with a woman as an adult ..." Rowen paused, awaiting assent.

"It is, you adorable little abomination."

"Then I'm sure that if they like me, there will be plenty of fireworks."

"I like that confidence. This next life is shaping up well

43

for you. How about physical features? What would you like to look like?"

"Handsome?"

"Rejected. I already told you, you'll be a man of great power."

"...Golden locks?"

"Rejected. In fact, you will be bald."

"...Strong?"

"Rejected. You will be scrawny and weak as a child, and fat and weak as an adult."

"...Really?"

"I grow tired of this. Meng Po," Delemor shouted suddenly. "Bring in the drink."

The adorable old lady emerged immediately with the beverage and hobbled over to Rowen.

"The negotiations are over," Delemor said, impatiently. "Drink and be gone!"

Meng Po handed over the concoction which was frothing over the rim of the cup. Rowen pinched his nose and chugged it down as fast as he could.

"Up we go," Meng Po said kindly, grabbing Rowen by the arm and helping him to his feet.

"Thank you," Rowen replied, groggily.

As he began to stagger, Meng Po clutched both of his cheeks and looked him dead in the eye. Rowen did his best to look back down at her but everything was hazy.

"It is better to have rubbed and rost than to have never rubbed at all," she said in a thick Asian accent that did not seem familiar. "Rub, Rowen. Rub!"

"Huh?" Rowen muttered unintelligently before his vision went completely haywire and everything went black.

XIANYANG, CHINA

MID-3RD CENTURY BC

The day that 11-year-old Prince Zhao Zheng Zhu, or Frank as he was known to his intimates, became king was at once glorious and regretful.

Glorious because his state of Qin had just defeated the state of Han, thereby taking the first of six steps to unify China.

Regretful because his father had just died, an unfortunate yet necessary condition to make the leap from prince to king.

"It is a bittersweet day," his mother, now Queen Dowager Zhao, said to him. "I am very sad that your father has perished, but once the sadness has passed, we will look back on this day as an auspicious one. It will go down as the day that the greatest leader in the history of mankind ascended to the throne. The hero that once and for all unified China and created an empire that shall stand and prosper for all of time. The Earth itself will crumble before your empire does. Great monuments in your honor shall decorate our magnificent land and our joyful subjects shall sing songs about you, the Son of Heaven, for eternity."

Frank's conflicted heart couldn't help but delight in his mother's words.

To add to this delight, young Frank received countless wonderful presents, his favorite of which was a 9-year-old boy named Rowen who had been captured during the taking of Han.

"I think he'll make an excellent companion for His Excellency," the lieutenant general said. "I'm sure you will find him quite resourceful. When I entered his dwelling, I heard the voice of a distressed girl calling from the corner. 'I am wounded,' she cried. 'And am in need of a strapping soldier from Qin.' I rushed to the corner but found nothing but an empty cask. That's when I felt a sharp sting in my back. I turned around to see none other than this waif. He had just shot me in the back with a blow dart. The scamp had lured me into the corner by throwing his voice. Quite a trick," the lieutenant general finished with a smile.

From that day on, King Frank and Rowen were inseparable. When they weren't studying or consulting with the Queen Dowager and generals about the unification campaign, they were happily at play.

They battled at chess using servants as pieces, making sure that when a piece was knocked out of the game, it was knocked out cold.

They engaged in blow dart competitions from atop the palace gates, using random passersby as targets.

And their favorite form of play was taking advantage of Rowen's ability to throw his voice to prank members of the royal court.

For instance, they pranked a maid by making her think that the Queen Dowager had requested that she wash the royal gowns in fire; they pranked a palace guard by making him think that the security general had told him to be on the lookout for flying monkeys; and they pranked a cook by making him think that a beautiful concubine had asked him to prepare her lunch with "a log of shit, for a friend."

It was during one of these shenanigans that Rowen came across the concubine Xera, a recent addition to Frank's ever-growing harem which would go into service upon his 15th birthday.

Despite being double Rowen's age, and despite being pledged to Frank and Frank alone for eternity, or perhaps because of those factors, at the precise moment that Rowen first laid eyes on Xera, Aphrodite—Goddess of Beauty, Horndog Love, and Shitty Dramas—pierced his heart.

From that moment on, not a day passed where Rowen didn't gush to Frank about Xera's beauty. He adored her porcelain skin, pouty lips, and silky black hair that she braided into a pair of sweeping loops behind her head and adorned with gold hairpins.

Frank was not nearly as smitten, but was happy enough to count her among his concubines and never ceased to be amused by Rowen's outpouring of emotion.

As the boys made the most of court life, several key developments occurred during the first year of Frank's reign.

A timely earthquake made for an easy conquest of Zhao, and a devastating hurricane helped make short work of Yan.

Both natural disasters were the work of their patron deity Dionysus—God of Mischief, the Drink, and One-Night Stands.

As a result, only three states remained and the outlook for unification by Frank's 15th birthday was rosy.

Further, ground had been broken on the Forbidden City, and thanks in part to the spoils of war, much progress had been made on what would be a massive complex of awe-inspiring buildings and gorgeous gardens.

Upon Frank's ascent to the throne, the Queen Dowager promptly began planning the complex which would include a luxurious royal palace, plush residences for concubines and other members of the court, and a stately building from which to govern.

On many occasions, the Queen Dowager boasted to Frank that the Forbidden City would be the most magnificent complex the world had ever seen, as befits the Son of Heaven.

"Unfortunately," Frank explained to Rowen, "as you are a commoner, you will not be able to live there with me. In fact, you won't even be allowed in. Hence the name."

This was obviously sad news for Rowen who loved

hanging out with Frank, and lived for glimpses of Xera.

Another interesting development was the pregnancy of the Queen Dowager, which she assured Frank was a good thing. Rowen, too, tried to convince him that it would be wonderful to have a younger sibling, but Frank couldn't help but feel suspicious, particularly since he had never trusted the father, a high-ranking official who always seemed to have the Queen's ear.

More progress was made in the second year of Frank's reign as Qin was able to defeat Wei with much of the credit going to a catastrophic landside that wiped out half of Wei's army.

In the following year, they were able to conquer their largest and most fearsome enemy, Chu. After their king was killed in a lightning storm, a power vacuum opened, leading to a brutal internal struggle which made them surprisingly easy prey.

At around the same time, the Queen Dowager gave birth to another child, giving Frank two adorable half-brothers to contemplate.

"Everything is going exactly as planned," Queen Dowager informed Frank as they entered the fourth year of his reign. "The Forbidden City will be finished by your birthday and because only the impotent state of Qi remains, unification is at hand."

The Queen was not wrong. By the time the construction of the Forbidden City was complete, Qi had fallen. While Frank's Qin army was on pace for an easy conquest, they were nonetheless aided by an epidemic of diarrhea that swept through the Qi army.

"I have wonderful news," Frank informed Rowen during the days leading up to his 15th birthday. "There's a way for you to live with me in the Forbidden City. Not only that, you'll be able to serve as one of my most trusted advisors."

Rowen was over the moon. Not only could he continue

to live a cushy court lifestyle, but he would be forever near the love of his life, Xera.

"It'll involve a small sacrifice on your part, but what do you say?"

"I say I'm in. I don't care what the cost may be."

A few days before the big ceremony to celebrate the unification of China, the crowning of an emperor, and the emperor's birthday, Rowen found himself in a smoky rowhouse adjacent to a small dirt courtyard.

"Your turn, little guy," a seedy yet shrewd looking gentlemen said to Rowen as he handed him a long pipe.

"What's this?"

"Opium," a round, droopy-eared fellow on the other side of Rowen replied. "It'll help you get through the procedure."

"What procedure?" Rowen asked.

The two men shot each other the-kid-has-no-idea-what-he's-in-for looks before letting out a bit of wry laughter.

"Best not to focus on it," the seedy gentleman said. "Just inhale."

"Yeah," the round fellow agreed as Rowen reluctantly filled his lungs with smoke. "Best to focus on the positive. Like what a life-altering opportunity this is."

The men snickered again as Rowen coughed violently when exhaling.

"I think you'll find that it's a relatively minor price to pay to be lifted out of poverty and into imperial robes," the seedy gentleman said. "Once we have the emperor's ear, it's simply a matter of learning his tastes and habits before being granted a plum position."

"Yes," the round fellow concurred. "Giving up one pleasure in return for so many is not a bad deal at all. Sure, we may start by doing menial tasks, but once we've gained the emperor's trust, we can even hope for power and wealth of our own. Not to mention that we'll be surrounded by beautiful gardens and lovely girls."

Rowen was not quite sure what they were getting at and as a wave of sleepy euphoria drifted over him, he was not all that concerned.

Upon being led out to the grim courtyard, they found a row of three chairs, each with a hole in the middle and were instructed by a kindly attendant to disrobe and sit.

Rowen followed the two men's lead, stripping down, and slumping drowsily into his chair.

"They're ready for you now, doctor," the kindly woman said.

His mind in a fog of happy relaxation, Rowen watched as the stone-faced "doctor" approached the round fellow from behind, steadied a pair of mighty sheers just below the seat, and with a look of great determination snipped the man's penis and testicles clean off.

Now in a state of detached confusion, Rowen stared as a torrent of blood gushed from beneath the round fellow's legs before he slumped to the ground with a great thud.

"Whoooooooa," Rowen gasped, languidly. "Is that guy gonna die?"

"Probably," the attendant replied, pleasantly. "At best, only two outta the three of you will live through the procedure and he's hemorrhaging pretty bad."

"That doesn't sound good."

"On the bright side, it probably increases your odds of making it."

Rowen watched in subdued horror as the doctor repeated the surgery on the seedy gentleman and then made his way over to him.

"But how am I gonna pee?!" Rowen said as the doctor prepared to strike.

The doctor paused momentarily, then gave his reply with great solemnity. "Sitting down."

***

"Is my new favorite eunuch finally awake?" Frank said as Rowen's groggy eyes began to open.

The sharp pain pulsating from his groin quickly prompted a recollection of what had transpired. "Why did they do that to me?" he asked, despondently.

Frank smiled down at him. "So that you may enter the Forbidden City. The only males allowed in are eunuchs."

"Why?"

"Because only eunuchs can be trusted."

"Trusted for what?"

"To be faithful to me. You wouldn't want me worrying about whether one of my concubines was giving birth to my child or to the child of one of my gardeners, would you? It's the only way to prove fidelity."

Rowen was still drowning in despair. "But I'll have to pee sitting down."

"Don't be so pessimistic, Rowen. This is a wonderful thing. Sure, it'll take some time to get used to your new facilities, but once you do, who knows, if you're able to arch your back just so and get a sharp stream going, you may even be able to pee standing up."

"…"

"Anyway, you're my best friend in the whole world. You wanted to live with me in the plush new palace, right?"

"… Yeah."

"And you wanted to become my most trusted advisor for life, right?"

"… Yeah."

"And you want to be around Xera, right?"

"Yeah."

"So cheer up, brother. This isn't something to pout about, this is something to celebrate. In fact, at my coronation ceremony, not only will we celebrate the Unification of China, but we'll also celebrate the Eunification of Rowen!"

Frank beamed down at Rowen who managed a weak

51

smile in return.

"Oh, and I have a delightful present for you," Frank said, fetching a ceramic jar from a side table. "It's your precious treasures. We've preserved them in alcohol so we can bury them with you when you die. And then when you're reborn into your next life, you'll be whole again."

***

As the birthday celebration that followed the imperial coronation was coming to a close, Frank took Rowen aside. "I've got wonderful news," he said, eyes sparkling.

"What is it, Your Excellency?"

"I'm appointing you scrivener to the imperial cherry-popping. As you can imagine, it's quite the honor and I'm happy to bestow it upon you."

"Thank you very much, Your Excellency. But I don't quite follow."

"You will have the distinction of recording the first time the Emperor of China has intercourse. You simply watch and write down everything that happens."

"Oh. ... Thank you very much."

Frank could hardly contain his delight. "And there's more."

"More?"

"Yes. I've chosen as my counterpart ..." Frank held his breath as he gave Rowen the quintessential wait-for-it look. "Xera!"

Rowen's heart dropped through his chest. "Xera?"

"Yes. Since you can't have sex with her yourself, I figure the next best thing is for you to watch *me* do her."

"..."

"While taking notes."

"..."

"I was a little surprised about the notes thing myself, but according to the Queen Dowager, it's something that must be done. Something about a scientific method to increase the imperial fertility ratio. Regardless, it's win win win."

"..."

"You get to see Xera in all her carnal glory. Xera gets the honor of being the Emperor's first. And as long as Xera doesn't fuck everything up, I get to sire an heir to the throne."

"..."

Frank apparently mistook Rowen's jaw-dropping shock for elated astonishment. "Isn't this great?! The perfect way to commence your service to the crown."

"..."

"I'll see you in the Chamber of Bumping Uglies in 10 minutes."

***

Despite failing his first assignment (Rowen's notes on the lightning-quick love-making session consisted of: "Awkward. Awkward. Awkward. Oh My God, he's hurting her!!!"), Rowen soon became a valuable advisor, and as the two boys matured into intelligent men, their successes mounted.

In addition to abolishing feudalism, they replaced hereditary rights with a meritocracy, standardized units of measurement, had networks of roads and canals constructed, and created a common currency and writing system.

When times were good, Frank would summon Rowen and a handful of gorgeous concubines to the Garden of Supreme Harmony and Intoxication where they would indulge in an artistic drinking game.

Floating along the gentle stream that meandered through the garden were cups of wine. If a cup stopped in front of you, you had to compose a haiku for the group. If the haiku displeased the emperor, you had to down the cup of wine.

Regardless of whether they were chugging wine in defeat or sipping it at a leisurely pace, the group would always give thanks and praise to Dionysus for the blessing.

As such, Dionysus greatly enjoyed witnessing the amusing events and when Yahweh expressed an interest in the region, he brought him to one as well.

"Life grows inside me
It kicks my belly with force
It must be a son"

"I like the sound of that," Frank said to Xera when it was her turn to recite a haiku. "But since the first two children you bore me were female ... Drink!"

"Garden of beauty
Full lips, breasts, and curvy hips
Care for a handshake?"

Frank burst out laughing at Rowen's poem. Almost nothing delighted him so much as Rowen's self-deprecating humor with respect to the frustration of being surrounded by beautiful women but not being equipped to do anything about it.

"That's rich," Frank said. "It makes me laugh, but it also makes me a tiny bit sad ... so Drink! Chug it down in honor of the almighty Dionysus."

Rowen obliged as a pair of elegantly dressed concubines comforted him.

"Well, these full lips will always be here to give you smooches," one of them said, rubbing against him and stroking his cheek.

"And these full lips will always be here to tell you how fat you've been getting," the other one said, patting his ever-expanding belly.

While Dionysus of course enjoyed the game immensely, particularly the praise, Yahweh was overcome with jealousy. When it was time for the next haiku to be delivered by a lovely young concubine, he took control of the words leaving her mouth.

"Don't forget Yahweh
Let us praise and bless His name
He is the one true God!"

"Drink!" Frank said in disgust. "Not only do we not know or care what you're talking about, but the last sentence had six syllables. So gulp that down in shame, you half-witted monkey fart."

Yahweh, needless to say, was not pleased.

In retaliation, he caused the Mongolians to the north of China to launch a series of raids so devastatingly brutal that anyone within 50 kilometers of the border who had not been raped or killed lived in constant fear of being so.

Completely clueless as to how to prevent further raids and at wit's end, Frank and Rowen decided to consult an oracle. They would ask the Gods for guidance to once and for all put an end to the barbarian raids.

The process was as simple as it was obvious.

They asked the diviner a clear-cut question: "How do we protect ourselves from the savages to the north?"

Next, the diviner carved the question into the back of a tortoise shell and placed it into a blazing furnace until it cracked.

Lastly, the diviner interpreted the response by reading the cracks and writing the answer on the underside of the shell.

At the precise moment that the shell hit 68°C, Apollo—God of Light, Prophecy, and Skinny Punks—gave his reply:

If you build it, they will stop coming.

The instant that Frank and Rowen read the response, they knew exactly what must be done.

A Great Wall!

"Perfect!" Frank said, a spark in his eye. "And you know what?! We'll make those rapist barbarians pay for it!!!"

Rowen furrowed his brow. "I'm afraid that just doesn't make any sense. I mean you no disrespect, Your Excellency, but while I have heard you say a lot of insanely idiotic things, this achieves a new level of stupid. If you inbred blobfish for a thousand years, the resulting blobfish would not be able to even conceive of anything so dumb, let alone say it out loud. Why in the world would our enemy pay for a wall to keep them out?!"

"Trust me," Frank said with a self-satisfied smile. "They're gonna pay for this wall."

***

While it was undeniable that having the Mongolians pay for the wall was an ideal solution, and while Frank maintained throughout construction that it was indeed the Mongolians who were paying for it, in practice, it was the Chinese themselves who paid the price.

Not only with their time and labor, but very often with their lives.

As to be expected, it was not easy to build an impenetrable wall with watchtowers every few hundred meters along an inconceivably long, treacherous border that extended through plains and precipitous mountains alike.

In fact, it was an unimaginably long and costly endeavor.

When possible, they procured raw materials from the immediately surrounding area, but more often than not, they had to transport the materials from far away on the backs of soldiers, peasants, and livestock.

Despite utilizing such technological wonders as wheelbarrows and rope, the amount of manpower necessary was astounding.

As such, Emperor Frank decreed that all males who were unable to pay a hefty Compulsory Labor Exclusion Fee, or a *get-out-of-wall-building fee* as it was commonly referred to, were required to donate two years of service to the effort.

In general, the construction consisted of building the sides of the wall with heavy stones and durable bricks, and then filling the space between with packed earth.

While the labor in-and-of-itself was extremely grueling, the harsh conditions were magnified by the fact that Frank was in an outrageous hurry to finish. Many surmised that the main reason behind this was that he was eager to have an everlasting symbol of the greatness of the man behind it, the Son of Heaven.

As a result, workers were often whipped and beaten when overseers deemed their effort to be lacking. It was not uncommon for them to drop dead of exhaustion, if not blunt force trauma.

In such cases, the corpse was simply dropped into the packed earth that filled out the inside of the wall.

"Why waste resources," Frank said. "Let them continue to serve their glorious empire."

So as the number of sons who failed to return home increased, so too did the number of distressed letters from grieving parents.

And as the number of farmers who struggled to feed their families grew due to the high taxes, so too did the seeds of civil unrest.

"We have a serious problem," Rowen said one day to Frank as they strolled through the Garden of Sublime Wisdom.

"Oh, please," Frank interrupted. "I'm not in the mood

to hear any more depressing updates about the wall."

"But Your Excellency," Rowen persisted. "Just yesterday, I encountered another grieving mother outside the Gate of Heavenly Peace. She was crying hysterically, tearing off bits of her ragged clothes, and bashing her forehead against the ground."

"Really, Rowen?! Is there nothing you can do other than rain on my parade?!"

"But Your Excellency, what's the point? With thousands upon thousands of our boys dying, who are we trying to protect?!"

"Me," Frank snapped back, before realizing that this might not be an appropriate reply. "The state. We are protecting the state. You need to look at the big picture. We are losing a few drops of blood from our pinky finger to protect our entire body. To protect our heart and our soul. And to sow the seeds of future prosperity."

As the confrontation reached a head, the two noticed what looked to be a vagrant charging headlong at them. He was screaming obscenities and brandishing a rusty blade above his head.

Never before had the walls of the Forbidden City been breached, and as such, the scene so confounded Frank and Rowen, that rather than flee for their lives, they stood as still as statues, mouths agape.

When it finally dawned on Frank that he was mere moments away from having his throat slit, he screamed in horror and soiled his drawers.

Yahweh, watching from Verixion, was pleased.

The vagrant, however, was tackled just short of Frank by a steadfast guard and before long he was being pummeled by a mob of them.

"Guard," Frank said as the beating subsided. "Have this man explain himself."

"What in God's name were you doing?" the guard asked.

"I was trying to put an end to His Majesty's life," the man said, scowling at Frank.

"Why on earth would you do that?" the guard asked.

"Because he is the bane of our existence."

"How dare this piece of street garbage speak of me this way," Frank said to the guard. "Give him a taste of the cane."

"Because we live in filth," the man continued through grimaces as he endured a barrage of blows to the ribs, neck, and head. "… while you live in luxury. We are unable to scrounge enough food to eat. All the crops we grow are taken as taxes. We have nothing."

"I do not believe my ears," the guard said. "If you are so miserable, why didn't you just kill yourself? How dare you bring your problems to the Forbidden City."

"Well said," Frank concurred. "If he thinks he had it bad before, he has no idea what the penalty for treason is. I sentence him to death by Surgical Incision Extravaganza."

Frank punctuated his proclamation by hocking a massive loogie in the man's face. Then he turned to Rowen and gave him a your-turn look.

While Rowen obediently spat at the man's feet, he took comfort in that fact that his spittle contained no phlegm whatsoever.

Frank beelined it for the nearest Chamber of Heavenly Bowel Relief to take care of some unpleasant business, but managed a smile as he visualized the punishment that the deranged criminal would receive: a meticulous surgical procedure where his body would be slowly carved up in such a way that his vital organs remained intact, ensuring that the torture would last as long as possible.

***

When times were bad, Frank would summon Rowen and a throng of gorgeous concubines to the Garden of

Supreme Harmony and Intoxication to drown his sorrows in wine and haiku.

Not too long after the assassination attempt, Frank had a case of the blues and was recounting the many reasons when the cup landed on him.

"Two little brothers
Too many eyes on the throne.
Two more fresh dirt homes."

"To my poor little half-brothers," Frank said while pouring half of his wine on the ground in tribute. "And to the supreme deity Dionysus," he finished, holding his cup in the air before downing the other half.

Dionysus, watching from within the courtyard, was pleased.

"It was a great tragedy," Rowen said, sympathetically. "But it was a necessary tragedy. There was nothing else that could be done, Your Highness, so do not beat yourself up about it."

It was clear to everyone that the father of Frank's half-brothers, and maybe even the Queen Dowager herself, wanted Frank out of the way so that the little brothers could reign. While Rowen was reluctant to shed blood, there was little else that could be done to extinguish the threat, so he had advised in favor of doing so.

As he did his best to comfort Frank, the ravishing concubines at Rowen's sides clung to him.

"You are so sweet," one of them said, staring at him almost dreamily.

"I could just eat you up," the other said as she placed a hand on his enormous belly. "It may take a couple of years," she continued, laughing. "But I swear I could just eat you up."

Frank smiled. A rare occurrence when playing the game in a melancholy mood.

The next time the cup landed on him, Frank turned his attention to the women in his life.

"Mother bore treason,
Xera bore only daughters,
Betrayal bred goodbye."

Frank again poured out half of his wine in tribute to the Queen Dowager and Xera, then chugged the other half in honor of Dionysus.

Rowen was aware that the Queen Dowager had been banished to a remote village in the corner of China. In fact, it was he who had advised Frank to do so. It was all he could do to save her life when Frank was convinced that his mother too conspired to see his half-brothers on the throne.

However, he was not aware that Xera had been banished and hearing the news was a shock. It almost felt like a dagger piercing his heart. Fortunately, he knew where to find her.

The third time the cup landed on him, Frank turned his attention to the topic that was most on his mind these days.

"A bum with a knife
Threatened my crown and my life
You too, Grim Reaper?"

After the assassination attempt, Frank had become more and more concerned with his mortality. Prior to the incident, he had been convinced that he was the Son of Heaven, and the thought that he might die had never even crossed his mind. But the bolt of fear that struck his mortal body the day of the incident had him scared to death of death.

"We must take measures to ensure my immortality," Frank said to Rowen after downing another cup of wine.

"Indeed," Rowen replied, racking his brain for a way to pacify Frank, whose paranoia and mental instability grew steadily with each passing day. "How about a shrine?"

"A shrine?" Frank echoed, letting the idea wash over him.

"Just like we do for the Gods, we can build you a shrine on sacred ground. And when your earthly body expires, your ashes can be enshrined there so that the people of China can worship you forever."

"Yes, yes, yesss," Frank said, nodding his head. "Wait. Shrine? Ashes? No, no, nooo."

"No?"

"No. A shrine will not do. We must think bigger. What we need is the Forbidden City."

"You want to turn the Forbidden City into a mausoleum?"

"No. I would be a sitting duck. We need a whole new Forbidden City. One that nobody knows of and that nobody will ever find. A secret complex of palaces, buildings, and gardens. With eternal rivers flowing in between. And the main palace will be of gold and bronze and will house my most valuable treasures. And to protect it all, a fully equipped army standing guard for eternity."

Frank's eyes blazed as he shifted his wild gaze from concubine to concubine. "And you, my pretties," he said. "You will be there for my delight. You and you and you."

Lastly, he pointed ominously at Rowen. "And youuuuuuuu."

"Of course," Rowen replied, reassuringly. "We will all serve you in spirit."

"Oh no," Frank said, shaking his head, wide-eyed. "You will be there in body. Much like we've preserved your precious treasures in alcohol, so too shall we preserve your entire bodies. All of you. And all of the army. We must start at once. Have someone begin preparation of the embalming alcohol immediately. Thousands of my most steadfast soldiers must be mummified in formation and stationed on all four sides of the Secret Forbidden City."

Rowen again racked his brain for a way to mitigate Frank's madness. "This is a brilliant idea. But first of all, if we start embalming our soldiers now, who's going to protect and fight for you in this life? Secondly, I'm afraid that embalming people will cause them to be trapped in this world. No one will be able to protect and serve you in the next one."

"What are you proposing?"

"As for the concubines, imperial staff, and myself, we will happy to be buried at your side. Our tombs can be constructed right next to yours and when we pass – of natural causes – we can be laid to rest at your service."

"I suppose that would do. But for the army?"

"Just like you want a replica of the Forbidden City, we can build replicas of thousands of soldiers. A terracotta army of ceramic statues each individually crafted based on individual soldiers. And not just soldiers, we can construct ceramic horses and chariots, too. A full and fierce army to stand guard for you for eternity."

"A terracotta army?"

"Yes. Each infused with the soul of its model to protect you and your empire in the afterlife."

Frank nodded in assent. "This does indeed sound promising. The protection of thousands. But we must ensure secrecy or they will come to destroy me. And we must ensure that the city and all its treasures are defended by live munitions that when triggered will strike whether in this world or the next. And once I have been laid to rest, surrounded by my treasure, the gates must be lowered and the city must be hidden underneath a great mountain such that no one shall ever become suspicious. Meanwhile, lurking underneath, shall by the greatest emperor the world has ever seen. Ruling for eternity! We must make it happen! You hear me, Rowen?! It is the only way! We *must* make it happen!!!"

"Oh boy," Rowen muttered to himself. "This is not gonna improve the tax situation."

***

Having hastily laid the groundwork for what would take nearly a million men over two decades to construct, Rowen swiftly made his way to the Garden of Dispossessed Favorites.

There, he encountered a scene that shattered his jaded heart. Seated on a bench staring wistfully at a magnificent sunset was his sweet Xera, who was now more forlorn than sweet.

She had failed the emperor by bearing him three daughters and zero sons. As such, Frank had deemed copulation with her to be a waste of time and severed ties.

However, since women who have laid with the Son of Heaven were prohibited from laying with anyone else, she was to idle the remainder of her days away here with the other concubines who were past their prime.

Hearing footsteps, Xera turned to see who was approaching and at the precise moment that her eyes met Rowen's, Aphrodite pierced her heart.

"Rowen, how wonderful to see you," she said, her eyes lighting up. "Come and have a seat. We've never really talked. Let's talk."

Rowen sat down next to her and was struck by the crow's feet encroaching the corners of her eyes, the strands of gray hair, and her suddenly twitchy manner.

Nonetheless, he still felt that ball of nerves in the pit of his stomach that had for all these years made speaking to her a near impossibility.

"So here we are," Xera said. "Quite a pair. An outcast and a eunuch."

Rowen smiled, sympathetically.

"I always had nightmares about winding up here," she continued, eyes darting all over the place. "Left alone in this ironically verdant garden. My youth and beauty gone. Replaced by wrinkles and gray hair."

Rowen's nerves subsided as he felt an overwhelming urge to comfort her. "Do not say such things, lovely Xera. You are still as beautiful today as you were the first day that I laid eyes on you."

Xera burst out laughing. "Oh, what a prankster you are, Rowen. Teasing a haggard old woman long past her prime. Or is it flattery? But a eunuch has no need to flatter a woman."

"As you say," Rowen replied, resolutely. "I have no need to flatter women. I never have. And as you must know, I have never flattered nor lied to a concubine."

The lack of ulterior motives had afforded Rowen the ability to develop intimate relationships with concubines on a level that your ordinary, fully-endowed man could not even imagine. But that ball of nerves in Rowen's stomach had always prevented him from developing one with Xera.

"I suppose this is true. I have heard many of them speak highly of you." Xera closed her eyes tightly while rubbing her forehead. "So what is your intent then? It is to torture me, yes?"

"No. What you said is simply not true. Yes, you have aged. We all have. But when I look at you now, I don't see your age. I see the vibrant beauty who took my breath away the first time I laid eyes on you."

Xera smiled, knowingly. "Oh. You must be speaking of your first duty as a scrivener after the Emperor's 15th birthday, yes?"

Rowen winced at the memory. "No. It was long before that. Back when I first arrived at court."

"Ahhh, yes. I remember those days. You were a scrawny little scamp always up to no-good." Xera laughed as she grabbed hold of Rowen's hands. "And now here you are. A pot-bellied eunuch flirting with a has-been concubine."

Rowen let out a chuckle as his face flushed red. "I must go, but may I visit you again?"

Xera's eyes lit up and her head cocked to one side. "Oh, yes! You may come at any time. What a wonderful thing that I've been banished here. Why I feel like the most popular girl in the empire. We are gonna have quite an affair, you and I."

Xera's words struck Rowen as both sarcastic and sincere. While he couldn't quite get a handle on her, he was ecstatic that they had finally sown the seeds of a relationship.

From that day on, whenever he had any free time, Rowen would visit Xera in the Garden of Dispossessed Favorites where their meandering discussions would last for hours. They bonded over their brief childhoods in the countryside, their lives within the gates of the Forbidden City, and the gradual mental decay of Emperor Frank.

"To be honest, I thought he lost it when he executed his brothers," Xera said one day, sticking her tongue out and tugging on an imaginary noose.

"Oh no," Rowen replied in defense of Frank. "He was still fine back then. That was more of a healthy paranoia. Without question, their father had dreams of establishing a dynasty and it was six of one, half dozen of the other for the Dowager, so Frank was right to get rid of them. Probably could have just banished them to the Land of Wa, though."

"This is true. Being banished is way better than being dead. You get to spend all your time thinking about the approaching blackness. It's a wonderful life."

"Oh, but it's not all bad, is it? I'm eternally grateful for all the time I've gotten to spend with you."

"Ah, yes. The silver lining. I really do cherish my time with you, too. I just wish things had been different. That we had met under different circumstances. Could you imagine if we had never been brought to the Forbidden City?"

Rowen smiled.

Xera gazed off at the horizon. "Could you imagine a normal life where you and I lived out in the countryside? Where we worked the land during the day. And where we dined on goose and wine at night. And where you had a penis."

As Rowen smiled wryly, Xera leapt on him and planted a wet kiss on his lips.

"What are you doing?!" Rowen cried, pushing her off. "You know we can't."

"It's just a kiss. What's more, a kiss with a eunuch. It's no big deal. Come on, give me some sugar!"

As Xera once again attacked Rowen, a shrill voice cried out from the other side of the garden. "Help! Someone Please Help! He's Trying To Rape Me!"

"Oh my God," Xera gasped. "Help her."

Once a source of wicked delight, Rowen's ability to throw his voice had this time allowed him to escape the garden without further damage.

"I'm going to need you to refrain from any further monkey business," Rowen commanded the next time he visited.

"But how can I restrain myself around the man who invented paper?" Xera countered, referring to Rowen's recent accomplishment

"You heard about that?"

"Of course, it's all that us discarded concubines can talk about."

As usual, Rowen was unsure of whether she was being sarcastic or sincere.

"It'll change everything," she continued. "Such an ingenious invention."

"Now it is you who is full of flattery. I simply switched up some ingredients."

"Don't be so modest. Going from bamboo and silk to

67

bark and hemp will save the empire a fortune and will likely allow even peasants to learn to read and write. It's quite an achievement."

"Oh, come on, you're being ridiculous. It will save the state funds when preparing official documents and that's about it. There won't ever be a time when commoners can read. There's no need for it."

"I'll bet the emperor is again showering you with riches," Xera said, eyes sparkling with mischief. "It's enough to drive a girl mad."

"Don't do it," Rowen warned, inching away from her.

Xera let out an unhinged giggle before grabbing Rowen's hand and forcing it on her breast.

"Stop it," Rowen persisted as Xera massaged her breast with his hand while moaning gratuitously.

"Stop! Thief!" A high-pitched voice suddenly cried out from the other side of the garden. "He's Getting Away With My Purse!"

While maintaining hand to hand to breast contact, Xera flashed Rowen a devious smile. "We have an old saying where I'm from," she said. "Fool me once, shame on you. "Fool me … can't get fooled again!"

Xera redoubled her effort and it took all of Rowen's strength to stand up and put some distance between them.

"Cut it out, Xera. You know that it is forbidden for anyone to lay with a former concubine."

"Lay with?! Who said anything about laying with me?! All I'm proposing is a cheeky kiss or two every once in a while, that's all. And maybe some breast-rubbing here and there. Just a kiss and some breast-rubbing, that's all. And maybe on special occasions, a finger bang. Just a kiss, some breast-rubbing, and a finger bang, that's all. I'm not talking about anyone laying with me!"

"I'm serious," Rowen persisted. "This won't stand. If we want to continue seeing each other, we can't have any monkey business."

Xera frowned and dropped her head. "You're no fun."

"Xera, you must know how much you mean to me. How much I treasure our time together. Every spare second I have, I want to spend with you. But there are lines that cannot be crossed."

Xera clicked her tongue.

"Don't you want me to visit you?"

"Obviously."

"Then please stop the shenanigans. Let us continue our discussions. Let us talk of the past and all that we've been through. And of what we as individuals and we as an empire are currently going through. And let us even indulge in fantasies of what could have been. Like if you and I lived the simple life along the Yangtze River. Where I spent my days fishing. And where you cooked delicious meals. And where our children would swim and laugh and play from dawn till dusk."

Xera smiled wistfully. "Or if we lived up high in the mountains. Where you would tend to our goats. And where I would turn their milk into cheese. And where you had a penis."

***

As Rowen and Xera continued their bittersweet trysts, growing closer and closer together, the empire grew closer and closer to self-destruction.

Many factors were at play, but it mainly boiled down to the heavy burden borne by the people as Frank continued to construct the most elaborate tomb ever built on Earth.

"He's really lost it," Rowen said to Xera one day.

"Still not letting anyone into his private quarters?" Xera asked.

"Yeah, he hasn't allowed a chambermaid in there in months. So when he was passed out after another opium binge, I took the opportunity to enter his sleeping quarters

69

and was shocked."

Xera squinted her eyes and wagered a guess. "Wall to wall jars of urine?"

"How did you know?"

Xera simply nodded.

"And he's got his fingernails and toenails preserved in alcohol. He's either analyzing everything for traces of poison or he's planning to take everything with him to the next world."

"Probably both. He's been executing people weekly on suspicion of treason, so he's probably studying that stuff for proof. And as far as bringing it to the next life, you really never can have too much."

"Well, the way things are going, that trip isn't too far off. His degeneration has really accelerated."

"But the plus side to that is that I'd be freed from this garden and you and I could actually live out one of our fantasies."

"I can't root for my best friend and our dear leader to kick the bucket, but living out our remaining days together somewhere far far away would be a dream come true."

"Oh, I can see it now," Xera said, staring off at the horizon as usual. "It'll be perfect. A little hut on a remote beach off the East Sea. Where we spend each morning admiring the sunrise coming out over the ocean. And where we spend our days drinking coconut milk on the soft sand. And where I spend our nights wishing that you had a penis."

***

As predicted, it wasn't long before their dream of living out their remaining days on a beach was on the cusp of becoming a reality.

According to the emperor's doctor, Frank died of natural causes.

More accurately, he died of dehydration, malnutrition, and self-neglect.

But even more accurately, he died because Yahweh, who had never gotten over the haiku slight, inflicted a slow and painful death upon him.

Yahweh, watching Frank exhale his last breath while surrounded by jars of urine, was pleased.

However, as soon as Frank's body was carried off to the mostly completed Secret Forbidden City, word spread of his demise.

The people's mob stormed the Forbidden City like wildfire torching a dry forest.

Rowen and Xera attempted to hide in the Garden of Benevolent Peace, but it was no use. They were found clinging to each other under a mulberry tree in the corner.

First, the mob ripped them apart from each other.

"Rowen!" Xera cried, reaching toward him with arms outstretched as they dragged her away.

"Xera!" Rowen shouted. "I love you!!!"

"I love you!!!"

Next, the mob ripped them apart literally.

"You fat, repulsive monster!" one of them roared as they pulled on all of his limbs at once.

The last thing that Rowen remembered before everything went black was the excruciating pain he felt as his arm was ripped clean out of its socket.

VERIXION III

"Is the cock-less wonder finally back with us?" Delemor boomed as Rowen slowly came to on the floor of the familiar gold chamber.

"What happened?" Rowen asked, groggily.

"They tore you apart limb by limb," Delemor replied. "It was electrifying."

"And Xera?"

"The same. I must say, there is almost nothing as riveting as the release of the pent-up rage of the masses. And boy did you guys know how to build up that rage. As the old saying goes, 'Oppression breeds entertainment.'"

"You lied ..."

Before Rowen could even finish his sentence, he felt the sting of the serpent's fangs tearing through his calf.

"Owww!!! I'm sorry! I'm sorry! I'm sorry!"

Delemor's tail slowly drew back beneath the table.

"You ... deceived me," Rowen said, tentatively.

In a flash, the serpent was back out from underneath the table, swaying menacingly in Rowen's face, fangs drawn, tongue flicking. "We would never deceive you," it hissed. "Just the thought of it breaks my heart."

Rowen was speechless, shocked not only by the sudden flare-up, but also by the fact that Delemor's snake tail could talk. Not to mention the mixed signals it was sending.

"Why so ever would you even say such a thing?" Delemor asked.

"You said that I would be surrounded by beautiful women."

"You were."

"Yeah but, ... you didn't tell me that ..."

"You were warned. And I didn't even have to go that far. I just happened to be in a generous mood that day."

"That's not fair."

Delemor let out a hearty laugh. *"That's not fair,"* he echoed in patronizingly high-pitched voice. "Who said anything about being fair?"

"That was torture. To be surrounded by gorgeous women my entire life, and then to be with the woman that I loved, and to not be able to ..."

"Yeah, that's another feather in your cap. Watching you squirm with those beauties draped all over you. Absolutely priceless. Right up there with watching the masses pummel you with your own arms and legs as your heart beat its last beat."

"Why did they do that?"

"They hated you."

"Me? Really? Why? I always did my best to have their backs. To keep the tax burden as low as possible. To keep the number of people forced to build the wall and mausoleum to as few as possible."

"And do you think you accomplished any of that?"

"Well ... I don't know ... I tried."

"Well even if you had been able to reduce their burden, they wouldn't have known to give any credit to you. To them, you symbolized the wealth and power of the Forbidden City."

"Really?! Despite being literally impotent, I symbolized power?"

"Yeah. Pretty rich, huh? ... Oh, that and monstrosity. You symbolized power, wealth, and monstrosity. Surely, you knew that they thought of you man-girls as freaks of outlandish proportion."

Rowen thought back on the events that led to the end of his life and could only shake his head.

"So how do you think you did?" Delemor asked. "Keep in mind that the people's judgment has no bearing whatsoever here. Most often, it's quite the contrary."

"Well ... I think I was a good and loyal friend and advisor to Frank."

"Fair enough. If that means something to you, anyway."

"And I think I was a loyal and loving companion to Xera."

"Loyal?" Delemor said, raising a reptilian eyebrow.

"You know what I mean. I feel like I was there for her. Through no fault of her own – through fate, really – she was forced into that deplorable situation. She was abandoned. Isolated. Anyone would lose it. And I'm just really glad that I was able to be there to comfort her. To make her feel loved. And to make her feel needed."

With each visit to the chamber, Rowen's eyes seemed to adjust a little better to the light reflecting off the gold walls, silver adornments, and crystal chandeliers, as well as to the light emanating from behind Delemor. And as Rowen poured his heart out, he could swear that Delemor was tearing up. That he was actually touched by Rowen's sincere feelings for Xera. And moved by her plight.

Despite Delemor remaining stone-faced throughout, Rowen felt that his suspicion was confirmed when a fist-sized diamond tear fell from the corner of Delemor's eye, rolled down his snout, and landed on the table with a thud.

"You can keep that," Delemor said, indifferently. "Anything else?"

"Well … I guess I failed, but I always tried to think of commoners."

"Yeah, you definitely failed there. But I don't feel the need to dock you any points for that. Anything else?"

"Ummm … No, I think that's about it. I tried to be good … and loyal … and loving …and compassionate. And I think I did a pretty good job?"

"Ummm … I'd like to say that this is a tough decision, my little ball-less wonder, but I'm afraid it's not. However, since I really enjoyed those times that Xera molested you – it's not every day you get to see a woman try to force a man to finger bang her – I'm gonna give you another chance. Get outside and wash that nauseating stink off and we can chat again."

As the door swung open, cool mist again flooded the chamber and Rowen did what was fast becoming the walk of shame down to the bathing facilities where he again contemplated the bottles of shimmering liquid.

"I guess I'm supposed to use the chocolate-colored one this time?" Rowen called out.

"It's up to you." Delemor replied.

"May I ask what it is?"

"What do you think it is?"

"Ahhh … chocolate-scented shampoo?"

"Well, if that's what you think it is, then why are you asking me? Go ahead and use it already."

Rowen squirted a small blob of the gooey liquid onto the top of his head and was instantly overwhelmed by a revolting stench.

"What the heck is this?" he shrieked.

"Sheep shit," Delemor replied, flatly.

"Why is there a bottle of sheep shit at a bathing facility?"

"I think the better question is: Why did you just dump a pile of sheep shit on your head? And the answer is: Because you have horrible judgment. You should listen to me more. And right now, my advice is to use the crimson or cream-colored shampoo to wash that shit off your head."

Once Rowen had washed the unpleasantness off of his head and was basking in the transcendent tingling of the cream-colored shampoo, he noticed a curious sight on the third lowest pine cluster of the miniature evergreen tree.

A cartoonish gecko-like creature with no hind legs was using its forelegs to force-feed its tail into its mouth. Further, it was chomping down on the tail, chewing, and swallowing. Chomp-chomp. Chew-chew-chew. Swallow.

Mid-chew on its third bite, the creature realized that it was being watched. After calmly swallowing, it looked Rowen dead in the eye and smiled. "Stop staring at me!"

Rowen immediately averted his eyes, pulling the old I-wasn't-looking-at-you.-Why-would-I-be-looking-at-you,-jerk?-If-anything,-you-were-looking-at-me.-Asswipe! maneuver.

He had picked a poor place to avert his eyes to though, as he found himself staring at the chocolate-colored – well shit-colored – shampoo and reliving the recent traumatic event.

As he reflexively turned away from the shampoos, he was met with the pleasant sight of Aphrodite sauntering down the path, tray in hand.

Rowen's breath was again taken away by her flowing blond hair, voluptuous curves, and teardrop beauty mark.

She smiled seductively as she reached him. "Care for a drink?"

"Yes, please."

About halfway through the delightful beverage, Rowen recalled the curious gecko-like creature. "Is that gecko eating itself?" he asked.

"What gecko?"

"That one," Rowen replied, pointing at the now empty tree branch. "He was right there. Munching on his tail. It was queerest thing."

"If you stick around here long enough, you'll see more oddities than you can handle," Aphrodite replied. "Anyhow, care for a dip?"

"Yes, please."

Rowen waded into the soothingly warm water and as he began drifting along a current, he felt Aphrodite's hands on his shoulders. "Can you give me a piggy back ride?" she breathed into his ear.

"Yes, please."

Rowen almost fainted at the touch of Aphrodite's hands, so when he felt her supple breasts rubbing against his back, he almost imploded in ecstasy.

He was so spellbound that he almost failed to notice

another mortal pass by on an opposing current at less than an arm's length away.

"Was that Sera?" he blurted out when the encounter finally registered.

"I don't know," Aphrodite replied, dismissively. "Who's Sera?"

"She's the girl that I've been with in all three of my lives so far."

"Hm. Never heard of her."

"She was the love of my life each time."

"Interesting," Aphrodite replied, flatly. "When you were with her, did she always have a look on her face as if she were passing gas?"

"… No."

"Probably wasn't her then."

Despite Aphrodite's brush-off, Rowen couldn't help but feel that that was indeed Sera. And further, that she too was floating along a current with a light-emitting being. A God.

"Oh, look," Aphrodite abruptly called out. "There's Zeus—God of the Sky, Lightning, and Non-Consensual Sex."

"Yikes," Rowen gasped. He looked up to find that they were approaching a small, circular island of pristine sand. In the middle, hovering over a giant crystal orb, was Zeus.

He looked like your everyday human grandpa, except that his muscles were absolutely ripped and he somehow managed to give off vibes of both magnificence and homelessness.

As Rowen walked up the beach, the picture came further into focus. Zeus had a full head of long, wavy white hair, but his face was clean-shaven. His piercing gold eyes were focused to the point of obsession on a vision inside the orb and he was licking his thick lips, slobbering all over the place.

"Hi, Zeus," Aphrodite said when it was clear that he wasn't going to notice their arrival. "This is Rowen."

Zeus looked up, smiling excitedly.

Rowen couldn't help but smile back at the exuberant God whose nose bulged as if it had been broken several times and whose smile revealed a large gap between his front teeth.

"Hi, Rowen," Zeus said. His voice was enthusiastically high. "I'm Zeus, son of Kronos—God of Ambition, Contradiction, and Eating Newborn Babies."

"Eating newborn babies?!" Rowen repeated, incredulously.

"Yeah, he ate all my older brothers and sisters. He thought he ate me too, but it turned out to be a rock in a blanket."

"He thought you were a rock in a blanket?"

"Yeah, my mother's very clever. After she gave birth to me, but before my father ate me, she wrapped a rock in a blanket and was like, 'Here's your newborn son to eat.' So he swallowed the rock down, blanket and all … you know, because he thought it was me. So he kinda presides over the whole baby-eating territory."

"…"

"Anyway, you came at a great time." Zeus pointed to the vision in the orb. "Check this out."

Rowen peered into the globe and saw a beautiful handmaiden attending an even more beautiful woman of high-standing.

"Isn't she a spectacle," Zeus said, enchanted. "Look at those long legs, that porcelain skin, and those seductive dark eyes. Not only is she the most beautiful princess of her time, but she's also the most virtuous and intelligent."

"Yeah, she's a vision of perfection."

"You wanna go down there, morph into a swan or bull or something, and rape 'em? You can have the handmaiden."

"… Ummm … I'm not really sure about that."

"C'mon, it'll be fun. Look how hot they are."

"I'm not sure raping them is the right thing to do."

"Don't be such a wet blanket."

"… But it doesn't even make sense. Why would you change into an animal to have your way with her?"

Zeus was stunned at the absurdity of the question. "What are you talkin' about?! If I went down there as Me, I'd never even get near her. Mortals aren't nearly as dumb as you'd think. They're wise to Our antics so you've gotta trick 'em."

"But as an animal?"

"Yeah, women love animals. They're all, 'Oh, look at this beautiful swan, lemme cuddle up with it.' Or, 'Oh, look how handsome this bull is, lemme get with it.'"

"Why don't you just take the form of her boyfriend or husband or whatever. Then you wouldn't even have to rape her. You could just have sex with her like a normal couple. She'd never even know."

Zeus' jaw dropped at this universe-shattering concept. "Holy Crap!" he cried, "You're a genius! Thanks, bud. Thanks!"

And with that, Zeus plunged head first into the orb, a surreal hum ringing out as he was sucked in.

"Rowen!" Delemor roared. "Enough ogling the talent. It's time to get down to business."

Rowen waded back into the soothing water, drifted to shore, and scrambled up the path to Delemor's chamber where he once again sat reverentially on his heels across from the awe-inspiring Delemor, perched high on his throne.

"So," Delemor said. "What can I do for you this time?"

Relatively used to the process, Rowen had been considering his last life while drifting along the current. "Well, to be honest, the way my last life ended is really eating at me."

"You didn't like being torn apart limb from limb?"

"No. It's not sitting well with me."

"So you'd rather be on the limb-tearing side then, eh?"

"No, not really. It would be great if there were no mobs ripping bodies apart at all."

Delemor snorted. "Sounds boring. But go on."

"I think I'd really like it if the people didn't hate me. If possible, I'd like to be a man of the people. ... Maybe even something like a folk hero."

"A folk hero?!"

"Yeah, where I'm able to do something great that the people see as an inspiration and tell tales and sing songs of."

"Wow. That is asking a lot. ... But since I'm in such a generous mood today, I think I can arrange it."

"Great!"

"How does being a hero in an epic civil war that changes the course of your country forever sound?"

"Outstanding!"

"However, during that war, you meet your demise. And it'll be pretty gory."

"Less outstanding..."

"But you'll be losing your life for your people, and songs will indeed be sung in your honor."

"Well, if the people are gonna love me..."

"But I'm gonna have to insist that you'll be cowardly."

"Why would the people love a coward?"

"I didn't say coward, I said cowardly. Listen carefully, you filthy crotchmite!"

"I'm sorry. But why would people love someone who's cowardly?"

Delemor's serpent tail emerged from underneath the table, hissing.

"Leave the minutiae to me, dingle. People don't need a hero to actually be heroic. Everything gets fudged with time. If you've lived a life that can be molded to someone's liking, they will sculpt you into a legend. Now do you want to be a folk hero or not?"

"I'm sorry. Yes. Yes, I do."

"Now since you've wasted my time, there will be pants pissing involved."

"I'm sorry?"

"Shut it. This is non-negotiable. You've pissed me off. As a result, your pants will be pissed. Anything else, or are you ready to go?"

"Ummmmm…"

"Women and looks, you mental midget."

"Ummmmm. I guess I'd like to have a beautiful girl and be pretty good-looking, but since you're allowing me to become a folk hero, I will humbly leave it up to you."

"Wow. You are finally getting it. Way to use all three of those limp neurons barely firing in your brain. You've earned a girl who will like you more than you could possibly want."

"Wonderful."

"As well as a torso to kill for."

"A torso to kill for?"

"Yeah, you will not be lacking in the torso department. Now enough of this, these negotiations are over! Meng Po! Your drink please!"

The sweet, hunch-backed Meng Po once again emerged with her concoction for Rowen.

As he downed the bitter beverage, she grabbed him by the elbow. "Seein' is believin' if you believin' what you seein'," she sung out animatedly as she helped him to his feet. "You can bet your momma on that!"

As the sweet old deity giggled, Rowen staggered and everything faded to black.

AIZU, JAPAN

MID-19ᵀᴴ CENTURY AD

It is common knowledge that your whole life flashes before your eyes when you are on the verge of death. What Rowen discovered at the tender age of 14 though, is that the exact same thing happens when you try to slice your best friend's head off with a samurai sword.

***

In the first scene that flashed by, Rowen was just three years old. He was holding a wooden sword known as a *shinai* over his head with both hands.

"Protect …" his father called out to him.

"Aizu!" Rowen replied, swinging the *shinai* down in front of him as if slicing an enemy in two.

His father smiled as young Rowen glared at the dead body of his imaginary foe.

As long as he could remember, there was nothing Rowen wanted more than to be like his father, who was as intimidating as he was kind. As usual, he was dressed in a long black robe of stiff silk with a matching overcoat bearing the Aizu crest. The top of his head was shaved clean and the hair from the sides and back, which he had grown out, was oiled and folded into a topknot on the crown of his head.

He was a high-ranking samurai and the family was privileged enough to have a nice plot of land with a *koi* pond and a two-story wooden house. The gabled roof was made of black *kawara* tiles and decorated with a pair of golden *shachihoko* ornaments at each end.

NEGOTIATIONS WITH GOD

While the *shachihoko*, a creature having the body of a fish and the head of a lion, offers protection and well-being, the deity whose patronage Rowen's family sought most was Ebisu—God of Good Fortune, Mucousy Foods, and Imported Beers That Aren't Really All That Good But Sell Well Because They're Exotic.

Behind his three-year-old warrior-in-training self, Rowen could see his family's statue of Ebisu on an altar built into the wall. In front of the pot-bellied deity with his huge smile and cartoonishly chubby earlobes was the daily offering of rice topped with *natto* (i.e., mucousy fermented beans), and a glass full of *sake*.

"Protect…" his father called out again.

"Tono!" Rowen cried, referring to the chief of Aizu, as he stamped his front foot down on the *tatami* floor while slicing another imaginary enemy in half.

***

In the next scene that flashed by, Rowen saw his eight-year-old self walking nervously down the dirt road in between his house and that of his next-door neighbor and best friend, Sean.

The two were playing hide-and-seek and as usual Sean was hiding behind a trio of Jizo statues guarding the roadway.

Sean's father was also a high-ranking samurai and the two boys were both being groomed to take up the family trade. They shared similar interests and had almost identical personalities except for one important trait. Courage.

Sean didn't seem to have a fear in the world whereas Rowen had his weaknesses and try as he might to hide them, Sean knew them all.

One of them was Jizo. In particular, the trio of Jizo statues between their homes. The stone statues were about the same height as the boys and looked like monks wearing

83

red bibs and red berets. However, time and weather had not been kind to them and all three were faceless. As such, they never failed to send a shiver down Rowen's spine.

"Okay, I found you," Rowen shouted out as he approached the statues, making a concerted effort to avert his eyes.

As his call went unanswered, Rowen was forced to take a few steps into the woods so that he could peer behind the frightful figures. As expected, Sean was crouching behind them with a gigantic shit-eating grin.

"Found you," Rowen repeated, anxious to end the game.

"You're such a scaredy-cat," Sean teased.

"I'm not afraid of them, they just give me the heebie-jeebies."

"Why? They're not bad guys, they're good guys."

"Why do you think they're good guys?"

"Because Jizo is a good God. He's the protector of babies and anyone vulnerable."

"You're crazy. He doesn't help babies, he eats them."

"No he doesn't, he protects them."

"Then why does he wear that creepy red bib?"

"Father says it's so that the babies he saves can eat in the next life."

"No, no. I don't think so. People don't wear bibs when they're gonna help someone eat. People wear bibs when they're gonna eat. Jizo definitely eats babies."

"Quit being such a scaredy-cat."

"I'm not scared, I just don't like them."

"Well if you're not scared, then I dare you to touch one."

"..."

"I double-dog dare you ... Samurai"

"..."

Rowen's lip started to quiver as Sean eyed him with wicked delight. It didn't take much to get to Rowen. All you had to do was question his courage and imply that he didn't have what it takes to become a samurai.

Fortunately, the test of courage was interrupted.

Unfortunately, it was interrupted by the one person in the world that creeped Rowen out more than the faceless Jizo statues. Sean's little sister, Fran.

"Can I play, too?"

To Rowen, the sound of her voice was like fingernails down a chalkboard. He couldn't stand her. Her face always seemed to be either covered in dirt or boogers, she smelled funny, she was always trying to touch him, and she never stopped pestering them with questions.

"No." Sean replied, dismissively.

"Why not?"

"No girls allowed," Sean said. "And it's time for training anyway."

"Why?"

"Because we need to train to become samurai."

"Why?"

"Because we need to protect Aizu."

"From who?"

"From enemies."

Sean and Rowen turned their backs on Fran and began walking back to Sean's home.

"Okay, fine. You go train. I'm going to town get some rice cakes. Bye byyyyyyyyyyye, Rowen!"

***

Next, a year later, Rowen saw himself in the front row of a group of samurai's children practicing *kendo*, the art of swordsmanship, at the local *dojo*.

The *sensei* was in the corner while young Sean led the session.

"Protect ..." Sean called out.

"Aizu!" the class responded, swinging their *shinai* down

and slicing their imaginary foes in half.

"That's right," the *sensei* said, sternly. "There is nothing in this world that is more noble, more righteous, or more heroic than protecting our beloved homeland."

"Obey …" Sean said.

"Superiors," the class responded, returning their *shinai* to attack position above their heads.

"That's right," the *sensei* said, stone-faced. "You must never disobey an order from a superior!"

"Protect …" Sean cried again.

"*Tono*," the class replied in unison, again striking imaginary death blows.

"That's right," the *sensei* said. "You must do anything and everything to protect our glorious leader."

"Obey …" Sean repeated.

"Superiors!"

"That's right. You must never disobey an order from a superior!"

"Kill …" Sean prompted.

"The Enemy!"

"That's right. Live with honor and glory! Fight with honor and glory! Die with honor and glory!"

***

On the way home from a particularly vigorous session, Sean once again playfully teased Rowen about his fear of the Jizo statues.

"Rowen, you show great spirit at the *dojo*, but I can't help but wonder if someone who's afraid of a stone statue will be able to fight in an actual battle."

"You know I will fight with honor and glory."

"Well if that's so, how about you show that spirit against Jizo?"

Rowen glared at Sean. "Fine. I'll touch one of the statues."

"Touch?" Sean repeated, his lip curling. "If you're really not afraid, how about you pee on one?"

"Pee on one?!" Rowen said in utter disbelief.

"That's right. I double-dog dare you ... Samurai."

Rowen had had it. He walked right up to the middle statue, dropped trou, and peed all over its faceless face.

What young 9-year-old Rowen and still pretty young 14-year-old Rowen watching his life flash before his eyes were completely unaware of was that at this very moment, Jizo, watching from Verixion, was incensed. "Nobody but nobody pees on the Jizo!" he yelled to no one in particular.

While even some Gods may consider Jizo's reaction extreme, Rowen's stream of pee set in motion a civil war in Japan that would exterminate every last member of the Aizu clan and change the way of life that the Japanese people had lived up until then.

**

The next scene that flashed by was that of a randy rite of passage. One that most boys and girls eagerly await and never forget. His first kiss.

While it is true that Rowen would never forget it, it wasn't due to lack of effort.

Rowen and Sean were horsing around with their *shinai* on Rowen's veranda while Fran, in her usual role as third wheel, was playing with a couple of dolls nearby.

Sean knocked Rowen's *shinai* out of his hands, sending it spinning across the veranda until it finally came to a stop just inches from Fran. The tip of the wooden sword was pointing right at her.

For reasons known only to Fran, her eyes lit up like she had just hit the lottery.

Rowen just shook his head at another bizarre Fran reaction, but as he bent down to pick up the *shinai*, she planted a huge wet one right on his lips.

Making matters worse, Rowen's mother happened to witness the incident and never let him hear the end of it.

She gushed on and on about what a cute couple they were gonna make, what a beautiful bride Fran was gonna be, and how lovely it would be when they were married and had a family of their own.

The first time Rowen's mother teased him about it, he felt the urge to end everything. Each time thereafter, that urge grew stronger and stronger.

***

The next scene that flashed through Rowen's mind was of a heart-wrenching goodbye.

The clans of Japan had recently fractured into two contingents.

One side was loyal to the Tokugawa shogunate, the feudal military government that had presided over a proud, prosperous, and peaceful Japan for the last two plus centuries. They valued their beautiful traditional way of life and refused to let foreign barbarians force their way into the country and destroy Japanese culture.

The other side was bent on restoring political power to the emperor of Japan and opening the country to the West.

The Aizu were members of the Northern Alliance who of course remained loyal to the shogunate. They were proud to do their part to preserve their beloved culture.

Rowen saw his 12-year-old self standing outside his home watching as his father, dressed in his finest samurai robes, emerged from their home. He had a curved, single-edge sword known as a *katana* strapped to his belt and was holding another in his outstretched arms.

"Aizu is in your hands now, son," he said, entrusting the shining sword to Rowen. "I have watched you grow and train, and I could not be more proud."

Tears welled up in Rowen's eyes, but he held them back

with all his might.

"With a little more time, you too will be a full-fledged samurai and I want you to have this so that you too may defend our home and our country with great honor and glory."

A wave of emotion crashed through Rowen's every fiber. He felt a deep sense of pride as he accepted the *katana* as well as a deep sense of sadness knowing that his father was leaving, possibly for good.

"When the time comes, you must fight bravely, and if necessary, lay down your life. There are things much more important than self, and there is nothing more admirable than fighting with honor and glory for your country, for Tono, and for your family."

Rowen was unable to utter even a single word in reply as he continued fighting back the tears.

His father, of course, sensed this and gave him a firm yet loving pat on the shoulder. "Goodbye, son."

Rowen then watched his father march, with his head held high, down the entrance path, through the front gate, and off to fight for their homeland.

As his mother embraced him from behind, a torrent of tears rushed down Rowen's cheeks.

***

In the next scene that flashed by, much like his father did two years prior, Rowen was marching out of town for battle.

The enemy was closing in and it was decided that the last lines of defense must go out to meet them.

Rowen was in a group of 20 sons of samurai known as the White Tiger Brigade. They were all supposedly 16 years old or over, but as Rowen had trained with them at the *dojo* for as long as he could remember, he knew that like him, many were just 14 or 15.

Nevertheless, they were steely-eyed and kept their composure as they paraded down the main street while the women and children shouted words of encouragement.

Rowen could not help but feel afraid of what lay ahead, but he also felt a strong sense of pride as he gripped his *katana* tightly and smiled at Sean marching next to him. They had shaved the tops of their heads together that morning, and for the first time sported budding topknots above their baby faces.

In front of the White Tiger Brigade marched the other last line of defense, the Black Tortoise Brigade, which was comprised of Aizu's last remaining adult males. Rowen and his cohorts had dubbed them the Gray Geezer Brigade because most of them were senior citizens in their 60s and 70s whose samurai hairstyles consisted of a few wisps of gray hair flapping in the wind on their naturally bald heads.

Nevertheless, both battalions marched with pride on their way to meet the oncoming enemy.

Like their sons and fathers, the women of Aizu maintained stoic faces as they cheered on Aizu's last hope.

"Fight with honor and glory," they cried. "There is nothing more heroic than dying for your country!"

It was only Fran who either was unable to put on a brave face or just didn't want to.

"Come home safe, Sean!" she screamed, tears streaming down her face. "You too, Rowen! I don't care what this is all about, the only thing that matters is that you two come back to us in one piece!"

***

In the next scene that flashed before Rowen's eyes, it was dusk. He saw himself crouched next to Sean behind some shrubs in a sparsely wooded area between Aizu and Lake Sanban.

They could see the enemy on the other side of a

clearing. At the forefront of their troops was a battalion of fearsome soldiers in full body armor who were sporting long, shaggy wigs of polar bear hair dyed blood red.

Rowen pissed his pants on sight.

"Is there a stream or something around here?" Sean asked.

"Huh?" Rowen replied, feigning ignorance.

"I swear I just heard the trickling sound of a stream or something."

"I have no idea what you're talking about. I didn't hear nothing. Anyway, those bastards outnumber us by like three to one. What are we gonna do?"

No sooner did the words leave Rowen's mouth than did the Gray Geezer Brigade commence the attack, beginning a brief scuffle that would become known as the Battle of Aidayua.

Screams of "Protect Aizu!!!", "Protect *Tono*!!!", and "Die you Motherfuckers!!!" filled the air as senior citizens charged, swords held high above their heads.

Sean and the rest of the White Tiger Brigade quickly followed suit.

Reluctantly, Rowen drew his beloved *katana* from its sheath, lifted it with both hands above his head, and charged with honor and glory.

Before they were even halfway to the enemy, the frightful blood-haired soldiers had drawn rifles and were firing upon them.

While one would have thought that Rowen's bladder was running on empty after voiding at the sight of the fearsome enemy, a further torrent of urine ran down his leg at the sound of gunfire. Rowen had never even seen a rifle let alone been fired upon.

"Run Away!!!" a number of Aizu fighters screamed as their comrades began to fall like ducks in a row.

Amid the chaos, Rowen did his best to follow Sean and the rest of the White Tiger Brigade as they fled back into the woods and randomly scrambled up a winding path toward Iimori Hill.

***

It was here that Ebisu intervened.

In the form of a pot-bellied bunny with golden fur and floppy ears, the benevolent God led the White Tiger Brigade to an irrigation tunnel near the summit of Iimori Hill.

To the boys' delight, not too far from the opening was a stockpile of rice, *natto*, and *sake*.

As such, they decided to fill their bellies, drown their defeat in booze, and sleep the night away with dreams of a more fruitful tomorrow.

***

The last scene to flash through Rowen's mind led him back to the present.

The boys rose at dawn, exited the tunnel, and found themselves on what appeared to be hallowed ground as a little wooden shrine and a trio of Jizo statues stood on a small clearing overlooking Aizu.

To their horror, in the distance they could see their beloved hometown ablaze.

Fire was ravaging the local shops and rowhouses, rifle shots rang out, and worst of all, the castle, which was the heart and soul of the town, was engulfed in ominous black smoke.

The boys gasped at the harrowing sight. "Our beloved Aizu is on fire!" one cried.

Along with the overwhelming feelings of grief and despondence, Sean and Rowen were overcome with rage.

Rage at themselves for their impotence.

Rage at the enemy for destroying everything that they

loved.

And rage at the Universe for allowing such a tragedy to occur.

"Fuck you, Jizo!" Sean screamed, giving the finger to the trio of Jizo statues.

As if on cue, Sean and Rowen marched over to the Jizo statues, dropped trou, and expressed their indignation and despair by soaking the treasonous statues in powerful torrents of urine.

"You're supposed to protect us!" Sean wailed.

"How dare you allow our innocent families to be slaughtered!" Rowen roared. "I hate you!"

After the boys had emptied their bladders and said their peace, the White Tiger Brigade discussed in desperation what they should do.

"Our castle is burning down," one of them sobbed. "The town, too."

"This is the end," another lamented. "The end of our castle. The end of Aizu. The end of us."

"Rather than die by the hands of our enemy, let's pray to the castle and end our lives with honor."

It didn't take long for everyone to agree and after holding hands and reciting a solemn Aizu prayer, the boys unsheathed their *katana* and daggers.

"Rowen," Sean pleaded. "I can't do it. I need you to do it for me."

"What?!" Rowen replied in disbelief.

"I can't do it, Rowen! I need your help." Sean forced his *katana* into Rowen's hands and knelt down before him.

Rowen couldn't do anything but stare at the sword in shock.

"Rowen, I need you to do this for me. You have to be brave and do me this honor."

Rowen continued to stare at the *katana*, dumbstruck.

A wave of calm washed over Sean and he gave Rowen a knowing smirk. "I double dog dare you … Samurai."

Rowen finally looked at his friend, tears welling in his eyes.

"Do it, Rowen! Please!!! Do it for me! DO IT!!!!!"

Rowen bit his lip, lifted Sean's *katana* over his head, and as he swung it down with all his might, his own life flashed before his eyes.

***

At the precise moment that Rowen began his downswing, a gust of wind blown by Jizo altered the strike ever so slightly such that the sword was driven deep into Sean's shoulder blade.

Falling back on his heels in great pain, but not mortally wounded, Sean glared at Rowen in exasperation. "Owwww, dude. What the fuck?!"

Jizo, giggling from near the wooden shrine, was pleased.

A wave of panic washed over Rowen and without thinking he regripped the *katana*, lifted it high above his head once again, and swung it down with all his might. This time, it was a clean strike.

Rowen averted his eyes as blood gushed from Sean's throat and his life quickly left him.

Weeping violently, Rowen grabbed a dagger, knelt down next to his fallen comrade, and plunged it deep into his abdomen.

As he slumped to the ground, everything faded to black, until he finally saw the light.

VERIXION IV

"Is the people's champ finally back with us?" Delemor boomed as Rowen slowly came to on the floor of the resplendent chamber.

Through the mist, he could see the crocodile-faced Delemor smirking at him.

"What happened?" Rowen asked.

"You did it, buddy. You're a folk hero!"

"Really?"

"Yeah. One of your tiggers survived that adorable mass suicide and told the world about your honorable demise. Way to not give in to the enemy and die with pride. Fantastic!"

Rowen couldn't tell whether Delemor was being sarcastic, but decided to take his words at face value. "Wow. I guess that's great."

"Without a doubt. Your story even touched some very impressive future world leaders like Mussolini."

"Who?"

"Never mind. Suffice it to say, your tale will be told in perpetuity."

"Awesome."

"Yeah. And you know what's even better? You kids were wrong."

"Wrong?"

"Yeah. The castle wasn't even on fire."

"What? That's impossible. It was covered in smoke."

"Yup. Smoke from nearby rowhouses that actually were on fire. Your precious *Tono* was alive and kicking in that phat hizzy."

"Phat hizzy?"

"The castle, buddy. Try to stick with me. He was in the castle and they both were doing fine. Sure, he eventually surrendered, but both made it through with hardly a scratch on 'em."

"Well ... I guess that's good, right?"

"Yeah, it added a little somethin' somethin'. But you know what was really neat?"

"What?"

"Your moms all did the same thing."

"What do you mean?"

"What do you think I mean, brain fart? I mean your moms all did the same thing. They gathered the little ones and rather than fall into enemy hands, everyone ritually disemboweled themselves. Well, I mean, first the moms ritually disemboweled the young ones – it would be too over the top if the little tykes were able to do it – but after that, the moms all ritually disemboweled themselves. Pretty great, right?"

"..."

"And the kicker is, no one's ever gonna tell their tale. I'm not sure whether it's not interesting enough or it's kind of a bummer or what, but the bottom line is, you guys are the only ones going down in history. They'll be singing the praises of the White Tiger Brigade, and only the White Tiger Brigade, forever. Pretty sweet, huh?"

"... That doesn't sound very good."

"Yeah. That's why it's great. And you know what's even neater?"

"... I don't really like where this is go—"

Before Rowen could even finish his sentence, Delemor's serpent tail had its fangs deep into Rowen's thigh. "Owwww!!!"

"How dare you not like where this is going!" Delemor roared, letting the serpent hold its bite a couple beats before slithering back under the table. "Now pipe down while I finish telling you the something that's even neater."

"I'm sorry."

"Zip it!"

Rowen nodded.

"There was absolutely no point to the entire episode. It occurred two months after the emperor decreed the foundational policy of the new government in Tokyo."

"Huh?"

"The outcome had already been decided. The war was over. You and your tigger buddies killed yourselves for nothing."

"…"

"Rich, right?"

"…"

"But don't be so down, little buddy. You're all still folk heroes. You and your tigger cohorts, that is."

"I … uhhhh … ummmm …"

"C'mon, don't beat yourself up. You'll be happy to hear that you've earned another chance. Sure, you had the personality and intelligence of a slightly retarded lemming, and for most of your life you were about as entertaining as a tree, but you scored some points by going out in that blaze of glory. With bonus points for the pointlessness. Now get outside and wash that revolting stink off so we can chat about your next shot."

The cool mist provided a modicum of relief as Rowen did the walk of shame down to the bathing facilities.

The cream-colored shampoo provided further comfort as Rowen felt near instant rejuvenation upon rubbing it into his scalp.

As he basked in the transcendent tingling, he noticed a tiny brown bear reclining on the middle pine cluster of the miniature evergreen tree.

While tiny, the jovial-looking creature was immensely fat and proudly displayed his cleanly shaven chest as he surveyed the area with bloodshot eyes, occasionally taking a swig from a ceramic jug that was close to twice its size.

Without warning, a mob of worker bees managing to collectively manipulate a club hammer, flew directly above the miniature bear and pounded his entire body with one sharp stroke.

Rowen's eyes almost popped out of his head as he watched the poor creature explode into a million pieces and the bees flew away as suddenly as they had come.

Dumbstruck, he sat there motionless until he heard the sultry voice of Aphrodite. "Care for a drink?"

"Yes, please," he replied, the bizarre scene already an afterthought.

"I've got some other things to attend to," Aphrodite said as Rowen savored the delectable beverage. "But I'm sure I'll see you again soon in some form or other. Feel free to have a dip by yourself when you finish washing."

Rowen couldn't help but ogle Aphrodite's curves as she walked back up the path and disappeared out of view.

After draining the remainder of the divine concoction, Rowen waded into the soothing water and drifted away on a tranquil current.

Before long, he came upon the same island as last time and again saw Zeus drooling all over the orb in the center.

"Hi Zeus," Rowen called as he walked up the beach.

"Rowen!" Zeus replied, smiling excitedly. "You are a Godsend. Your rape strategy could not have gone any better!"

"..."

"I morphed into that fair wench's husband and made sweet, resistance-less love to her all day and all night."

"Wow. Well, I guess it's good that she didn't feel like she was being raped ..."

"Yeah, why not. Anyhoo, she even bore me a son. He's a wonderful boy. Cunning and powerful. The little dude killed two poisonous serpents at the tender age of two. The wife's a little pissed about it, though. In fact, she's the one who sent them."

"Your wife sent snakes to kill a 2-year-old?"

"Yeah. Oh shit, here she comes now. Her name's Isis— Goddess of Revenge, Forgiveness, and Unfortunate

Homonyms Such As Those That Make You Sound Like A Terrorist. She's a total nightmare. I suggest you get the fuck outta here as quickly as possible."

"But she's your wife. Are you saying that you don't like her?"

Zeus snort-laughed. "Wow, you haven't been around long have you, boy?"

"But then why did you marry her?"

"Because I'm a face man. And she had the prettiest face out of all my sisters."

"Your sisters?!"

"Sorry, kid. Can't get into it now. Toodles."

Zeus disappeared in a flash as Isis floated toward the island and ... well ... beached herself.

Rowen's jaw dropped as he took in the sight.

Isis' head was that of one of the most beautiful women he had ever seen. Long, lustrous auburn hair, dazzling sapphire blue eyes with thick, dark lashes, and glowing, rose-colored cheeks.

The rest, however, was a completely different story. She had the body of a manatee, the dorsal fin of a shark, and the skinny legs of a feeble goat.

Rowen couldn't help but stare as she laboriously pulled herself onto the beach before slumping over into what Rowen imagined was her sun tanning position.

Once settled, she turned to Rowen and gave him a listen-and-obey-you-little-shit look. "Don't ever talk to Zeus again."

"Rowen!" Delemor boomed. "How dare you harass a divinity, you impudent puke! Get back in here so we can get down to business."

"Goodbye, ma'am," Rowen said, nervously. "I mean, goodbye Mrs. Isis. I mean, Goddess Isis." Rowen bowed profusely as he backed into the water. "I'm very very sorry."

After drifting to shore and scrambling back up to the chamber, he once again sat reverentially on his heels across from Delemor, seated high on his throne.

"What can I do for you this time?"

"I'm honestly kind of at a loss. I keep trying to live good lives, but I don't seem to be making any progress."

"You've got that right."

"So I'm not really sure what I should do."

"Right again. How's about we play a little game. I say a word and you say the first thing that pops into your teeny tiny little brain."

"… Okay."

"Aphrodite."

"Gorgeous."

"Boobs."

"Delightful."

"Sex."

"Yes, please."

"I think we're onto something. Even your pee brain must see it by now."

"I … I'd like to become an adult."

"Done."

"And … I'd like to try sex."

"Hell yeah, little buddy. I think you'll even like it."

"And … if possible, I'd like to enjoy being an adult."

"I like the sound of that. How so?"

"I … I guess I'd like to be popular with the ladies. Naturally."

"A ladies man, eh? I'm in a generous mood today, and if little Rowen wants some charm and confidence, how's about we give little Rowen some charm and confidence. Anything else?"

"Well, I don't know if it's much different, but I'd like to enjoy adult life, adult parties."

"Gotcha. Kinky orgies with gorgeous co-eds on ecstasy fisting you. Done and done."

"No, no. I don't mean that. Just partying. Like at bars and stuff."

"Oh, okay. I hear you. Just your average partying with booze, bitches, and music, eh?"

"Well, I'm not sure I'd put it like that, but yeah. Just normal adult partying."

"Sure. I can't see how that could go wrong. Done and done. Anything else?"

"Well … if possible, maybe I could have a connection to Verixion?"

"A what?! A 'connection'?! What do you mean by 'connection'?"

"Maybe I could call on the Gods every once in a while if I need some help."

"You can always call on the Gods every once in a while if you need some help. Whether we answer or not, that's a different story."

"Well … Maybe you could answer?"

"I'm afraid that will depend on you, your situation, and whatever mood we're in that day."

"So, …"

Before Rowen could even begin his response, Delemor's serpent tail was hissing in his face.

"Okay, understood. Hopefully, I can do the right things to merit an answer."

"Good luck with that. But back to the topic at hand. While I am in a generous mood today, you're asking to be a rock star with special powers to channel the Gods, so I'm gonna need some serious concessions in return."

"…"

"Let's move on to your physical traits. You're gonna be wall-eyed."

"What's that?"

"It's like cross-eyed, but the opposite. One of your eyes is always gonna be looking out."

"Can you still see okay like that?"

"I think so. To be honest, I'm not sure. But you're gonna be partying so hard you're not gonna care."

"..."

"And you're gonna be exceedingly tall and lanky."

"Exceedingly? Like, I'm gonna stick out?"

"Hell yeah, you're gonna stick out. That's what you want, right? Popularity? To go along with that monster personality, you're gonna have to accept the monstrous body that goes along with it."

"..."

"And how's about we throw in a busted, bulbous nose for kicks?"

"But I thought I was gonna be a ladies..." Rowen cut himself off sensing that a snake bite was imminent if he dared question Delemor.

"What's that?" the reptilian deity bated.

"Nothing. Perhaps it's time for Mrs. Po's drink?" Rowen asked, hopefully.

"Yeah, I guess that's enough. You're lucky you caught me in such a good mood today. The cards are really stacked in your favor this time. Meng Po! Your concoction please!"

As usual, Rowen received the bitter drink from the darling old hunchback and dutifully dug in.

Meng Po hovered over him as he drank. "Be careful what you wish for, Rowen," she said. "Cause you just might get it." She punctuated her warning with ominous cackling.

For what seemed like the first time, Rowen felt like he might be able to grasp what Meng Po was getting at, and as a wave of understanding began to wash over his face, Meng Po leaned in close, removed her coke-bottle glasses, and looked Rowen dead in the eye.

He was taken aback not only by her seriousness, but also by the fact that one of her eyes was neon pink, and the other was made of glass and filled with swirling white smoke.

"Seriously, Rowen," she said. "Don't be wishing for no gonorrhea of the throat."

As everything went black, Rowen once again heard the

maniacal laughter of the sweet old deity.

ST. PETERSBURG, RUSSIA

LATE 19TH CENTURY AD

The day that Nicholas II and his wife Alexandra, commonly known as Sandra, were crowned Tsar and Tsarina of Russia was at once glorious and tragic.

Glorious not only because of the pomp and circumstance of a royal wedding, but because the young emperor and empress were truly in love.

Tragic because during the celebration, when rumor spread that there was not enough beer and pretzels for all the commoners outside the banquet hall, a stampede ensued and 1,368 people were trampled to death.

Many saw this as an omen of things to come.

Some said it was a premonition of the fall of the royal family.

Others said it was a premonition of the fall of Russia herself.

But most just viewed it as a really crappy day.

***

Grigori Rasputin, who would go on to be known as the Mad Monk, the Holy Devil, and the Miracle-Working MaleWhore, but in his day went by the nickname Rowen, was born to a peasant family in a remote Siberian village.

Growing up, he had always had a keen interest in three particular subjects: Morals, the supernatural, and vodka.

Morals because the principles behind right and wrong seemed so subjective and malleable. So debatable. And thus, so intriguing.

The supernatural because he had always felt the

presence of, and a connection with, the many deities inhabiting this world.

And vodka because it makes everything more fun and getting what you want a lot easier.

As a young man, Rowen set out on his first pilgrimage to the Holy Monastery of Abalak where he spent nearly three years learning to read and write, as well as studying sacred text, prayer, and the monastic lifestyle.

While he enjoyed learning contemporary religious and spiritual thought, he found the monastic life to be too restrictive and dogmatic, and was put off by the habit of certain monks to engage in extracurricular activities among themselves.

He decided to become a wandering monk and it was on this second pilgrimage that he began tapping into his mysterious power of healing.

At the third holy site that he visited, he came across a young man and his father as they were being consoled by a priest.

"I'm very sorry, my sons," the priest said. "God works in mysterious ways."

"But there must be something we can do," the young man pleaded.

"You have done everything there is to do," the priest answered as soothingly as possible. "You have consulted all the doctors, tried all the medications, and most importantly, you have come to us. We will pray for your mother."

"And all we can do is pray, too?" the father said in desperation.

"Yes. It's in God's hands now."

Rowen took a swig of vodka from his flask and staggered over to the group. "What's the trouble here?"

The three men looked up at him in surprise. Rowen made quite the figure. He was a head taller than all of them, wore a long, greasy black robe, and had a long disheveled black beard to match his long, disheveled black hair.

"It's his wife," the priest said, patting the father on his shoulder. "It appears that God will be welcoming her into Heaven soon."

Rowen glared at the priest, sizing him up. "Hooey," he said, waving his hand in the priest's face and turning to the young man and father. "Take me to this woman. I will fix her."

At first, the men were taken aback, but having no other alternative, they quickly decided to lead Rowen back to their home.

"I'm not sure whether this man is a healer or a hobo," the young man whispered to his father. "But there's something in his eyes."

"Is there anything we can get you?" the father asked as he ushered Rowen into their old wooden house.

"Vodka," Rowen replied.

Without hesitation, the young man brought him a glassful.

"Where is she?" Rowen blurted out.

"Upstairs," the father replied, leading the way to the master bedroom where his wife lay in bed, her unblinking eyes glued to the ceiling, her hair damp, and her cheeks glistening with sweat.

Rowen stood over the bed and appraised her condition.

The woman continued to stare at the ceiling, apparently unaware that anyone had entered the room.

Rowen turned to the young man and father. "I will take the sickness from her."

He then turned back to the woman, held the glass of vodka to his chest, and mumbled the following in a language that clearly was not Russian. "Great God, Dionysus, thank you for this drink. I receive it in your honor. Please heal this woman so that we may drink and sing and drink and dance in your honor and glory. Praise be to you."

Rowen then downed the vodka, dropped the empty

glass on the floor, and leaned over the woman.

As he gazed fixedly into her vacant eyes, he put one hand on her forehead and the other on one of her boobs.

Suddenly, the woman seemed to snap back to life and she locked eyes with Rowen. Her head and torso shook, and her eyes began to twitch. An expression came over her that was pure fear.

At the precise moment that she opened her mouth to let out a blood-curdling scream, Dionysus—God of Mischief, the Drink, and One-Night Stands—sucked the illness clean out of her.

As Rowen lifted his hands from her, a look of relief washed over the woman's face and she gave him a big smile before conking out.

Rowen turned to the men. "She will be fit as a horse come morning."

"It's a miracle!" the father cried out, rushing over to his wife's side, falling to his knees, and clutching her hand to his cheek.

"How can we ever thank you?!" the young man asked.

"Vodka."

***

Rowen's supernatural relationship with Dionysus was a kind of virtuous cycle. The more praising and paying tribute to Dionysus he did via songs and toasts, the more he was able to cure the sick and feeble, and in turn the more he was able to drink and pay tribute and so on and so on.

Clearly, Rowen had the ideal relationship with God. Not an institutional one, or a vicarious one, but a personal one made all the more enjoyable by their mutual interest in vodka, dance, and women.

As Rowen wandered around Siberia from holy site to holy site, word quickly spread of his healing power, charisma, and booze-fueled celebrations.

No sooner did he arrive somewhere than did the townspeople ask him to perform a miracle. At the same time, not only did they make preparations at the local tavern for a celebration, but they also readied the town's holding cell in case Rowen's voracious sexual appetite led him to target an unwilling party. However, after one look into his hypnotic, penetrating eyes, even the most faithful of wives were up for a roll in the hay. So in practice, the cells generally wound up being occupied by drunk, jealous husbands sleeping one off.

It wasn't long before his reputation grew to the point that the Bishop of Siberia sent a letter of recommendation to the Bishop of St. Petersburg who welcomed Rowen to the nation's capital.

While many thought it odd for the bishop to give him such a warm welcome considering that he declined to take an official position in the Russian Orthodox Church, Rowen nevertheless captivated countless clergymen with his incredible feats of healing.

And he captivated countless socialites with his incredible feats of drinking.

After one of his first medical miracles in St. Petersburg, a particularly poignant one where he brought the seven-year-old daughter of a duke out of a coma by whispering into her ear, festivities were held at a posh tavern.

With the exception of Rowen, who still dressed in greasy black robes and was reluctant to run a comb through his long, disheveled hair, all of the patrons were dressed in the latest high-society, urban fashion.

After a quick succession of shots and beers, Rowen slammed his stein on the bar, called out for music, and marched to the center of the establishment where he proceeded to dance.

Well, calling it dancing may be a bit of a stretch. He mostly ran around in circles with his palms up and arms outstretched while occasionally stopping to fold his arms across his chest and bounce up and down like a toddler just learning to stand.

Nevertheless, the crowd was enthralled. Particularly the ladies, who clapped and cheered and squealed with delight.

Among those ladies was a pair of sisters known as the Pink Doe Princesses. Some said they were called "doe" because they had big beautiful doe eyes. Others said that it was not in fact "doe," but "dough," a slight on their curvy figures. And still others did not give a shit one way or the other.

Regardless, both Tatyana and Svetlana were enraptured by the mysterious wandering monk they had heard so much about. More importantly, at this particular moment, Svetlana's body was inhabited by Aphrodite—Goddess of Beauty, Horndog Love, and Shitty Dramas.

When the tune ended, Rowen was drawn to the Pink Doe Princesses, feeling in particular an uncanny, inexplicable attraction to Svetlana. After looking her up and down, he abruptly grabbed the drink out of her hand, downed it, and gave her a slobbery kiss on the lips.

"Goodness me," she swooned as Rowen released her from his embrace, tilted his head back, and let out a roaring laugh.

"You dance so beautifully," Tatyana said.

Rowen gazed deep into their eyes. "I know. I'll bet you ladies can really cut a rug, too. You're not too bad on the eyes." Rowen grazed their collarbones with the back of his hands. "And these pearl necklaces really suit you."

"We've heard so much about you and I must say, the rumors do not disappoint."

"Quiet woman, I'm trying to think." Rowen swayed back and forth as he struggled to regain his train of thought. Suddenly, his head snapped back as he remembered. "Ah," he said, raising a finger in the air before grabbing Tatyana's drink out of her hand, downing it, and giving her a slobbery kiss on the lips.

"Mr. Rasputin!" an official-looking man called out as he made his way through the crowd toward Rowen who was again roaring with laughter. "Mr. Rasputin," he repeated, putting a hand on Rowen's shoulder.

"What is it, dwarf?!" Rowen barked.

"Did you see his eyes?" Tatyana said to Svetlana under her breath as Rowen responded to the intruder. Both women were weak-kneed and blushing.

"Magnificent," Svetlana replied, starry-eyed.

"I am a messenger of the Tsarina," the man replied.

"Well, why didn't you say so, smidget?! Come, let's have a drink." Rowen gave the Pink Doe Princesses a fork-over-those-drinks-bitches look, but was met with blank stares.

"I'm afraid there's no time for that," the man said.

Rowen frowned.

"You are hereby summoned by the Tsarina. She requests that you visit the Winter Palace tomorrow."

"So she's heard of my prowess, has she?" Rowen asked with a smug smile.

The man cupped his hand around Rowen's ear and whispered. "It's the crown prince, Alexei. The sole heir to the throne. I'm afraid he's been ill and neither doctor nor priest has been able to do anything about it. You must come to the palace first thing tomorrow."

A swell of satisfaction surged through Rowen.

This was the culmination of all that he had accomplished thus far, a reward for his pious endeavors.

Yet at the same time, this was a mere starting point. The campaign to capture the most powerful seat in the world would begin the next morning.

"Do not fear, little fellow," Rowen said. "I will visit the palace tomorrow morning. Tell the Tsarina that her troubles are over."

The man nodded and rushed out of the tavern.

Rowen marched to the bar and demanded a pencil and one last drink.

110

After scribbling something down on a napkin, he downed the vodka and strode back over to the Pink Doe Princesses.

"There will be cause for great celebration tomorrow," he said, holding the napkin out to Tatyana, who quickly identified it as an address. "Round up some more beauties and meet me at my apartment tomorrow evening."

Wide-eyed, the women nodded and once Rowen turned for the exit, they collapsed into each other in a fit of giggles.

Upon reaching the exit, however, Rowen spun back around and lifted a finger in the air.

The ladies leapt to attention.

"Oh yes," he called, again remembering something of great importance. "Bring booze. Lots of it."

***

Rowen strode into the crown prince's room as if it were his own.

Flanking both sides of Alexei's bed were St. Petersburg's foremost doctors and clergymen. Without even so much as glancing at them, Rowen could feel their impotence.

"Thank you so much for coming," Tsar Nicolas II said, extending a hand.

"Thank you for having me," Rowen replied, shaking the Tsar's hand. "It is a great honor."

"No," Tsarina Alexandra interjected, extending a delicate hand. "The honor is all ours. We have heard many tales of your wondrous healing power and we are grateful for your visit, Mr. Rasputin."

"Please," Rowen replied, embracing her hand with both of his. "Call me Rowen. I am at your service, Tsarina."

"Please," she replied, almost blushing. "Call me Sandra."

"Well then, Sandra," Rowen said, releasing his grip and waving his hands flippantly around the room. "Other than the ineffectuals littering the room, what seems to be the problem?"

"It's our boy," Tsar Nicholas said. "They say he has hemophilia. Even the slightest knock can cause severe bruising and agonizing pain."

"I'm afraid I'm at my wit's end," Sandra said. "The doctors and priests can do nothing to soothe my poor boy's distress and they say it's only a matter of time before he leaves us."

Rowen surveyed the room. "Get out! All of you! Out! Out! Out!"

With looks of consternation and indignation, the doctors and priests streamed out of the room. Even Tsar Nicholas took a few steps toward the door.

"Not you, Tsar Nicholas. Please remain."

Rowen approached the boy, who was sitting up in his bed eyeing him apprehensively.

"Hello, young prince," Rowen said, as affably as possible.

Alexei smiled weakly.

"How are you feeling?"

"… My chest hurts."

"Come now, my love," Sandra said, gently pulling the boy's shirt over his head. "Let's show the nice man what has happened."

Rowen stared down at an array of bruises from light blue to dark purple. "Well, this certainly is a mess, isn't it? How about we clean it up?"

Alexei smiled again.

"What is it that you like to do when you're feeling good? Drawing? Sports? Writing poetry for your girlfriend?"

Alexei giggled meekly and Sandra was overjoyed. It had been a long time since she had seen her only son laugh, and even though it was a weak one, she could not have been happier.

"You love riding your bicycle, don't you Alexei?" Tsar Nicholas said.

"Wow," Rowen exclaimed. "So you're a thrill seeker, are you? A speed demon, eh?"

Alexei smiled again.

"But it's too dangerous," Sandra said. "With his condition, I'm afraid it's just too risky."

Rowen leaned toward the boy and spoke in a hushed voice. "Never mind your mother. She doesn't understand what it's like to be a man. I'll have you up and speeding around the palace grounds in no time."

"Really?"

Rowen stared fixedly at the boy. "You believe me, right?"

Alexei's face tensed up and his lower lip began to quiver. He had never seen such intense eyes.

"You must believe me," Rowen said. "You must be brave. I can see what a brave boy you are. Are you ready?"

Alexei mustered all of his courage and gave Rowen a determined nod.

"I'm going to take these bruises away so that come tomorrow morning your chest will be good as new." Rowen placed one hand on the boy's forehead and the other on his sternum.

In a language that was clearly not Russian, Rowen chanted, "Great God, Dionysus, please heal this boy's wounds and allow us to once again sing your praises and celebrate your glory as you would have us."

Then, in a language that was Russian, he whispered in Alexei's ear. "This is the spell to take all of your pain away. Rest today and tomorrow we play. Bicycles, sugar tarts … tiny little fairy farts."

Rowen stood up from the boy, extended his palms outward, and gave a self-satisfied, Jesus-himself-couldn't-have-done-any-better look.

"How do you feel, my sweet?" Sandra asked.

"Better, mother. I feel better."

Sandra turned to Rowen and clutched both of his hands.

"By the grace of God, you have done it! He's gonna be okay! You're a miracle worker!"

"Yes, he'll be just fine. He will feel much much better tomorrow. But now, we must let him rest. Make sure that no one disturbs him. In particular, no doctors. No more poking or prying or probing. Nothing that will cause our brave boy any further stress. Have an attendant bring him cabbage soup and crackers for lunch and string beans and pheasant for dinner. Other than that, leave him in peace."

"Understood, my good sir," Tsar Nicholas said.

Upon exiting the room and closing the door, Sandra once again clutched both of Rowen's hands. "You must be rewarded."

"I require no reward."

Sandra looked at her husband. "He is so modest. A true man of the cloth."

"The crown prince's return to health is my reward," Rowen said.

"First, we will set you up with an apartment worthy of your capabilities," Sandra said. "It will be across from here so that you can attend to Alexei at a moment's notice."

"If it will allow me to better assist your family, I humbly accept."

"Second," Sandra continued. "You are hereby appointed the official Caretaker of the Crown Prince."

"And third," Tsar Nicholas said. "You are hereby appointed Special Advisor to the Tsar of Russia. We need a man like you, a man with preternatural insight and mystic abilities to help guide our glorious empire to unprecedented prosperity."

Sandra smiled at Rowen warmly. "We have always been faithful servants of our Lord and we knew that He would send someone like you to us one day."

***

"To Dionysus!" Rowen shouted, raising a glass of chilled vodka high in the air. "The most magnificent of deities. All joy and pleasure is born through Him. Hallowed be His name!"

The throng of gorgeous women in revealing dresses that filled Rowen's living room clinked glasses and cheerfully downed their champagnes, wines, and vodkas.

After pouring himself another, Rowen crashed down onto a mahogany sofa, pulling a pair of ladies onto his lap.

"You really did it?" asked the one with blond curls, delighting in Rowen's attention and touch.

"Do not doubt, woman," Rowen replied, stroking her hair. "The boy will live to see another day."

"You're incredible," said the one with cupid bow lips.

"And you're so kissable," Rowen declared, planting his lips on hers.

"How did you do it?" the one with blond curls asked.

"If only you could understand," Rowen replied, brushing her hair aside and sucking on her earlobe.

"Try us," the one with cupid bow lips entreated.

"I intend to," Rowen said, smiling devilishly before planting another slobbery kiss on her.

Svetlana, again inhabited by Aphrodite, sauntered over and stood above the sofa. "The Tsar and Tsarina are forever in your debt," she said, her seductive doe eyes expressing both respect and desire.

Rowen looked up and was pleased to see her looking ravishing in her glittering gown. "There's my bright-eyed doe," he said, clutching her hand.

"Alexei is the only heir to the throne," she continued. "After their fourth daughter was born, Russia feared the worst, but when a boy was finally born, we breathed a collective sigh of relief that the empire would continue. And now that they have you and your mysterious powers to protect him, we are assured that the future of the crown is bright."

"Indeed," Rowen said, staggering to his feet. "And now, we must give praise to Dionysus in the form that delights Him most. Come."

Upon downing his drink, he pulled Svetlana into the adjacent bedroom. Swaying back and forth, he surveyed every inch of her with his mystifying gaze.

Her knees buckled ever so slightly when his eyes finally met hers. "You're a very impressive man," she said, regaining her seductive confidence. "It really is astounding how quickly you've managed to appear out of nowhere and work your way all the way up to what may be one of the most powerful positions in Russia."

"You're a clever one, aren't you, Svetlana?" Rowen said, continuing to admire her doe eyes.

"Not nearly as clever as you."

Rowen leaned back and let out a boisterous laugh. "You know, of all the girls I've met here in St. Petersburg, you just might be my favorite."

Svetlana blushed. "Well, I'm flattered that you think so. Because you are my absolute favorite man in St. Petersburg. Your swagger ... Your charisma ... Your *je-ne-sais-quois*. I couldn't be more happy to have come here. My sister and I ..."

"If only you didn't talk so much," Rowen said, cutting her off and again leaning back and letting out a rambunctious laugh.

Svetlana's cheeks flushed crimson.

"Come now, woman," Rowen said, grabbing the straps of her dress with his great paws and pulling them down over her shoulders. "Let us engage in a euphoric union with the divine."

Svetlana let out an impassioned sigh as Rowen pushed her onto the bed and buried his face in her voluptuous breasts.

***

"Rowen," Tsarina Sandra said. "May I present to you Prince Felix Yusupov and his lovely wife, Princess Irina."

Rowen studied the couple.

Felix had expressive eyes, effeminate lips, and jet black hair parted meticulously to the left.

Irina was a knockout. While the upper echelon of St. Petersburg society was in attendance at this celebratory ball, Rowen found her to be by far the most elegant and enchanting woman there.

"Felix," Sandra continued, "is the scion of one of the wealthiest families in Russia."

Felix gave Rowen a self-satisfied smile and offered a limp hand. "It's nice to make your acquaintance, Rowen. We've heard so much about your mysterious powers and ... *unusual* habits."

Rowen reluctantly shook his hand.

"Irina," Sandra said, "is the Tsar's only niece."

Irina curtseyed. "It's a pleasure to meet you."

Rowen smiled.

"I'll leave you three to get acquainted," Sandra said, exiting.

Rowen snatched a couple glasses of champagne from a passing waiter, downed one, and then continued to size up the couple.

"Doesn't he have the most remarkable eyes, darling?" Felix said to Irina. "It's just like they say. Absolutely transfixing."

Rowen grimaced. While Felix hadn't overtly said anything insulting, there was something lurking beneath that rubbed him the wrong way.

"I agree," Irina said, smiling at Rowen. "You have the most hypnotic eyes I've ever seen."

This was much more to Rowen's liking.

"And what is most fascinating of all," Felix said, "is your ability to look both my wife and me in the eye at the same time. How *do* you do that?"

Rowen glared at him. "Well, Prince Fuckoff, I have a medical condition known as googly eyes, and if you're making light of them, I suggest you don't. They are a divine gift that allow me to see things that others don't, and to enjoy certain views while still enduring small chat with pompous imbeciles."

...

Rowen winked at Irina. "And by 'certain views,' I mean your wife's cleavage."

"Thank you, I got that."

"Just making sure. You know, in case you don't pick up on subtle social cues from people that you're speaking with who are at this moment contemplating a game of hide the kolbasa with your spouse. Incidentally, fine lady, not only are you a treat to the eyes, but you're wearing some of the finest jewelry I have ever seen."

Rowen caressed her earlobe, allowing her diamond earring to dangle in the palm of his hand.

Irina blushed. "Thank you. These are my favorite earrings. They belonged to Marie Antoinette. They're called the Tears of Paradise."

After admiring the sparkling orbs, Rowen grazed her collarbone while appreciating her necklace, a crisscrossing of diamonds and rubies with drop-shaped pearls hanging down. "Was this also Marie Antoinette's?"

"It was. It's such a lovely piece, isn't it? The Venus Infinity. Absolutely to die for."

"It's just some shiny stones stitched together. But when placed on you, it's radiant."

"Thank you," Felix chimed in. "I picked them out myself and even gave her Marie Antoinette's veil to wear to our wedding."

"It doesn't surprise me that your taste in accessories is so refined," Rowen replied, sarcastically. "But hush now, the adults are talking."

Felix winced. Failing to capture Rowen's attention, he

grabbed him by the elbow and began leading him toward the bar. "My good sir, I'm afraid we're getting off on the wrong foot. Come, let me freshen your drink."

While being pulled away, Rowen turned his head back toward Irina and flashed her a your-husband-is-a-twat,-I-can't-wait-to-make-him-a-cuckold smile.

"Listen," Felix said, grabbing two glasses of chilled vodka from the bar and handing one to Rowen. "I'm terribly sorry if I offended you with my comment about your eyes. That was not my intention. It came out all wrong. The truth is, you have the most intense eyes I've ever seen. I find you fascinating."

Rowen downed half of his vodka. "That's nice, little man, but I'm not here to mesmerize or entertain the likes of you. I've got a much higher calling."

"Yes. I know. Of course. I just mean that with my social and economic standing and your mysterious abilities ..."

"I don't care about your family's money." Rowen gulped down the other half of his vodka and placed the glass back on the bar.

"Yes, but there are many things that we can do for each other. Once you get to know me," Felix said, brushing his hand against Rowen's, "you'll see."

"You naughty boy!" Rowen said, retracting his hand. "I've seen your ilk before at the Monastery of Abalak and it's not my cup of tea. Vodka, that's my cup of tea. Not backdoor shenanigans. If you're looking for a man of the cloth to indulge your depravity, you should be attending Sunday School. But frankly, you should be paying more attention to your wife. She is an exquisite piece of ass."

***

"What catastrophe has our courageous crown prince suffered this time?" Rowen asked, striding into Alexei's bedroom yet again.

"He took a nasty fall while ice-skating," Tsarina Sandra said, panicked. "I knew we shouldn't have let him do it. It's just too dangerous."

"Of course you should," Rowen replied as he made his way to Alexei's bedside. The poor boy was in considerable pain and his breathing laborious. "Training to play center forward for our hockey team, is it? Or is figure skating more your fancy? Did you take a spill while working on your double axel?"

Alexei smiled weakly.

"Let's have a look," Rowen continued, having a seat on the bed and gently pulling Alexei's shirt up.

Once again, his chest and arms were covered in ghastly bruises as he was suffering severe internal bleeding. "A fine mess, indeed."

"He can barely breathe," Sandra said. "You've got to save him!"

"Fear not," Rowen replied. "God will once again come to our aid."

Rowen stared fixedly at the boy. "Ready to clean it up?"

Alexei nodded determinedly.

"That a boy," Rowen replied, placing one hand on Alexei's forehead and the other on his sternum.

After invoking Dionysus, he leaned in close to the boy. "I've got the perfect spell for this one," he whispered. "Rest today and tomorrow we play. Slapshot, loop de loop … unicorn poop."

No sooner did Rowen finish uttering the charm than did Alexei's breathing return to normal and a peaceful smile settle over his face.

"How do you feel, my sweet?" Sandra asked.

"Much better, mother."

"Come now," Rowen said to Sandra. "We must let him rest. No one is to disturb him for the rest of the day. Have an attendant bring barley soup in an hour and then broccoli and pheasant for dinner. Other than that, leave him in peace."

Upon exiting the room and closing the door, Sandra as usual clutched both of Rowen's hands. "You really are a miracle worker! We would be absolutely lost without you."

"Oh, come now. I'm simply a conduit for God's will. He is the one who deserves the credit."

"That's exactly it. God speaks to us through you." Sandra let go of Rowen's hands and wrapped her arms around him. "My sweet sweet man. You are a blessing"

Once Sandra finally released him from her embrace, Rowen looked deep into her eyes. "Is there anything else I can do for you?"

Sandra sighed while staring back into his hypnotic eyes. After a moment though, she shook her head slightly as she recalled the plight of her country. "Yes. I'm afraid that there is a lot more that we will need from you in the coming months. As I'm sure you're aware, the hostilities to the west escalate with each passing day. War seems to be an inevitability. The Tsar will need your blessed advice on who can lead us to victory abroad and who can bring us prosperity at home.

Rowen smiled. "I am at your service, madam."

***

"To the most profitable prophet in St. Petersburg!" Svetlana said, holding a glass of vodka high in the air and batting her gorgeous eyelashes at Rowen. "You've done it again and all of Russia is in the palm of your hand!"

"Here here!" Rowen said, pointing at the palm of his hand and laughing heartily. Once he was able to compose himself, he too held up his glass. "To the Tsarina!" he boomed, clinking glasses with Svetlana, her sister Tatyana, and the rest of his harem of fervent followers.

They were once again celebrating in a cozy lounge off to the side of the bar at Rowen's favorite tavern.

"Can we have a celebratory dance, too?" Tatyana pleaded, wrapping her arm around Rowen and nudging him toward the middle of the room.

Rowen finished his vodka, handed the empty glass to Tatyana, and took position in the center of the open space.

"Music!" he called, clapping his hands together high above his head.

As usual, with the smuggest of faces, he circled the floor briskly with his arms outstretched and palms up, stopping now and again to fold them across his chest and bounce up and down like a human toilet plunger.

And as usual, the ladies ate it up, clapping and cheering and squealing with delight.

Satisfied and thirsting for another drink, Rowen strode over to the bar to find an unpleasant surprise.

"Congratulations, Rowen," Prince Felix said. "I heard that you once again summoned your mysterious powers to heal Alexei."

"What are you doing here?" Rowen replied, brusquely.

"Why, I'm here to celebrate with you," Felix said. "Your miraculous feats never cease to amaze. You just keep getting more and more impressive."

"..."

"And your dancing is ... how shall I say ... arousing." To emphasize his sentiment, Felix brushed his hand over Rowen's hip.

"You bad boy!" Rowen growled, grabbing the offending hand and tossing it aside. "I thought I told you that you are barking up the wrong tree. Now, if it's a three-way we're talking about, I'd consider it. But on two conditions."

Rowen held up his right pointer finger in Felix' face. "One: the third party in this three-way is your wife."

Rowen held up the adjacent middle finger, pushing even closer. "And two: your role will be confined to taking notes and/or sketches on a sofa across the room."

Felix smiled, deviously. "Oh my, you really are the Holy

Devil. Wicked to the core."

Rowen leaned back and let out a hearty laugh. As he regained himself, he noticed a couple of attractive young ladies whom he'd never seen before looking his way.

"Go home, Felix," he said, pushing him out of the way and making a beeline for the women.

He penetrated them with his eyes as he strode over and could feel them falling under his spell. They swooned as he kissed one of them on the lips while grabbing the other one by the pussy.

The ladies in his harem giggled and cheered, entertained by his shenanigans.

"Girls," Rowen said upon releasing his lips from one and his grip from the other. "Come and meet some of my devotees. Tonight is a night of celebration and salvation."

He led them to the lounge at the side of the bar and quickly handed each a drink, then grabbed a couple for himself.

After clinking glasses, he downed one for each woman.

"Girls," he said, addressing his entire harem. "In the midst of this celebration, I feel inspired to preach. Let us head back to my apartment and to the Holy of Holies."

As Rowen marched toward the exit, his regulars clapped their hands in anticipation as they scrambled to catch up.

Svetlana and Tatyana could barely contain their excitement. "You girls are in for a treat," Svetlana said to the newcomers. "Tonight, you're gonna learn something that will stay with you for the rest of your life."

"If you're lucky," Tatyana added, "you'll discover what it feels like to be saved."

***

Rowen indulged in a glass of red wine as his harem flowed into the living room adjacent to his bedroom.

Once the girls had a fresh drink and were sitting

attentively on a sofa or leaning attentively against the wall, he plunged into his sermon.

"I will make this short and sweet," he declared, eyeing the newbies. "I want to talk about sin and salvation.

"Those feelings that are pulsing through you at this very moment, burning in your loins," he continued, gazing deeply into their eyes one at a time. "Those sexual urges. Are they sin?"

Dumbstruck, the girls were unable to reply. With each second, they fell deeper and deeper under Rowen's spell and did not want to disappoint him with the wrong answer.

"Yes," Svetlana chimed in, taking a step forward.

Rowen's head snapped in her direction. Slowly, he took a drink. Then a step toward her. "That's right, my little mouse." Rowen wrapped his arm around her and squeezed her behind. "And what a wicked sin they are."

He turned back to the newcomers. "And so what are we to do?"

"…"

"The clergy would have you repress those feelings. Push them way down into the bowels of your being. Lock them up and throw away the key.

"But is that the path to salvation?! Will ignoring your primal urges save your soul?! Or will it simply lead to a life of self-torment and emotional constipation?!"

Rowen let the rhetorical questions hang in the air as he drained the remainder of his wine and beckoned Svetlana for a refill with a nod of the head.

Once his glass was again full, he continued. "The clergy will tell you that the path to salvation runs through the church. Put your trust – and your money – in them and they will take care of it for you.

"Blasphemy!

"Salvation cannot be obtained through an institution. Salvation is only obtained through the individual."

Rowen surveyed the room, locking eyes at random.

"Through you … and you … and you … and you. Salvation is obtained by seeking the spirit of God within oneself.

"So what are we to do with these sexual urges? These sinful thoughts and feelings?"

Once again sensing that the newcomers would be unable to answer, Svetlana took another step forward. "Yield to them," she said, her voice burning.

"Correct," Rowen replied, once again wrapping an arm around her, but this time awarding her an impassioned kiss. Perhaps too impassioned as it took a few gulps of wine to recover his train of thought.

"Yes, yield to those urges. But why? To what purpose?"

Rowen again eyed the newcomers who were spellbound by his sermon but again at a loss for words.

"It is because by engaging in sexual intercourse, we consciously sin together, and in this way the power of the sin is nullified.

"It is through sin that we attain divine mercy.

"Sin and repentance are the conditions necessary for salvation. Just like there can be no good in the world without evil, there can be no salvation without sin.

"Only when we yield to temptation and repent are we saved.

"The clergy will tell you to stay away from Rasputin. They will tell you that if you lay with Rasputin, you will defile your soul.

"This could not be further from the truth. When you lay with Rasputin, he is not polluting you, he is purifying you.

"He is saving your soul!"

At the precise moment that Rowen uttered these words, Delemor, in Verixion, knowing how the night would proceed, inscribed the names of the two newcomers into his register entitled, Humans Not Going To Hell After This Life.

And at the exact same moment, Aphrodite crossed into this world like a bolt of lightning and entered the body of

Svetlana.

Rowen ran a finger down the cheeks of both newcomers. "Tatyana will inform you of the ceremonial washing you can look forward to."

He then turned his attention to Svetlana. "But first, me and this sinner have some cleansing to do in the Holy of Holies."

Rowen grabbed her by the wrist and led her into his bedroom, or the Holy of Holies, as he called it.

***

"Time to go home," Rowen said, pushing Svetlana out of bed with his foot.

In the name of purification, they had tangled tongues, bobbed for apples, and bumped uglies, but none of it was to Rowen's satisfaction.

Svetlana fell to the floor with a thud. "What?!"

"I grow tired of you, woman. Get out!"

"You're literally kicking me out?"

"Something about you tonight irks me. I no longer wish to see you. Out!"

"I thought I was your favorite."

"Favorite?! Hah! Even your sister has surpassed you on that list. In fact, send her in on your way out."

Despite her insides seething with rage, resentment, and humiliation, Svetlana reigned in her emotion while putting her dress back on.

Emerging into the living room with a seemingly satisfied smile, she nodded to Tatyana. "Your turn, sis."

Tatyana giggled and hurried into the Holy of Holies. As she crossed through the doorway, the entire room overheard a cheerful Rowen greet her.

"Ahhh, there's my 68th favorite girl."

***

126

In what was becoming more of a regularity, Rowen was summoned to the Tsar's palace for advice completely unrelated to Alexei.

The Tsar was despondent behind his desk and Sandra, standing beside him, looked equally forlorn.

"The war is out of control," Tsar Nicholas said. "We have already lost more than a million men and there's not a ray of hope to be seen."

"You must tell us what we should do," Tsarina Sandra said. "What does God wish us to do?"

Rowen frowned. "I'm afraid there is no easy solution."

"Has He spoken to you?"

"… He has."

"Then you must tell us. You must tell us what He would have us do."

"… I cannot. In good conscience, I cannot pass on His message. It's too dangerous. It's … it's madness!"

"Dammit!" Tsar Nicholas screamed, uncharacteristically losing his temper and slamming his fist on the desk. "Tell us, good sir!"

"The troops cannot win without their leader."

"What are you saying?" Sandra replied, disoriented.

"He would have you, Tsar Nicholas, go to the front and take command of the troops yourself."

"What?!" Tsar Nicholas cried out in shock.

"He says that the army has no chance without you. But with you, with the presence of their glorious leader, they will be inspired to fight like a pack of crazed wolves. For their emperor, for Russia, they will win the war. I'm very sorry, but it's the only way."

***

Many factors contributed to the outbreak of World War I.

It was partly because of political, territorial, and

127

economical conflict;

Partly because the Germans were being dicks;

Partly because the French were being cunts;

Partly because there were simply too many human beings on Earth;

Partly because massive amounts of people decided to worship no Gods other than Yahweh, drawing the ire of the rest;

But mostly, it was so that Rowen could have a clear, unobstructed shot at Tsarina Sandra. With Tsar Nicholas off playing war, it was like shooting fish in a barrel.

***

"There are rumors that you and I are having an affair," Sandra said, laying back on her pillow and pulling the sheets over her bare breasts.

"Let them talk," Rowen replied, clambering out of bed and pouring himself a glass of red wine.

"It's just adding fuel to the fire. First, they were grumbling about your undue influence over us and now this."

"Undue?!" Rowen repeated. "Now that hurts. My influence is nothing if not due."

"Perhaps we've been a little too cavalier in letting you handpick the ministerial cabinet."

"*Me?*" Rowen replied, incredulously. "I only advise based on what God instructs."

"This is true. But the war effort has not improved."

Rowen drained his wine and crawled back into bed. "Give it time."

"But the more defeats we suffer, the more ammunition they have against us. And they're just itching to come after you."

"That would not be good, my fair Tsarina," Rowen said, kissing her neck while massaging one of her breasts. "For if anything were to happen to me, I'm afraid the royal family would be wiped from the Earth."

***

"The Tsar's ministers have been turned into marionettes," Purishkevich, a lifetime politician, said. As an assemblyman of the Lower House, he had uttered the exact same line to an agitated crowd of hundreds the day before. Today, he delivered the line to a group of three in Prince Felix' upstairs study. "Marionettes whose strings are being manipulated by the contorted fingers of Rasputin."

Felix felt a surge of adrenaline and rage course through his body. Purishkevich left quite the impression. Despite his baby face, prominent widow's peak, and pointed ears, when it came to politics, he was as knowledgeable as anyone, and he spoke with charisma, passion, and fury. Felix was certain he had invited the right person to get the ball rolling at his secret meeting.

"He has an excessive and undue influence over the royal family," Purishkevich continued. "And an unpatriotic influence over the courts. He simply must be stopped."

Bishop Palovick, head of the St. Petersburg church, nodded. "I agree," he said, his ruddy jowls jiggling. With his long grey hair, ruby robe, and hippopotamus-like frame, it would not be out of line for someone to mistake him for Saint Nicholas. "Rasputin is immorality incarnate. He is a false prophet … nay, he is the Antichrist. With his incessant drunkenness, sexual promiscuity, and willingness to accept bribes, he is the antithesis of all that is good. He is the bane of a righteous Mother Russia."

"Yes," Purishkevich agreed. "I can forgive drinking and womanizing to a degree, but it is those bribes that will be the downfall of our entire society. They grease his palm and he uses his undue influence to get them appointed anywhere they want. And those that speak up, he has dismissed from their posts. Mother Russia is crumbling."

Felix' lips curled into a suitably evil smile. He had invited the right people. Purishkevich and Bishop Palovick fueled each other's fire, and the inevitable conclusion was a conflagration to engulf and consume that beast of a man, Rowen.

"We cannot allow him to continue," Felix said, scowling. "His excessive influence over the Tsar … his dissolute ways … his utter refusal to engage in rumpy-rumpy. We must put an end to him!"

"I'm sorry?" Bishop Palovick said. "What was that last one before the 'put an end to him'?"

"Hm?" Felix replied, with an oh-fuck-I-did-not-mean-to-say-that look.

"We got the first part about the excessive influence," Purishkevich said.

"And the second part about his dissolute ways," Bishop Palovick followed. "But the third part …?"

Purishkevich furrowed his brow. "Something about rumpy-rumpy?"

"No," Felix replied, backpedaling. "Not rumpy-rumpy. I said … uhhh … lumpy-lumpy. You know … like with the marionettes. Lumpy-lumpy."

"I do not see what lumpy-lumpy has to do with marionettes," Purishkevich replied.

"You know … with the manipulating strings … and … they get all … lumpy-lumpy …" Felix was desperate to get the conversation back on track and abruptly turned to his third guest. "Gentlemen, may I present the solution to our problem. That problem being Rasputin's excessive influence, moral depravity, and the tremendous threat that he poses to the survival of our beloved Mother Russia. Here he is, Doctor Lazovert."

Felix pushed the doctor into the middle of the circle and the other two gentlemen sized him up. He was bald, bespectacled, and wore a knee-length white coat so that there was no doubt about his being a doctor.

And while the good doctor felt more or less indifferent toward Rowen, it was not as if he liked him. So he was more than happy to go along with any plan where he would be able to unload a batch of pharmaceuticals at an absurd profit.

"Doctor Lazovert," Felix explained, "will provide us with the proper medication to eradicate the disease."

Catching Felix' drift, Purishkevich and Bishop Palovick smiled and nodded. "I'm in," they said, simultaneously.

"Then it is settled," Felix said, rubbing his fingertips together. "I have the perfect bait: my lovely wife Irina. As that brute has been so insolent as to make insinuations about her to my very face, there is no doubt that she will be able to lure him here without him suspecting a thing."

***

At the precise moment that Felix began to unveil his plan to Irina, Aphrodite happily took control of her body.

"And so you see," Felix said, "because of Rasputin's undue influence and moral depravity, he must be stopped."

Aphrodite, needed no further persuading. "I see, my sweet," she said. "It will be no problem. I'll simply put on an enticing dress and my favorite jewelry to seduce him, and I will bring him here."

"Excellent," Felix replied, once again rubbing his fingertips together.

***

"I had a feeling you'd come knocking," Rowen said, greeting Irina at his door. "What can I help you with?"

"I only wish it had to do with me," Irina replied, looking ravishing in Marie Antoinette's Tears of Paradise pearl earrings and Venus Infinity necklace. "But it is my husband.

I know that you two have not got along, but I need you to save him. I'm desperate."

"Hmph," Rowen sighed, disappointed that she had not come for a lesson in salvation. "What is it that you wish me to do for the fruit?"

"As you have discerned, he is not well. He never has been. From before I met him, he had always lived a morally dubious life. At the age of 12, he began wearing his mother's gowns. At 15, he started putting on lipstick. And at 19, he traveled to England. Need I go on?"

Rowen shook his head no in disgust.

"I desperately need your help," the beauty continued. "Please. Come to our home and cure him of his disease."

Rowen gave her an I'm-not-really-sure-it's-worth-my-time look.

"He needs a miracle that only you can perform."

Rowen responded with a still-not-interested look.

"I'll do anything. If you can straighten him out, I am yours for a night."

Rowen immediately flashed her a shit-yeah-I'm-in look. "You'll indulge my every desire?"

"Yes. For one night. Anything you want. Your wish is my command."

Rowen leaned back and let out a hearty laugh. "I have the distinct sensation that a trap has been laid." He looked deep into her eyes. "Baahhhh, I'm sure it's nothing."

***

At roughly the same time, Felix and his three conspirators were busy setting the trap.

Dr. Lazovert put on rubber gloves and ground cyanide potassium crystals into a fine powder.

Felix instructed him to sprinkle a dose on the vanilla pudding cream cakes.

He did so with a perverted smile. "This dose is big

enough to kill a full-grown elephant almost instantly."

Next, he doubled the dose and dropped it into a decanter of 1902 chianti.

***

Irina led Rowen through their palace entrance and into the dining room where Felix was waiting. "I'll be back in a moment," she said. "I need to … wash my hair."

"Oh, what a pleasant surprise," Felix called out.

"I am happy to be here," Rowen replied, eyeing Irina's rump as she exited.

Felix sidled up next to Rowen and whispered into his ear. "I will give you one last chance."

Before Rowen could even comprehend what Felix had said, Felix planted a kiss on him.

"You bad boy!" Rowen replied, shoving Felix away. "But it's nothing. I am here to help. Your wife and I, when she returns, will sort you out."

Felix, spurned yet again, took a defiant yet pleasant tone. "Some pastries while we wait?" he said, offering Rowen the vanilla pudding cream cakes.

Rowen eyed them suspiciously. "I am more of a chocolate pudding cream cakes man."

"I'm afraid we're all out."

Reluctantly, Rowen snatched a vanilla pudding cream cake, but before eating it, he eyed it suspiciously. "This pastry looks a little poisony to me."

Felix' eyes widened.

"Baahhhh," Rowen blurted out, leaning back and letting out a great laugh. "I'm sure it's nothing."

Felix smiled with anticipation as Rowen wolfed it down. "How about some fine chianti?" he offered. "To wash it down?"

Without hesitation, Rowen assented.

"It's from '02," Felix boasted, handing Rowen a full

glass.

Rowen took a deep sniff. "This smells quite a bit poisony."

Felix flashed an oh-shit-he's-on-to-me look.

"Baahhhh, I'm sure it's nothing," Rowen said, leaning back laughing yet again. "To good health!"

Felix watched with glee as he downed the wine and held out his glass for a refill.

***

"You will not believe it," Felix cried to his conspirators in the upstairs study. "He has eaten all the pastries and consumed both decanters of wine. It's been at least a half an hour and yet nothing. He just sits there gloomily, waiting for my wife to return. I can discern no effects from the poison whatsoever. He just belches every now and then and dribbles a bit. What shall we do?"

Purishkevich nodded resolutely and handed Felix one of his nine revolvers. "Finish him."

***

Upon returning to the living room, Felix pointed to an expensive painting of the Messiah. "You'd better have a look at the crucifix and say a prayer."

Rowen stood and took a few steps toward the depiction. "Looks painful."

No sooner did the words leave his mouth than did Felix shoot him in the back, twice.

Rowen fell to the floor.

After what seemed like an eternity had passed, Felix approached Rowen's motionless body and reached his hand out to check his pulse.

As Felix was just about to touch Rowen's neck, Rowen rolled over and grabbed hold of Felix' wrist. "You naughty boy!"

Felix tried desperately to withdraw his hand.

"I'm not gonna let you stop me from taking what is mine!" Rowen roared.

Through the grace of God, or, to be more specific, through the grace of Aphrodite, Felix was able to free his hand and flee upstairs.

"You'll not believe it!" he cried. "I've registered two shots into his chest and yet he still lives."

"He is the devil," Bishop Palovick replied as Purishkevich swiftly distributed fresh pistols to everyone.

As the group raced down the stairs, they heard the front door slam shut.

"After him!" Felix shouted needlessly as everyone was already in full chase.

As Rowen neared the courtyard gate, a flurry of gunshots rang out. The majority were true to the mark and Rowen collapsed in the snow.

Purishkevich, being the fittest, arrived at Rowen's limp body first and unleashed a hurricane of kicks and punches to Rowen's chest, neck, and groin.

Felix pulled Purishkevich off and the assassins sat in silence hoping that Rowen would move no more.

After what seemed an eternity, Felix returned inside to retrieve a throw rug. The group then wrapped Rowen in the carpet, carried him to the nearest bridge, and flung his limp body into the freezing river.

***

Within the year, Tsarina Sandra and the entire royal family were shot, bayoneted, and clubbed to death at the direction of political revolutionaries dedicated to creating a classless society that would not only afford prosperity to everyone, but do so in exactly equal measures.

They managed to do so in just a shade under seven

centuries.

VERIXION V

"Is the Miracle-Working MaleWhore finally back with us?" Delemor boomed as Rowen rubbed his eyes, slowly reacclimating to the resplendent chamber.

Through the mist, Delemor's crocodile face was beaming at him, most likely in irony.

"What happened?" Rowen asked, racking his brain for details of his demise.

"What happened was that all your moral and political corruption ticked off people from all walks of life. The range was quite impressive. In the end, a priest, a politician, an aristocrat, and a doctor banded together to assassinate you."

As bits and pieces of his life slowly but steadily came back to him, Rowen winced. It was like he was watching someone else. Someone with whom he had absolutely nothing in common. Not mentally, not physically, and certainly not emotionally. He was instantly questioning how he could have been such a person.

"So how did you enjoy that ending?" Delemor inquired, smiling wickedly. "I thought it was quite riveting."

"I'm glad you enjoyed me getting shot in the back like 20 times," Rowen replied, dispiritedly.

"Only six, your Holy Devilness. Only six. But it was more than that. First, you ate and drank enough cyanide to kill a brigade of black bears."

"Really?"

"Yeah, really. Someone up here must have been looking out for you. Cause it wasn't the poison, it wasn't the gunshots, and it wasn't the wanton ass-whoopin' that killed you. It was the water … You died from drowning."

"Really?"

"Yeah, check the autopsy. It was one of the most epic deaths ever. Clearly, all those people you provoked really wanted you dead."

Rowen's head slumped down as he recalled the backlash against him. It seemed as if anyone not under his spell found him morally repugnant and politically corrupt.

"Ahhh, don't be so glum, kid. There were areas where you showed enormous growth."

Rowen's head shot up and his eyes widened, desperate for even a dash of virtue to cling to.

"When you were young," Delemor explained, "you could hardly even talk to a girl. But by the time you arrived in St. Petersburg, without even saying a word you would walk up to a woman and just kiss her on the lips. And once you made it to the top, you'd just walk up to one and grab her by the pussy. Re-markable!"

Rowen sighed deeply and clutched his head with his hands. His entire being was engulfed in shame. "Did I … did I do anything right?"

"Right?! What are you talking about?"

"I feel utterly awful. I feel so ashamed of everything."

Rowen heard a loud thud on the table in between him and Delemor, and he watched as a diamond tear rolled off and onto the floor.

"I mean, I feel completely different now and wouldn't be caught dead doing half of those things."

"Yeah, the dancing was pretty bad."

"But … did I … was there anything that I did right?"

Delemor eyed him for a beat. "Do you really want me to answer that?"

"… No."

"Yeah," Delemor replied, his voice now thick with disappointment. "I didn't think so."

"Do I … ummmmm … do I at least get another shot?"

"Sure, buddy. If that's what you want."

Rowen let out a huge sigh of relief. "Thank God!"

"You're welcome. Now go have a wash so we can discuss your next shot."

Rowen did the usual walk of shame down to the bathing facilities with mixed feelings. He was demoralized by the person he had been, but at the same time felt grateful for another chance and was eagerly awaiting the revitalization that the shampoo brought.

As he basked in the sublime tingling of the crimson suds, he felt a pair of eyes staring at him from the third highest pine cluster of the miniature evergreen tree.

At first glance, he saw in the reflection of a hand mirror the cartoon face of an extremely good-looking man with wavy blond hair, bright blue eyes, and a chiseled chin. Upon making eye contact, the cartoon face smiled at him and his teeth sparkled like the stars.

Rowen shifted his eyes ever so slightly to the cartoon creature that was holding the mirror and was astounded to see a gap-toothed donkey with bloodshot eyes and what seemed to be a few strands of pubic hair hanging down over its forehead.

"Nice, right?" the donkey said, nodding its head up and down in self-satisfaction.

Rowen furrowed his brow as he tried to make sense of the bizarre creature before him.

"Care for a drink?" a sultry voice sounded.

"Yes, please!" he replied, spinning around expectantly.

While Rowen took in the beautiful vision that was Aphrodite, a bizarre sensation washed over him. He felt as if his mind was being warped by radiation as Aphrodite's face transmorphed in and out of familiar faces from his previous life.

"Oh my God, it was you!" he exclaimed as the strange sensation almost overwhelmed him. "I mean, *they* was you."

Aphrodite smiled. "I enjoyed seeing you down there."

"The first time I saw you there, you were like no other. So dazzling. It was like … I got the same exact feeling then that I have looking at you now."

"Oh, Rowen," Aphrodite replied, coquettishly. "You're

such a sweetheart."

"Oh my God!" Rowen yelped, as his recognition deepened. "But then that other time! I'm so sorry! I can't believe I pushed you out of bed with my foot."

"You naughty boy!" Aphrodite replied, teasingly. "But it's fine. To be honest, I liked the way you were. So kind and flattering and hypnotic sometimes, and so unpredictable and cruel and revolting at others."

"Wait a second," Rowen blurted out, the full picture coming into focus. "It was you! You set me up! You led me like a lamb to the slaughter. If you liked me, how could you do that?"

Aphrodite flashed a wicked grin. "Revenge."

"… Yeah, I guess I had it coming."

"To be honest, it was more pride than revenge. After you *kicked* me out of bed, I never heard the end of it from the other Gods. I had to do something."

"But we're okay now? You don't hate me?"

"Of course not. How about you? How do you feel?"

"I feel … fine. No ill-will whatsoever. This is great! It's like another fresh start."

Aphrodite nodded toward the water. "Shall we take a dip?"

"Yes, please!"

Rowen's mind wandered as they drifted along a soothing current. He had been in this situation before but everything felt different. It was strange how quickly he could change from self-conceit in his prior life to self-loathing in Delemor's chamber to complete and utter serenity upon bathing.

"Rooooowen! You the man, baby!"

Rowen was brought back to reality by a group of girls screaming his name.

He looked up to find a small luxury yacht cruising by. From the second story deck, a throng of gorgeous, bikini-clad women were waving and calling out to him.

"Thank you so much for getting us on the list!" one cried.

"We totally owe you one, big cheese!" another screamed.

The girls were difficult to make out not only because of the mist, but because they were encircled by a horde of deeply tanned males with glistening muscles and little circles of light radiating behind them.

There was one exception, however. Rowen barely made out a male mortal at the back of the yacht who was mooning him. "Hey Rowen!" he screamed, slapping his cheeks. "I put the 'asses' in assassinate. See you around, bitches!!!"

Rowen turned to Aphrodite. "Was that the Pink Doe Princesses?"

"Yup. Among others."

"And that last guy, was that Felix?"

"Yup."

"Wow. Felix seems to be the same old douche, but the ladies sure seemed happy to see me."

"How could they not be?"

"Hm?"

"You saved them. Don't you remember?"

"Really?"

"Yeah, you got them on Delemor's list. If not for that, they'd be burning in Hell right now."

Rowen couldn't believe what he was hearing. "So I actually did some good."

"It depends on how you look at it."

"What do you mean?"

"Among other endeavors, Tatyana went on to run a sleazy brothel in her later years while Svetlana swindled a fortune out of her husband and fled to France with another man."

"Yikes."

"Perhaps. It doesn't really matter though as they already

141

had get-out-of-Hell-free cards."

Engrossed in the conversation, it took Rowen a second to realize that they had just washed ashore. He looked around to discover a tiny, picturesque island with black sand, a scattering of white conch shells, and a pair of reclining beach chairs facing a translucent orb.

"Care to have a look?"

"Yes, please!" Rowen replied, exuberantly. "At what, exactly?"

"At Hell. How does the 4th Circle sound?"

Rowen was unsure how to reply. "Good?"

"Care for a drink?" Aphrodite asked as Rowen settled into the heavenly recliner.

"Yes, please!"

Aphrodite handed him a frozen pina colada-looking drink complete with mini-umbrella decoration.

As Rowen took a sip of the divine beverage, what appeared to be a live feed of a small section of the 4th Circle of Hell began streaming on the orb.

The first thing that grabbed Rowen's attention was the river. Or what at first glance appeared to be a river, but instead of flowing with water, was raging with fire. It was gushing with liquid flames that whirled and seethed, lashed and spewed.

"Pyramos," Aphrodite said. "It means river of flames. This one encompassing the 4th Circle is called the Pyramos Culus."

Rowen nodded blankly.

"There are some unspeakably bad people here," Aphrodite said.

Rowen's eyes widened as he finally nodded in understanding.

On the bank of this section of the river was a steep hill. Three quarters of the way up, a tortured soul was pushing a boulder that was at least three times his size.

"I don't deserve this," the flabby, balding man lamented

as he inched the boulder up. "I was just trying to be cool."

Beads of sweat gushed out of every pore in his body as a hot sun beat down from directly overhead.

He groaned with each step. "Ouch," he cried, stepping on a jagged thorn. "Fuck," he cried, stepping on a rusty nail. "Ouch," he cried again, stepping on barbed wire.

In his wake was a stream of blood trickling all the way down to the river of fire.

Making matters worse was a flock of vultures hovering around him, pecking at his legs, back, and neck whenever his pace slowed.

"This isn't fair," he whined.

His attitude changed, however, when he finally saw the ray of hope that was the top. "Take that!" he cried, giving the boulder a final push over the ridge and onto the nearly flat summit.

The boulder came to a stop on the edge and the desperate soul let out an enormous sigh of relief.

Respite, however, was not in the cards as an ever so slight gust of wind blew, causing the boulder to teeter back over the edge and before the tortured soul could react, it was too late.

"No! No! No!" he cried, fruitlessly holding up his hands.

As the boulder slowly rolled over the pathetic soul crushing every inch of him, he let out a torrent of profanities and blood-curdling shrieks.

Rowen couldn't help but wince and feel pity. "What did he do?"

"Well, it might be difficult for you to understand at this point in your journey," Aphrodite replied. "But here goes. Whenever a scandal takes place on Earth, there are certain people who name it by attaching the word 'gate' to the end of a key word relating to the scandal."

"Gate?"

"It's a reference to a famous scandal known as Watergate."

143

Rowen nodded blankly.

"Anyway, even though it's been done to death, they think they're being extremely clever. Like they've just coined a new phrase and everyone's gonna fall down at their feet and start worshipping their brilliance."

"You're right," Rowen said. "I don't really follow, but I have a feeling that guy is exactly where he should be. Is it okay if I go down there and spit on him?"

"Your heart is in the right place, Rowen," Aphrodite said, patting his knee. "But I'm afraid that's not possible at this time."

A little further down the Pyramos Culus was an absolutely horrific sight.

At first, Rowen thought that he was looking at a hulking demon dancing by himself. The enormous being had the head of a black bull with massive gleaming horns made of obsidian, the body of a herculean giant with bulging sinewy muscles, and the powerful hind legs and surprisingly silky tail of a great steed.

Upon further inspection, Rowen noticed that the beast was having its way with a tortured soul a mere fraction of its size.

With each thrust into the man's backside, the demon let out a fearsome grunt as steam shot out of its flaring nostrils and its rippling muscles flexed.

Despite looking like a rag doll devoid of all life, with each thrust he received, the tortured soul let out an ear-splitting cry.

"Oh my God, this is awful," Rowen gasped.

"Hold on," Aphrodite said. "It looks like he's about to climax."

As the beast gave a final thrust and let out a long, satisfied grunt, the man was launched high into the air and landed half a football field away.

Upon recovering from its orgasm, the demon retrieved the limp soul, dragged him back to the designated area, and tossed him on the ground. "Your turn, Meezlebub."

It was at this point that Rowen realized that there was a line as long as the eye could see of demons of all shapes and sizes waiting their turn.

The one called Meezlebub was in the form of a degenerate human with long oily hair, salt-and-pepper stubble, and a tattered hoody zipped halfway down.

"Wow, this is truly horrible," Rowen said as Meezlebub began his session by fondling the tortured souls' genitalia. "Is this one of those ironic punishments where the guy is being raped in Hell because he raped people while on Earth?"

"No," Aphrodite replied, flatly. "This guy is here because he wore one of those irritating fedora hats all the time."

Rowen was taken aback. "A fedora hat?"

"Yeah, you know fedora hats, right? The ones with soft brims and indented crowns that are pinched on both sides near the front?"

"Oh yeah, I saw some pictures of those."

"They were repulsive eyesores when they were first invented and grew even more repugnant with time. By the early 21st century, not only were they painful to look at, but only the douchiest of douchebags wore them."

Rowen nodded. "Makes sense."

"Yeah," Aphrodite continued. "Now you'll find many of those fashion/personality offenders living out eternity here in the 4th Circle."

Further still along the Pyramos Culus was a gangly teenager with a curly red afro. He was lounging on a couch in front of a TV.

"It doesn't seem like this guy's got it too bad," Rowen observed.

"Just watch."

The rangy redhead was watching a professional basketball game and out of nowhere he went ballistic, standing up and screaming at the television.

"You're such a loudmouth, pompous, self-absorbed douche!"

"Whoa," Rowen gasped. "Where'd that come from?"

Aphrodite smiled. "He's being forced to watch games nonstop with the most irritating commenter ever."

"Nobody gives a shit how you did things in your day!" the lanky ginger shouted, spittle flying everywhere. "You weren't a God. You were just really fuckin' tall!"

Rowen couldn't help but snicker at the boy's over-the-top indignation.

The kid stood up and kicked the TV. "A nice cross-over move is NOT one of the true marvels in the history of Western Civilization, you half-witted bigfoot!"

Aphrodite smiled again. "The poor bastard doesn't even see the irony. As punishment for a lifetime of atrocities, Bill Walton the brash, young teenager is being forced to watch his future self, Bill Walton the abominable color commentator, and he's so blind to his own ugliness that he can't tell that he's watching his future self."

"No, asswipe!" the boy screamed, bashing his head against the TV, blood trickling down his face. "You're the sad human being! You're the embarrassment to basketball!! YOU'RE THE DISGRACE!!!"

"Rowen!" Delemor boomed. "Quit wanking it to the deplorables. They're not there for your enjoyment. They're there because they were human excrement. Now get back in here so we can discuss your next life."

Rowen flashed Aphrodite a that-dude's-gonna-beat-my-ass-with-a-switch-if-I-don't-get-back-there-asap look. "I'd better get going," he said, scrambling out of the lounge chair, down the beach, and into the water.

As he drifted toward Delemor's chamber, he contemplated his most recent life as well as what he had seen in the 4th Circle of Hell.

It was clear to him that he had lived a morally

questionable life. Yet at the time, he had not felt in the least like a sinner. If anything, he had felt that he was honest while almost everyone else was a hypocrite. Further, neither he nor the ladies from his harem had wound up in Hell.

Sure, he had only seen examples of three people suffering in that wretched place, but none of them seemed to be there for debauchery. But of course it was a very small glimpse of the 4th Circle, and there were at least three more most likely for other types of sinners.

It was too little information to draw any conclusions, but at least he had done something right to avoid Hell this time and to have another crack at life and therefore another crack at Empyrean.

Finally back in the chamber and sitting reverentially on his heels across from Delemor, Rowen squinted at the luminous God trying to make sense of his physical and mental makeup.

With each trip to Verixion, Rowen was able to acclimate to his surroundings a little better as he became familiar with the environment, creatures, and Gods.

Yet Delemor was an enigma.

Through the radiant light beaming from behind him, Rowen was now able to make out rough scales on Delemor's snout as well as fearsome, jagged teeth jutting out in seemingly random directions. And perhaps it was the randomness of those razor-sharp chiclets that made them so fearsome.

But on the other hand, the look in Delemor's eye seemed to be one of compassion. And it seemed that every time they met, Delemor was overcome with emotion and wept a diamond tear.

"Quit staring at me, clown!" Delemor roared.

Rowen averted his eyes to the floor underneath the table, praying that he would not be faced with the serpent coming out to punish him.

Fortunately, all was calm.

But one thing seemed certain about Delemor's disposition. No way was he in Rowen's corner.

"So what is it that I can do for you this time, buddy? What would you like to get out of your next life?"

"I have to be honest, I'm again a little perplexed. I wanted to be an adult and do fun things that adults do, but apparently I went overboard."

"Did you now?"

"To be honest, I'm not sure how I ended up that way. I can't identify with the person that I just was in the slightest."

"I'm sure he'd say the same thing about you."

"Who would?"

"You would, you brain fart. The former you. The Rasputin you. I'm sure he'd shake his head at you like you're shaking your head at him."

"I just … I just don't know what I was thinking."

"Well, when you're down there, there are a lot of factors influencing your development. You and I can work out a few of the big picture items and even some of the details, but in order to make it interesting, a lot of who you become and what you do depends on your circumstances and your decisions."

"So then it's like half destiny, half free will?"

"Nope."

"No? Then like 75% free will?"

"Look, stinky cheese," Delemor said, getting frustrated with the conversation. "It all depends. It depends on you, your surroundings, and Us. And it depends on which life you're living. Sometimes we don't give a shit and you're free to do whatever the fuck you want, to the degree that your situation allows. And sometimes there's a whole lotta celestial interest and almost everything you do and encounter is because of Us."

"Wow. I don't know if I'm happy to hear that or sad."

"No one cares whether you're happy to hear that or sad.

Your emotions are irrelevant. But what I do care about – albeit not that much – is discussing your next life. So what can I do for you?"

Rowen furrowed his brow. "Maybe that's it. Maybe that's what I'd like to do."

As Rowen thought out loud to himself, he heard hissing underneath the table and his eyes widened with fear as he saw Delemor's serpent tail swaying back and forth, ready to strike.

"I'm sorry! I mean, maybe I could live a life where I care more. Where I put a little more thought into what living a good life really means. In this last life, all I was concerned with was fame and success. I wanted to be popular. I wanted to stick out; at the tavern, at the royal court, everywhere."

"But in hindsight, you'd rather not stick out because the nail that sticks out gets hammered down, is it?"

"Yes," Rowen replied without thinking.

"But at least you got to do your fair share of hammering, no?"

"No. I mean, it's not that I regret being a target if that's what you mean. It's that, I didn't really consider what it means to live a full, just life. All I cared about was women, booze, and power."

"I thought you cared about salvation."

"Did I? Looking back, I can't even tell. Maybe that was just an unconventional, rebellious outlook used solely to attract the attention and affection of women. I think I may have been a sham."

"I know you were a sham. You're always a sham."

"And that's the point. I think I'd like to live a life where I continuously contemplate what it means to be good. Where I'm not just concerned with my own ambition, but with right and wrong. A fully-examined life where we all work hard to debate and discuss our morality, and where justice is served."

The more excited Rowen got, the more disinterested Delemor became. "Hmph," Delemor groaned, slumping back into his throne. "Some kind of age of philosophy, is it?"

"Yes!" Rowen replied. "That sounds perfect!"

Delemor yawned. "Okay, I'm growing bored of you already so I can make that happen to speed things up. Anything else?"

"Well, last time I was extremely blessed to have the help of Dionysus so often."

Delemor raised an eyebrow.

"This time," Rowen continued. "I don't want to ask too much, but would it be possible to just communicate with a God at some point if needed?"

Delemor sighed. "At some point?"

"You know, like if I'm at a critical crossroad and really need some advice or to know the answer to a question or something."

"Well, if you're willing to put the effort in, I know just the right place for you."

"Thank you so much!"

"So while I am in a charitable mood, I'm still gonna need some concessions in return for all this generosity."

Rowen sighed. "Ummm … I'm not really concerned with looks this time so you could give me like a huge nose and a unibrow and stuff like that."

"I guess," Delemor agreed reluctantly, as if doing Rowen a favor.

"Or maybe some unforeseen negative consequence or two that comes from living a fully-examined life?"

Delemor seemed amused by this. "Well, you know, when you start questioning everything, you start doubting everything."

"Yeah, that sounds pretty bad."

"So in that vein … you will never trust a word that comes out of the love of your life's mouth."

"Not a word?" Rowen replied, meekly.

"Okay," Delemor said patronizingly, as if granting a major concession. "Since I'm in such a generous mood today, I won't make it *everything* she says ... just the important stuff. Oh, and you're gonna have a gummy smile."

"A gummy smile? What do you mean?"

"You know, excessive gingival display."

"..."

"When you smile, your pearly whites are gonna be vastly overshadowed by your gums. Basically, all anyone is gonna see when you smile is a mouthful of gums."

"... Well, I guess if ..."

"Also, you're gonna have a tic."

"A tic? Like my face will suddenly twitch for no reason?"

"Face, shoulders, legs, arms, back, ass, throat ... let's not limit ourselves here. All options are on the table."

Rowen grimaced.

"Meng Po!" Delemor called. "Can we get this seeker of light a drink, please?!"

The sweet old lady once again brought in a cup of her special concoction and handed it to Rowen.

She smiled affably as he chugged it down. "Shit happens."

"I'm sorry?" Rowen asked while being helped to his feet.

"You go ahead and think your ass off, but all the knowledge you need is crammed into those two little words. Shit happens."

As the adorable old deity cackled, Rowen's vision went haywire and his entire world went dark.

POMPEII, ITALY

1ST CENTURY AD

"It is a beautiful day for a dump, is it not, my good friend?" Rowen said to Francesco as the two young men entered the public latrine.

"It sure is," Francesco replied, patting Rowen on the back. "I cannot wait to empty my bowels with you and all these other fine folk."

The sun was shining brilliantly upon the open-air, horseshoe-shaped toilet facility located in the city center. It was an engineering feat able to service over two dozen defecators at any one time.

Along the perimeter was a stone bench with holes cut into it every few feet on which to sit upon and do your business. Water flowed steadily underneath, swiftly washing the excrement away.

In front of the bench was a footrest with a small trench of running water to scoop and rinse with when your business was finished.

As they stepped through the entrance, Rowen admired the marble elephant head and ran his hand down the smooth trunk from which water gushed underneath the benches.

The entire city was decorated with beautiful stone carvings and statues which served as ever-present reminders of Pompeii's culture and sophistication.

"I can't go anywhere in this city without feeling an enormous sense of pride," Rowen said to Francesco.

"Indeed," Francesco replied, as they squeezed past a string of gentleman and overheard a symphony of plops into the water below.

They found a couple of empty spaces toward the back of the U, lifted their togas up, and let out contented sighs as they took their seats.

"I can't imagine not having this," Rowen said, unable to wipe the grin from his face.

"Yeah," Francesco agreed. "If you're not relieving yourself at an open-air public facility, you're not living your life right."

"There's just nothing better," Rowen said, briefly able to wipe the grin from his face as a slight grimace took its place while he helped push his business along. "Here we are, united together in a glorious celebration of nature's most basic of needs."

"True intimacy," Francesco said, nodding. "And all the while we get to converse and debate the matters of the day. Anyone not doing it like this is doing it wrong."

"And not just with our friends," Rowen continued, surveying the multitude of gentleman crapping in their vicinity. "But with everyone. Regardless of whether one is rich or poor, we come together here as one, all with an equal voice."

"Indeed," Francesco replied, pondering this last bit. "While this wondrous human experience is enhanced by discussing politics with strangers …" Francesco lowered his voice and gave a sideways glance at a long-haired, emaciated young man in a tattered tunic. "Perhaps we needn't hear everyone's opinion."

"Nonsense," Rowen replied, emphatically. "Lending an ear to everyone is what has made this city great."

"So you don't think we've gone too far?" Francesco asked. "You don't think that despite there being clear differences among us, that this notion of equality hasn't gotten carried away?"

"Not in the least. I think we have the perfect amount of equality. In fact, I think that this is the golden age of equality."

"Certainly, our women would all agree with you. They've never had it so good. They're clearly the weaker sex in just about every category, and yet they're treated as if they're practically our equal."

"Do you really think so?"

"Of course."

"Are you sure? While men engage in romantic affairs with impunity, women can be exiled for doing so."

"Oh, come on. Affairs are a natural part of male behavior. It's how we're constructed. It can't be helped."

"Also," Rowen added. "They can't vote or hold political office, and they're raped quite frequently with no means of recourse."

"Phooey on that. It's not like we force them to marry their rapists or burn them to death when their husbands die like they do in some cultures."

"Phooey on that!" the emaciated fellow chimed in, glaring at Francesco. He had light skin, light eyes, and a rather high-pitched voice. "Do you understand the kind of hardships our society puts upon women?! It's outrageous! Women are integral parts of our society, as much as, or even more than men are. They should be treated as fully equal to men. Including the right to vote, the right to hold political office, and the right to not get raped all the time!"

While Rowen was taken aback by the stranger's sudden outburst, Francesco burst into laughter. "You think women should be fully equal?!" he asked, condescendingly.

"Yes," the frail-looking fellow replied, defiantly. "Not only do I think it, but one day it will happen. Mark my words!"

"How could that possibly happen?" Francesco replied, turning to Rowen. "How could the inferior sex become equal? It's not natural, is it, my good friend?"

Rowen pondered the idea for a moment. "I suppose it doesn't make much sense, does it?"

"You see?" Francesco said, turning back to the young

man. "You're talking nonsense!"

"But," Rowen interjected. "What if someone had been trying to get laid?"

"What do you mean?" Francesco replied.

"Like, in order to sleep with a woman, what if a man in political power offered up equality?"

Francesco was incredulous. "What?! To get pussy? Who would decide to do that?! Just take it!"

"You'll see," the emaciated fellow again chimed in, ominously. "Maybe not today ... maybe not tomorrow ... but someday. Someday, society will wise up and women will be treated as equal – as they should – and they'll look back upon fellows like you as brutes."

Francesco laughed, dismissively. "Sure, why not?! And then maybe not that day ... or the day after ... but someday. Someday after that, society will wise up again and look back upon those people as pussies. Now would you get out of here you rabble-rouser, you're ruining my crap."

In a huff, the young waif scooped a handful of water from the small trench, splashed his butthole with it, and stormed off.

"What do you think, Gilgamesh?" Francesco said to his head slave who was sitting attentively at his side. "Do you think women should be treated as fully equal?"

"Women?! Fully equal?!" Gilgamesh replied, flashing a did-you-just-go-full-retard-on-me? look. "Now that's a notion I can wash my ass with."

***

"Zeus' tit!" Francesco cried out in consternation. "Would you look at this?!"

After finishing their business, Rowen and Francesco decided to head to the Colosseum to take in the early afternoon wild beast feeding. As they made their way along one of the main thoroughfares, Francesco came face to face

155

with some horrifying graffiti:

Francesco is mediocre

"Can you believe this? How dare some scoundrel drag my good name through the mud!"

"It is an outrage," Rowen sympathized.

"Gilgamesh! Have that one clean it off at once," Francesco shouted, pointing to one of his other slaves.

Gilgamesh promptly slapped the man on the back of the head. "Find some supplies without haste and remove that monstrosity!"

***

"The end is nigh!!!"

As Rowen and Francesco approached the entrance to the Colosseum, they encountered a disheveled man screaming the phrase at passersby careless enough to make eye contact.

"What do you suppose that vagrant is on about?" Francesco asked Rowen.

"Why, I think he means to preach to us."

"For what? To inform us that the end of the world is coming?"

"I believe so. I think he means to warn us so that we can prepare."

"But it doesn't even make sense. What's there to prepare for? If the end comes, it's over. … It's literally the end."

"I agree, my good friend."

"What can possibly be done once everything has ended?! Nothing! It's all over!"

"Perhaps he means that the end of this world is coming, but he knows a way to get a leg up in the next one."

"The *next* one?! If there's a next one, then it's really not an end at all, is it? Sounds more like some kind of checkpoint or intermission. This lunatic is really testing my patience … and my patience is *failing!*"

Francesco grabbed his head slave by the shoulder. "Gilgamesh," he shouted, pointing to another one of his slaves. "Have that one give that schizoid a stern kick to the groin."

Gilgamesh promptly slapped the subordinate slave on the back of the head. "Shake a leg and go punt that man's twig and berries!"

***

"It is a beautiful day for an exotic animal feeding, is it not, my good friend?" Rowen said to Francesco as they settled into their seats.

"It sure is," Francesco replied, patting Rowen on the shoulder. "I hope the beasts are famished."

The sun was still shining brightly, and the atmosphere was electric at the city's crown jewel. A packed house of over 6,800 people were chomping at the bit for some much-anticipated entertainment.

Even more so than the open-air public latrine, the Colosseum was an engineering marvel adored by all.

The magnificent limestone structure was three stories high with terraced bleachers from the ground-level up. The main field was made of sand and concrete and was built a full 15 feet underground. Along the perimeter wall was a series of openings with sliding steel-barred gates allowing entrance and exit as desired.

Beyond these openings, as well as below the main field, was an elaborate labyrinth of halls and holding cells unseen by the spectators.

However, what made the Colosseum stand out as a true architectural masterpiece was not the size or the sight, but the sound. The ingenious design allowed for even the slightest peep from a competitor to ripple through the bleachers all the way up to the highest row. As such, nary a last breath went unheard by even those in the cheapest of seats.

Another testament to the culture of equality.

"They had best not bring out any herbivores like that buffoon giraffe they peddled out there last time," Francesco said.

"Ladies and gentlemen," the announcer called out from the broadcast box in the first row. "From the House of Titus, I give you Dungi, a lethargic slave who was more interested in eating than working."

"Booooooo!!!!!!!" the crowd shouted as a heavy-set man was pushed through one of the gates onto the field.

"Dungi," the announcer called. "Since eating is your favorite thing in this world, perhaps you'll enjoy an exotic beast eating you!"

Wide-eyed, Dungi back-pedaled toward the center of the field, anxiously surveying the grounds.

Without warning, a tiger burst through a gate across the field and beelined it for Dungi.

"Also from the House of Titus," the announcer called, "a Bengal tiger all the way from India. Ladies and gentlemen, say hello to Peaches!"

The crowd erupted in applause as the tiger leapt at Dungi, knocked him to the ground, and quickly went to work ripping him apart limb by limb.

"Take that, Dungi!" Rowen screamed as Peaches bit into his abdomen, growling as she ripped out his entrails.

***

"Ladies and gentlemen," the announcer called once they had removed a sated Peaches from the field. "From the House of Romulus, I give you Nabu, a whiny slave who couldn't take a beating without back-talking incessantly."

"Booooooo!!!!!!!" the crowd shouted as a defiant man

with an abundance of scars on his back and legs was pushed through a gate onto the field.

"Nabu," the announcer called. "Since back-talking is your favorite thing to do in this world, feel free to sass this African hippopotamus as it mauls you to death! Go get him, Chompers."

The crowd erupted in cheers as an enormous hippo charged Nabu at an alarming speed. Paralyzed by shock and fear, Nabu failed to even attempt to move out of the way. At top speed, the hippo plunged its head square into Nabu's chest, sending him flying into the wall and shattering practically every bone in his body.

"Take that, you whiny bitch!" Francesco jeered as Nabu's gray matter seeped out of his cracked skull and onto the ground.

"This sure takes the stress out of life, doesn't it, my good friend?" Rowen said to Francesco as the Colosseum workers made their way onto the field to escort the hippo out and clean up the mess that was Nabu.

"It sure does," Francesco concurred.

"While I can't imagine a more satisfying form of entertainment, do you suppose it might be a bit overboard?"

"Overboard?! Don't be ridiculous. These soulless monsters aren't just slaves, they're criminals. Haven't you been listening to the introductions?"

"I suppose you have me there," Rowen conceded. "But what about the practice of slavery in-and-of-itself? Perhaps subjugating human beings is not the right thing to do?"

"Oh, come now. It's as natural as breathing. For as long as there has been civilization, there has been slavery. In fact, without slavery, civilization itself would not be possible. How do you think our glorious empire was built?"

Assuming this was a rhetorical question, Rowen waited for Francesco to continue.

"… Well?" Francesco asked, intent on receiving an

answer.

"By massive amounts of unpaid labor."

"Precisely. They're the backbone of our economy. Without them – and without the keen oversight of intellectual superiors such as you and I – we'd still be living in the Stone Age."

"But still, now that we've advanced this far and have a more refined and enlightened ideology, shouldn't we reconsider whether it is just to enslave fellow human beings?"

"Nonsense," Francesco replied without missing a beat. "They are the spoils of war. We are not simply picking people out at random, we are putting our defeated foes to good use. I'd go so far as to say that we're doing them a favor. Taking them from the ashes of some backwater hellhole and bringing them to the pinnacle of sophistication."

"I suppose you're right in that they're going from no civilization to the greatest civilization in history, but the fact that they're branded, whipped, and sometimes even killed seems a little questionable. Perhaps we should treat them a little more fairly?"

"More fairly?!" Francesco repeated, incredulously. "They're treated more than fair. They're only beaten when they're not working hard enough or when we need to get them going. Like whipping an ox when ploughing a field."

"Are you suggesting that they're on the same level as livestock?"

"Yes, most of them are indeed as useful as farm animals. … Oh wait, you meant that the other way, didn't you? In that case … ummm … sorta? I suppose some of them might not be as low as a beast of burden – the ones who are able to speak a word or two of our language anyway – but there's no denying that they're a vastly inferior ethnicity. I mean, c'mon, they're savages. Have you heard of some of the Gods that they believe in?"

"…"

"For instance, they pray to some bizarre God called Mithra. And when they gather together to worship, they somehow eat his flesh and drink his blood to become one with him. Can you think of anything more disturbing or more barbarian?"

"My goodness, no."

"And have you not heard of some of the food that they eat?!" Francesco turned to his head slave. "Gilgamesh, isn't it true that the people of your home country eat stews containing dung beetles?"

Gilgamesh smiled sheepishly. "It is true."

"You see?" Francesco said, flashing Rowen a self-satisfied smile.

At the precise moment that Francesco finished speaking, Ganesha—God of Reason, Intellect, and Outlandishly Phallic Noses—struck.

Rowen's left eye began to twitch and his cheek muscles spasmed uncontrollably.

"Oh boy," Francesco sighed. "Do you need to have an epileptic seizure every time you think of a decent counter-argument? Your face is hard enough to look at as it is."

"S-s-s-s-sorry," Rowen replied, as the convulsions came to a halt. "I've got it. It's so simple."

"Go ahead, spit it out."

"If you were born there, you'd do it to."

"What do you mean?" Francesco said, furrowing his brow.

"If you had been born where Gilgamesh was, and were raised by his parents, and had grown up in his community, you'd probably eat the flesh of that God and drink his blood, too. I don't know how, or why, because it's the most insanely disturbing thing I've ever heard; I mean, it sounds like something only a serial killer would do, but nonetheless, you'd probably think it natural. And if you'd grown up eating dung beetles, you'd probably think them sweet.

161

Right, Gilgamesh?"

Gilgamesh shook his head furiously. "Oh no, they are not sweet. They make vinegar look like sugar. But they give you great energy."

Francesco nodded as he contemplated Rowen's point. "I think you may be onto something there, my good friend. And if you are, then certainly the case must apply in reverse. If they were born here, they'd do it, too."

Rowen tilted his head, not quite getting Francesco's gist.

"If Gilgamesh had been born in my place, and I in his," Francesco continued, taking hold of the broad leather belt that was wrapped around Gilgamesh's waist, "it would be me wearing this belt with Gilgamesh's name on it."

Gilgamesh smiled.

"Yeah, I bet you'd like that," Francesco said. "He wouldn't think twice about it. It would be as natural as breathing, because that would have been the culture he had grown up in. There's nothing that can be done, really. Anyone growing up in our shoes would of course believe the same things that we do, and eat and drink the same food and wine that we do, and beat the living shit out of one of their slaves if the dimwit brought out a fruit tray containing green grapes instead of purple grapes. Hell, even if something that we engage in were hypothetically immoral, it couldn't possibly be our fault because it's simply a product of the time and culture that we live in. Isn't that right, my good friend?"

Rowen thought hard on Francesco's argument before breaking into a giant, sheepish grin. "I suppose so."

"Good lord!" Francesco cried at the sight of Rowen's uber-gummy smile. "How many times do I have to tell you to keep those lips zipped when you smile?! How many children must be frightened? How many babies must cry?! When will this end, my good friend?!!!"

"Sorry," Rowen replied, buttoning his lips.

"Ladies and gentlemen," the announcer called, once

again gaining everyone's attention. "From the House of Flavius, I give you Suzub! He's not particularly foul-tempered or the like, but he does have a terribly unsightly mole on his back."

"Boooooooo!!!!!!!" the crowd jeered as a slender man with a very confused look on his face was pushed through a gate onto the field.

"Suzub," the announcer called. "Since unsightly things are your bag of tea, how about this black mamba!"

As the announcer finished his line, a black mamba was launched through a gate a quarter of the way onto the field.

"Ladies and gentlemen," the announcer continued. "All the way from Africa, I give you the deadliest snake in the world! Say hello to Smooches! Give him a kiss will you, Suzub?!"

The crowd erupted in applause.

Wide-eyed, Suzub sprinted back to the wall next to the gate he had just come out of, pinned his back up against it, and stared at the snake in fear.

The black mamba slithered toward the middle of the field, coiled itself up into a defensive position, and waited.

Suzub, unable to move, also waited.

After what seemed like an eternity but was probably more like five seconds, a spectator in the first row looming over Suzub dumped his wine all over the slave's head.

The crowd erupted in cheers and a few others followed suit, prompting Suzub to find a spot toward the center of the field that was out of striking distance of both the black mamba and the ornery spectators.

After what seemed like an eternity but was probably more like ten seconds, the announcer intervened, desperate to get the action going.

"Suzub," he called. "Quit being a coward and approach that snake!"

Suzub's eyes almost popped out of his head. He couldn't help but shake his head in disbelief.

"Gentlemen," the announcer called. "We have a live one. Please take your positions."

At the announcer's instruction, impossibly muscular guards in steel helmets with gladius swords hanging from their hips emerged from each gate and closed in on Suzub.

"Suzub," the announcer called. "Quit being a coward and approach that snake or these gentlemen will cut you into a thousand pieces one stroke at a time."

Suzub gulped nervously. Having no other choice, he slowly walked toward the snake.

The black mamba's jet black eyes, pulsating scales, and flickering tongue glistened in the sun. It made for a petrifying sight, but for the moment Smooches remained calm.

Suzub came within a few footsteps of the snake and tread carefully in a circle around it while it eyed him suspiciously.

"Suzub!" the announcer roared. "You quit being a coward and give that snake a kick in the face!"

Suzub's eyes once again almost popped out of his head as he flashed a this-is-God-damn-ridiculous look.

A metallic sound cascaded through the Colosseum as the guards unsheathed their swords in unison and began marching toward Suzub.

"Okay, okay," Suzub muttered. He bit his lip in determination, planted his left foot halfway toward the black mamba, and punted it with all his might.

Smooches hissed violently as he flew through the air and the crowd fell silent as its venomous fangs sunk deep into the thigh of one of the guards.

"Suzub, you coward!" the announcer called. "You weren't supposed to use the snake as a weapon!"

As Smooches dangled by its fangs from the guard's leg, the adjacent guard fearlessly sliced him in half.

"Guards!" the announced roared. "Finish the job!"

The crowd went berserk.

"Take that, you snake charmer!" Rowen screamed as the legion of guards slowly cut Suzub to pieces.

***

"Ready to head to the Classy Cat?" Francesco asked Rowen as the last of Suzub's remains were carried off the field.

"But it's time for the gladiators," Rowen whined.

"Come now, you know I can't stand the gladiator bit. It makes me uncomfortable."

"But it's even more popular than the wild beast feedings. The people love it. Some of these guys are real heroes. Men of great virility."

"Exactly," Francesco said, shaking his head in frustration. "You know that the word 'gladiator' is based on the word 'sword,' right?"

"Yes."

"Which you know also means 'penis,' right? I can't just sit here and watch these virile penises cross swords, it's extremely distressing."

"Well, I find it inspiring!" Rowen said, defiantly.

"Are you coming with me to the Classy or not?" Francesco finished, heading toward the exit before even hearing Rowen's reply.

Defeated, Rowen gathered his belongings and scrambled after his good friend.

***

Before ducking through the entrance curtain of Pompeii's most notorious entertainment establishment, Francesco and Rowen took a moment to admire the emblem stitched into it.

A busty, scantily clad personified cat in the middle of a seductive belly dance was beckoning passersby with a

165

come-hither wink.

"You can't help but dive right in," Francesco said, pushing through the curtain and into the reception area where they were greeted by a charismatic woman with graying hair.

"Welcome, gentlemen!" she said with a smile. "How are you doing this fine day?"

"Very good," Rowen replied, feeling a little anxious as usual.

"Fantastic!" Francesco chimed in. "But not as fantastic as one lucky lady will be doing in a few minutes. Just look at the specimen I've brought with me today."

Francesco was of course alluding to Rowen as if he were male beauty incarnate. He rarely missed an opportunity to give his good friend a good ribbing.

"Just look at that nose," Francesco continued. "It makes Vesuvius look like an anthill."

Rowen blushed.

"Well, I like it," the hostess said. "I think it makes you look dignified."

"And how about that unibrow?" Francesco said. "Clip that thing and we could make you a sweater."

"Well, I like his eyebrows, too," the hostess replied, gracefully. "It makes you look distinguished."

Rowen's eyes lit up and he couldn't help but smile.

"And there's our winning smile," Francesco said.

The hostess made a face as if she had been jabbed in the gut. "Yeah, you probably shouldn't smile."

"At any rate," Francesco said, rubbing his hands together, eager to get down to business. "What's the vacancy situation looking like?"

"It's wide open. You guys have beaten the postgames rush and are the first ones here. You have your pick of the litter."

"Fantastic," Francesco replied, rubbing his palms together. "I don't suppose that a certain 'Wolf Girl' of shall we say 'high standing' is on duty today, is she?"

Francesco and Rowen had long heard rumors that Empress Valeria, wife of Emperor Claudius, would often sneak off to the Classy Cat to indulge her insatiable sexual appetite. She reportedly performed under the alias, Wolf Girl.

"Ah," the hostess replied, leaning in close and speaking in a hushed tone. "You mean Lyciska. Unfortunately, she is not here at the moment."

"Do you have any idea what kind of hours she keeps?"

"I'm afraid I do not. She comes and goes when the mood strikes. She is like a fiery comet shooting through the night sky; passionate, and impossible to predict."

Francesco nodded. "I see."

"But since you are the first here, please feel free to have a look at the murals above the doorways and select whichever kitty cat strikes your fancy."

"Thank you," Francesco replied respectfully before heading down the candle-lit hallway.

"Thank you," Rowen echoed, giving the hostess a tight-lipped smile.

As they wandered down the hallway, stopping to inspect each woman's specialty, they were often able to peer into the room and catch glimpses of the ladies lounging seductively on beds covered in fine blankets and furs.

"This one looks quite enjoyable," Francesco said, pausing in front of a painting of a woman lying over the armrest of a sofa chair with a male taking her from behind.

Rowen blushed and kept moving.

"How about this one?" Francesco asked, pointing to a mural of a woman lying down on her shoulders with her arms flat on the ground and her buttocks raised high in the air. Her legs were folded back over her such that her knees were on the ground next to her head and her shins on the ground above her. Kneeling directly over her head was the male with his pelvis pressed into hers.

"I don't even understand what's going on," Rowen mumbled.

"Well, I'm sold," Francesco said, as Rowen scurried down the hallway to the next one.

After inspecting a few more specialty positions that he deemed too dangerous, too complicated, or too ambitious, Rowen finally found the perfect one. A woman lying on her back with the man lying on top of her.

***

"To the good life!" Francesco said, raising his mug of wine.

"To the good life!" Rowen repeated, clinking jugs but saying a silent prayer of thanks to Ganesha, his favorite six-armed God, before drinking.

The two were seated at the bar of their usual drinking establishment, the Lotus Pad, a damp hole in the wall with a musky smell.

"Is there anything better than that first sip of wine after some profoundly satisfying exercise?!" Francesco said, basking in the afterglow of another gratifying trip to the Classy Cat.

"I'll drink to that," Rowen replied, having another gulp while surveying the clientele. "Don't look now," he said in a hushed voice, "but I think that guy from our morning BM is here."

Francesco immediately turned to find the emaciated young man from the public latrine glaring at him over his drink.

"What is that rabble-rouser doing here?!" Francesco said to Rowen in obvious irritation.

"It's nothing," Rowen replied, soothingly. "He's just having a drink like you and I."

"Well, he's ruining mine."

"Don't give it any thought."

"I don't want to, but now that I think about it … I bet … I bet …" Francesco stood up abruptly and marched over to the young man. "It was you, wasn't it?!"

The young man flinched. "What are you talking about?"

"You've got it in for me, don't you, you miscreant?!"

"Leave me alone."

"You're the one dragging my good name through the muck."

"I don't know what you're talking about."

"You graffitied that wall with that outrageous, that slanderous, that injurious phrase, 'Francesco is mediocre.' How dare you?!"

"I've got nothing to do with it."

Francesco turned to Rowen who had run up to his side, hoping to keep things calm. "Do you believe this, Rowen? First, he tries to destroy my reputation, and now, he lies about it. To my face!"

"It might not have been him," Rowen replied.

"Oh, it was him, alright!" Francesco slammed his hands on the table and leaned over it staring daggers at the young man. "And I'm not gonna stand for it like some garbage plebeian! No, I've got a mind to … I've got a mind to … I've got a mind to call Gilgamesh in here and have him smash this scoundrel upside the head with my jug of wine."

"Francesco, no!" Rowen cried, desperately. "Let's not resort to violence. We can settle this like gentlemen."

As Francesco turned his head toward Rowen, the young man took the opportunity to plunge a knife into the top of Francesco's hand and flee as Francesco screamed in pain.

"Ahhhhhhhhh!!!" Francesco shrieked. "He stabbed me! The delinquent stabbed me! Pull it out! Pull it out!!!"

In a panic, Rowen braced Francesco's arm with one hand and pulled the knife out with the other. Blood oozed from the wound.

"It hurts! It huuurrrrrrts!!!" Francesco screamed in agony. "That bastard! He's crippled me! I'm done for! My

169

hand is crippled!"

The owner came around the bar and gave Francesco a cloth to wrap the wound in.

"This is all your fault!" Francesco yelled at Rowen. "If you hadn't distracted me, I would've had Gilgamesh in here to glass that son of a bitch and it would be his blood all over the table and not mine. You're gonna pay for this, Rowen!"

"I'm very sorry," Rowen pleaded. "Let's get you home to recover. Hopefully, your hand will heal."

***

"I may never be able to use my hand again," Francesco said to Rowen the next day as he lay in bed recuperating. "I demand satisfaction!"

"I'm very sorry, my good friend," Rowen replied. "If there's anything I can do, please just say the word and I shall do it."

"While I'm still extremely angry at you, I like your attitude. Clearly, we can agree that since you distracted me and allowed that bastard to mutilate me, you bear responsibility and must therefore provide compensation."

"I didn't intend to distract you, and I'm absolutely sick about it, but do you really think it's my fault?"

"Yes. How could it not be? If you hadn't distracted me, that fatherless hemorrhoid wouldn't have stabbed me. Therefore, it's 100% your fault."

"But what about him? He's the one who stabbed you."

"It's 100% his fault as well. And I fully intend to have him fed to a wild beast at the Colosseum, but right now we're talking about you. I demand compensation!"

"Well, what would you like me to do? I'd be more than happy to help you to recover. Perhaps I can buy some salve or ointment from town and apply it to the wound each day?"

Francesco burst out laughing. "The punishment must fit the crime, you dolt, and that doesn't even begin to scratch the surface. No, the penalty must be much much stiffer." He lowered his eyelids and stroked his chin for a moment in thought. When the solution came, his eyes popped open. "You will be my slave."

"What?"

"As compensation, I demand that you become my slave for the remainder of your days."

"You want me to be your slave because I tried to prevent you from getting in a fight?"

"No. Not because of what you tried to do, but because of what you did. It was because of you that I was assaulted. What you did was tantamount to aiding and abetting a violent criminal. I will have my satisfaction."

"But surely, that is too far. I'd be happy to provide compensation in a reasonable fashion, but that would not be fair. Not at all. I cannot agree to this."

"No? Then we are at an impasse. How would you suggest we resolve this?"

"Well, we could ask Pliny the Elder. He is renowned for his wisdom and surely he could provide us with a just resolution."

"Pliny the Elder?! That senile old windbag?! I wouldn't trust him to judge a game of rock, paper, scissors. No, there must be a better way. We need a determination from a much higher source, one with actual knowledge and authority."

"Well, we could go to the Oracle at Delphi. There's no higher source than an actual God."

"The Oracle at Delphi? In Greece? But we're Roman." Francesco pondered this for a beat. "Ah, I guess when you think about it, we're pretty much the same. I'm in. Let's do it."

***

171

The journey to Delphi was a long and arduous one, but along the way Rowen and Francesco were able to discuss a number of topics that they hoped the Oracle would give them answers to on behalf of Apollo—God of Light, Prophecy, and Skinny Punks. Ideas such as whether slavery was immoral, whether everyone should have the right to vote, and whether females shouldn't be raped all the time.

"I probably should have asked this before we set out on this long and arduous journey," Rowen said as Delphi was finally in their sight, "but what do you think of the Gods in general?"

"What do you mean, my good friend?"

"Well, some philosophers have raised questions about their behavior. With all their vengeance, violence, and backstabbing, perhaps they don't make the best of role models for those of us striving to live a just life."

"I don't think it's for us mere mortals to question Gods."

"But take Zeus, for example, and his habit of coming down to Earth and sexually assaulting our women."

"Yeah, that Zeus is quite a character."

"Don't you think it's super weird and super creepy how he always inhabits an animal when doing so?"

"Yeah, that's pretty odd. But I think he caught on to the fact that you can just take on the appearance of the target's boyfriend or husband."

"Well, that's good news, I guess. It removes the bestiality aspect anyway."

"Perhaps a better question is whether the Gods even exist in the first place."

Rowen flashed Francesco a what-you-talkin'-bout-Willis?! look. The notion that the Gods might not exist had never even occurred to him.

As the idea washed over his brain, Ganesha struck, and Rowen's left eye and cheek muscles spasmed uncontrollably.

172

Francesco flinched. "Leave it to the guy whose face has an epileptic seizure whenever he has a rational thought to call Zeus weird."

"The Gods have to exist," Rowen declared. "How else can you explain water pouring out of the sky, molten lava spraying out of a mountain, and the entire world shaking suddenly?"

Francesco nodded. "This is true."

***

After a good night's sleep at the edge of Delphi, Rowen and Francesco awoke at dawn and headed to the Oracle.

Built around a sacred spring on the side of a mountain, the temple consisted of soaring marble columns encircling an open-air altar. In between the columns were ornate sculptures of Apollo, depicted in various phases of charioteering the sun across the sky.

Inside, Pythia, the high priestess of Apollo, was perched on a stool above a fuming crevice. She was surrounded by priests who took care of her and interpreted her cryptic answers from Apollo for the petitioners.

The sun shone beautifully above the temple and Rowen and Francesco were fortunate to have only a couple of groups waiting in line in front of them.

At the precise moment that Rowen first peered into the temple and caught sight of Pythia, Aphrodite—Goddess of Beauty, Horndog Love, and Shitty Dramas—pierced his heart.

Rowen then watched in rapture as she received the first group.

"This way, Your Highness," the head priest said to the leader of the first group as he guided him through the entrance and onto a standing area close to the altar. "What is it that you would like to ask?"

The dignified man turned toward Pythia. "We wish to

173

know whether we should attack the great Kingdom of Arrichion. We know that it would be a great struggle with great sacrifice. And in order to do so, we beseech you, please let us know if we will be able conquer them."

Upon finishing his question, the leader eyed Pythia with bated breath, anxiously awaiting the divine response.

Holding out his bare hand, the head priest made a little coughing sound.

Realizing his blunder, the leader quickly untied a bag full of coins from his belt and dropped it into the head priest's hand where it let out a pleasing jangle.

"Pythia," the head priest said, approaching her and gently putting a hand on her back. "Convey the message of these blessed men to our most sacred and hallowed God, Apollo, and humbly entreat Him for His holy prophesy."

The head priest then knelt in front of her stool, cupped his hands over the fuming crevice, and wafted a few handfuls of smoke toward her face before quickly retreating so as not to accidently inhale any of the forbidding gas himself.

As Pythia breathed the fumes deep into her lungs, she waved her arms rhythmically while rocking her head back and forth. Slowly, her graceful movements became increasingly stilted and her eyes rolled back into her head. It looked as though she were experiencing a slight seizure.

The main priest rushed back toward her, grabbed her shoulders, and pulled her away from the crevice. "What has He told you?"

Pythia's head flopped backward limply and Rowen could see the whites of her eyes. "Het mythr si nogna teg uyo."

"I see," the priest said, nodding as he handed her off to a couple of subordinate priests who helped her to a bench away from the crevice.

The priest approached the lead petitioner. "The illustrious and all-seeing Apollo replies as thus: 'If you wage war, a great kingdom will meet its demise.'"

A look of absolute glee spread over the leader's face as he raised a fist in the air and jumped for joy. "Hurrah!" he cried.

"Hurrah!" the rest of his group echoed.

"We're gonna win!" he screamed in pure bliss.

"To the end of Arrichion!" his men hollered, hugging and slapping one another on the back as they exited the temple full of joy and determination.

"How fantastic," Rowen said to Francesco.

"Yeah, sounds like great news," Francesco replied. "As long as it's not their kingdom meeting its demise."

"Right this way, gentleman," the priest said to the pair of handsome young men next in line.

"Here you are, Father," the senior of the two said, handing over a small bag of coins. "It's all we could muster."

"Thank you, my sons. Now what is it that you would like to ask?"

"My little brother's in a bit of a pickle. Our parents have promised him to the daughter of the Dominus of Hideos. While he would still rather sow his wild oats, she is not so bad to look at that you would castrate yourself at the first sight of her. Further, her family is quite wealthy. As such, even if he were to abandon bachelorhood and wed the girl, I think he could still live a happy life. But obviously, we have our doubts. Could you please let us know whether he should go through with the marriage?"

The little brother fidgeted nervously with his hands as he waited for the answer.

"Oh shit," Rowen said to Francesco as they watched the scene unfold. "We may have made a huge mistake in coming here."

"Why's that?"

"It seems that everyone is asking for visions of the future, whereas we're looking for a judgment. Oh man, we may have gone through that long, arduous journey for nothing."

"Don't worry about it," Francesco replied, dismissively. "The Pythia communicates with Apollo. She'll get us our answer."

"I hope so," Rowen replied, somewhat relieved. "Hey, do you think she's alright?"

"Yeah, why do you ask?"

"Look at her. Huffing those fumes can't be good." After a few more deep breaths from above the steaming crevice, Pythia's whole body again began to convulse.

"Seems about what we should expect for a conduit to a God, no?" Francesco said.

"I suppose," Rowen replied, unconvinced. "But look how out of sorts her breathing is, and how sweaty she is, and how her eyes keep rolling back in her head. I think she's huffing poison, my good friend. If she keeps this up, I think she could die."

"Oh, stop being so dramatic. She's fine. She's literally talking to a God right now. If anything were to happen, He'd save here."

"Veren nogna vieg uyo pu!" Pythia shouted, spasmodically.

"I see," the priest said, once again nodding his head in understanding as the subordinate priests helped her to the bench away from the fumes.

The priest approached the brothers. "The illustrious and all-seeing Apollo replies as thus: 'If you marry the daughter of Dominus of Hideos, a great fortune will be devoured.'"

The brothers turned to each other and locked eyes for a moment blank-faced, before their eyes lit up and huge smiles broke over their faces.

"I'm getting married, big brother!"

"You certainly are, little brother! You have a fortune to consume!"

After a jubilant embrace, the brothers leapt up and down as they exited the temple.

"Wow," Rowen said to Francesco. "Everyone's getting such good news."

"Yeah, as long as they're interpreting it right."

"Right this way, gentleman," the priest said as they entered the temple and took the designated spot a few paces from the Pythia.

Francesco elbowed Rowen.

"Here you go, Father," Rowen said, pulling out a bag of coins and handing it to the priest.

"Go ahead and ask what you'd like to know."

Francesco bowed his head to the priest, then turned to Pythia. "Your High Priestess, my good friend here Rowen and I got into a bit of a verbal scrap with a local thug and at the moment I was about to call in some protection, Rowen distracted me, creating an opening for the thug to attack. Of course, the thug seized the opportunity and plunged a razor-sharp dagger into my hand which not only caused me grave pain, but as you can see has rendered it near useless." Francesco held his hand out limply before continuing. "As punishment for his part in this criminal offense, we humbly ask the awe-inspiring Apollo what kind of restitution I am owed from Rowen. He should be my slave, right?!"

The priest once again put a gentle hand on Pythia's back while asking her to commune with Apollo, then cupped his hands above the crevice and enveloped her in fumes.

"It doesn't smell right in here at all," Rowen said under his breath to Francesco.

"I must admit," Francesco replied. "It does smell a bit poisony."

"The poor thing. They're torturing her."

"It's not that bad."

Pythia's body once again began to writhe violently as spittle flew from her mouth.

"Okay," Francesco conceded. "I suppose she could have it a little better."

"We've got to save her!"

"Kewa em pu rofeeb uyo og-og…" Pythia began in an eerily low voice.

"Indeed," the priest said, helping Pythia up and bending an ear toward her as she continued mumbling while being helped to the bench.

"Gentleman," he said, taking position in front of Rowen and Francesco. "The illustrious and all-seeing Apollo replies as thus: 'My domain is not judgments, it is prophecies.'"

"Oh crap, I knew it."

"Nevertheless," the priest continued. "Since He is in a generous mood today, the illustrious and all-seeing Apollo judges as follows: 'The unsightly one shall provide restitution to the self-absorbed one in the form of the unsightly one's favorite possession.'"

Upon hearing the word of Apollo, Rowen and Francesco turned to each other and locked eyes for a moment blank-faced, before they both broke into smug I-told-you-so-douchebag smiles.

***

"Good morning, Sunshine!"

Pythia awoke with a start to find a blurry stranger hovering over her.

Watching the scene unfold was Aphrodite, who couldn't help but be moved by the romantic situation. A damsel in distress rescued by a budding knight in shining armor coming to underneath a persimmon tree in a picturesque orchard just outside of Delphi.

"I've got some fruit for you," Rowen said, holding up a basket. "There's persimmons, apples, and grapes … just the purple ones."

At the precise moment when Pythia's vision began to focus, Aphrodite unleased a sharp arrow into her heart causing her to fall madly in love with Rowen.

She's all yours, Aphrodite whispered to Rowen, who of

course was unaware of her presence.

Pythia could hardly believe the passionate emotions coursing through her. She was no stranger to crushes, but she had never felt anything like this. While she had never been attracted to someone with such an enormous schnoz and bushy unibrow, she somehow found him irresistible. She was drawn to him.

"Who are you?" She could hardly speak, but the words managed to float from her lips.

"I'm Rowen," he replied, eyeing her curiously. He had never been looked at in such a way and chalked it up to brain damage.

"What a beautiful name," Pythia said, dreamily. "Rowen."

Rowen had never received such a compliment and the fact that it was coming from the object of his affection made his heart race as he broke into an overjoyed smile.

Pythia's bubble burst the moment she caught sight of Rowen's uber-gummy smile. Her expression of enchantment instantly transformed into one of repulsion. She couldn't help but let out a deep groan as if she had been kicked in the stomach by a giant.

Aphrodite sighed in frustration. *You're on your own, little buddy.*

"Are you okay?" Rowen asked.

"Please … please … just give me a moment."

"How you feeling, Sleeping Beauty?" Francesco chimed in.

"Terrible. No, fine. I'm … I'm a bit confused. What's going on? Have I been kidnapped?"

"Not kidnapped, Silly Goose," Rowen said. "Rescued."

"Rescued?"

"Yeah, rescued. From those horrible men that were poisoning you."

"You mean the priests at Delphi? How did you manage to steal me away from them?"

179

"Oh, it was easy," Francesco replied. "At the end of the day, when you were … how shall we say … comatose, we simply entered the temple, picked you up, and carried you off."

"The priests just let you carry me off? Carry the Pythia off? Without trying to stop you?"

"Yeah, it was no problem at all. The main priest was like, 'What are you doing?' And we were like, 'They told us to pick her up and bring her back, so that's what we're doing.' And that was that."

"That was that?! The priests didn't even ask who it was that told you to bring the Pythia back?!"

"Nope. Rowen raised the same issue beforehand, but I told him it would work. Just act like you're supposed to be there and they'll assume you are."

"Isn't it cute how she refers to herself in the third person?" Rowen said to Francesco.

"Not so much cute as weird. Why do you refer to yourself as 'the Pythia'?"

"Because Pythia's not my name. It's the title of the high priestess of Delphi. My name's Sera."

"It's lovely to meet you, Sera. I'm Francesco."

"Wow, I'm really taken aback by the priests' nonchalance, but I guess they'll replace me without much of a problem."

"Really?" Rowen asked. "There are more women in Delphi with your ability to channel Apollo?"

"There's not much need for that, they just need a female to sit above the crevice, breathe in the fumes, and breathe out nonsense. Then the head priest just makes up an ambiguous reply satisfactory enough to keep the petitioners, and more importantly, their bags of coins, rolling in."

"Those frauds!" Rowen exclaimed.

"The irony is, I actually have the power of prophecy, granted to me by Apollo. I suppose the rumors of such is why I became a candidate to become Pythia in the first place. But they kept me so high on that noxious gas that I never had a chance to use it. It took everything I had just to produce a few garbled sounds let alone show people the future."

"Apollo actually gave you the gift? How did that happen?"

"You won't believe me."

"That's not fair," Rowen replied, his feelings hurt. "Please give us a try."

"Okay, but I'm telling you, you won't believe me." Sera took a deep breath before beginning. "When I was 14 years old and just becoming a woman, Apollo visited me. I was caught completely off guard when bathing by myself under a small waterfall near my home.

"'Young maiden,' he said suddenly, causing me to make a mad dash for my clothes. 'You are the most beautiful creature I have ever laid eyes on.'

"While I enjoy a compliment as much as anyone else, when someone, be it a God or otherwise, appears out of nowhere and starts gushing like that it's … it's just too stalkery. It sent shivers down my spine.

"I tried to ignore him, but he wouldn't stop. 'You are the most graceful, most attractive, most vivacious being I could ever hope to have the pleasure of meeting.'

"It was a downpour of compliments, each one creepier than the last. I told him that I had to go home and begged him to leave me alone, but that only made things worse.

"'I must have you. Please, I will do anything. Even for just a touch of your hair, I will do anything. Can I have a touch? Can I just run my fingers through your lustrous curls? Anything! I'll do anything!'

"I almost vomited all over myself. He was so whiny. So grating. It got to the point where I was ready to agree to almost anything just to get him to leave.

"And that's when he offered me the gift of prophesy. A power like that changes everything. My family was just barely scraping by and this was a chance for a better life for all of us. He knew he had me.

"'Yes, I will give you the gift of prophecy. You will be able to see the future and profit from it greatly. Your family will no longer just eke by. And all that I ask in return is that you let me know you, just once. Just one roll in the hay. Oh please, allow me just one roll in the hay with you!'

"So to be able to provide for my family – and to escape that horribly unpleasant situation – I agreed. But on two conditions.

"One, that he would grant me the power immediately.

"And two, that he would wait until my 17th birthday to collect. I told him that this was because I wanted to wait until I was a full-grown adult, but in reality, this was to allow me time to make sure that I could actually go through with it with such a repulsive, persistent creep."

"So you're saying he gave you the power right then and there?" Francesco asked, dubiously.

"Yeah. And over the next three years, I was astounded by what I was able to see. While I kept the gift a secret for the most part, when my town was on the verge of being attacked, I had to let everyone know. As a result, rumors of my ability must have spread, ultimately leading to the priests bringing me to Delphi.

"But on my 17th birthday, I couldn't go through with it. Apollo was just too off-putting. I mean, he's literally a God so physically, there were no issues, but his personality was just too icky."

"So you're saying you reneged on the deal?" Francesco asked.

"Yeah. I refused to let him lay even a finger on me. And as punishment for this, he declared that while I would forever have the gift of prophecy, no one would ever believe me."

Francesco and Rowen gave each other she-doesn't-seriously-think-we're-buying-this-crap looks, and burst into laughter.

In between laughs, Francesco managed a reply. "Do you really think anyone's gonna believe that Apollo visited you in person and offered you divine powers to get it on with you?!"

"That's so insane," Rowen added, still chuckling. "No rational person is gonna go for that. Like you can really see the future. C'mon, quit jerking our chain!"

"Why wouldn't you believe me?" Sera asked, defiantly. "Just yesterday you believed that I could speak with Apollo thanks to some special fumes."

"Yeah, but that's the Oracle," Francesco countered. "The *Oracle at Delphi*. Not some peasant girl Sera who bullshits about breaking the hearts of Gods. It's ludicrous!"

The guys again burst into laughter and all Sera could do was shake her head. "I told you you wouldn't believe me."

When the guys finally settled down, they looked at her in amusement, and in a tone dripping with condescension said, "You're too cute."

"So what's the plan here anyway, guys? Where are you taking me?"

"You mean you don't know?" Francesco teased. "I thought you could see the future."

"It doesn't work like that."

"Oh, really? Then how does it work?"

"I get premonitions. They can come at any time and be about anything, but in general, they either involve a personal experience concerning the people I'm with or a major event or catastrophe affecting a whole population. And it's not like I can channel them. They just come to me."

"Well, we're taking you to Epidaurus," Rowen said with a reassuring yet tight-lipped smile.

"Epidaurus? Like where the Asclepion Sanctuary is?"

"Exactly," Rowen replied.

"Why're you taking me there?"

"To heal you, you silly goose. The Asclepion Sanctuary is renowned for the quality of its medical treatment. It's the only place in the world where you get proven results."

"Do you really think I'm in that bad of shape?"

"He thinks you have brain damage," Francesco chimed in. "He thinks all those fumes from deep within the Earth poisoned your brain and will slowly turn it into mush if you don't see a qualified medical expert."

"I didn't say 'brain damage,'" Rowen countered, turning to Sera. "I'm just worried about you. About your health. If you could have seen the state that you were in … it was horrifying. If they kept doing that to you, it would have only been a matter of time before you... Anyway, I just think it's really important that you get examined, and why not arrange an examination from the best?"

As Rowen finished his thought, Sera froze up suddenly and a glazed look settled over her eyes.

"Sera?" Rowen called, emphatically. "Are you okay?! What's going on?! Sera?!"

As Rowen put a hand on her shoulder, she snapped out of it. "I know you guys aren't gonna believe it, but I just had a vision."

Both Rowen and Francesco perked up. Rowen was eager for the chance to hear one of her prophecies while Francesco was eager to crap all over it.

"Do tell," Francesco said.

"I saw three things. All of them at the Asclepion Sanctuary. I saw a hound gorging on the intestines of a young boy. I saw a father feeding his daughter to a fanged serpent. And I saw a woman give birth to a 5-year-old."

Not that they tried very hard, but the guys were unable to hold back their laughter as they once again burst into hysterics.

"A 5-year-old?!" Rowen repeated, cracking up.

"He must have come out with a full blown goatee," Francesco said, delighted with his joke. "Or even a couple kids of his own!"

It took a while for the guys to settle down, but when they finally did, they once again looked at Sera in amusement and in unison said, "You're too cute."

***

The journey to Epidaurus was a semi-long, semi-arduous one, but it gave Sera an opportunity to get to know Rowen and Francesco.

"I would have left you for dead," Francesco informed her. "But good old Rowen here wasn't having it."

Possibly in an effort to build Rowen up in the eyes of Sera, but more possibly in an effort to embarrass him to death, Francesco decided to tell Sera their thought process when stealing her away.

"I've never seen my good friend so shaken up. As he watched the reaction you had to those fumes, *he* actually started shaking. It was like he was in worse shape than you were. He just couldn't bear to see you like that. He kept mumbling, 'We've got to save her,' 'We've got to rescue her,' 'We can't leave her like this!' Isn't that right, Rowen?"

"You were in very bad shape," Rowen said to Sera, as if defending himself for a crime.

"And what did I tell you, Rowen?"

"What do you mean?"

"About rescuing her."

"You said you had no interest whatsoever in rescuing her."

"That's right. And?"

"And that she'd just be another mouth to feed and an all-around added burden."

"That's right. And do you know how he replied to that, Sera? He said that you could have his food and that if it came to it, he would carry you on his back. Can you believe what a fool this guy is? I just don't understand what's gotten into him."

Feeling Sera's gaze, Rowen blushed.

Suddenly, Sera found Rowen's outlandishly big nose to be stately and his bushy unibrow, macho. She felt her heart melting again. "That's so sweet of you, Rowen."

And with those five simple words, a wave of euphoria crashed through him. Nothing could please Rowen more than learning that he had pleased Sera. "Really?" he said, turning toward her, grinning from ear to ear.

In a flash, Sera's heart-melting feeling was replaced by the violent urge to vomit. The moment she caught sight of that uber-gummy smile, the bubble once again burst.

"Are you okay?" Rowen asked.

"I'm sorry," Sera moaned between dry-heaves. "The seafood must have been spoiled. Please don't look at me."

"She'll be fine, my good friend," Francesco said, patting Rowen on the shoulder. "Just give her time."

"But we haven't even eaten any seafood."

***

"I will be happy to show you around," the cheerful young medical priest said, leading them into the sanctuary grounds, which were a mixture of lush greenery with expansive views of the sea and pristine ivory temples and dormitories.

Not long into their tour, Sera stopped short, gasping. "A hound gorging on the intestines of a young boy," she whispered, ominously.

Rowen and Francesco traced her line of sight.

"What's going on over there?" Francesco asked the medical priest.

"Oh that?" he replied. "No need to be alarmed. That poor boy was injured in a hunting accident. He got his stomach cut up pretty bad and he's being treated by one of our medical dogs."

186

"Treated?"

"Yes, it's licking the wound to help it heal. Saliva not only aids blood clotting, but it also contains a bacteria-fighting enzyme that helps prevent infection."

"I see," Francesco said, nodding before making eyes at Rowen and laughing at Sera. "You're too much. Hounds eating boys?! C'mon, the kid's just having his wound treated."

The guys were still chuckling when they entered the Abaton, which according to the medical priest was the holiest part of the sanctuary.

As they walked down the hall past a series of rooms, Sera once again stopped short, gasping. "A father feeding his daughter to a fanged serpent."

"What's going on in there?" Francesco asked the medical priest.

"Oh that? They're just treating that poor girl. Apparently, she suffers from anemia. The snake is used in the purification ritual prior to the ingestion of beetroot which contains high-quality iron that is easily absorbable and will increase her red blood cell count."

"I see," Francesco said, nodding.

The guys once again snickered. "A father feeding his daughter to a serpent?! That's rich. You really are priceless!"

A little further down the hall, they passed a room where a small naked boy covered in placenta and crying at the top of his lungs was being handed over by a pair of medical priests to an outstandingly overweight and extremely exhausted woman.

Sera once again came to a halt and gave the guys a you-know-I-nailed-this-prophecy look.

"What happened here?" Francesco asked the medical priest.

"Oh, how wonderful!" he replied, clapping his hands. "That poor woman had been pregnant for five years and she's just now been cured. Needless to say, the result is that adorable five-year-old boy."

Sera gave the boys a self-satisfied nod. "It's exactly as I said. I hit this one right on the nose."

Francesco raised an eyebrow while Rowen raised half a unibrow.

"Not so fast," Francesco said. "First of all, you didn't get it 100% correct…"

Sera butt in. "Yes, I did."

"I'm afraid she did," Rowen concurred.

Francesco continued without acknowledging either of their statements. "Second of all, even a blind squirrel finds a nut every once in a while. And that's what happened here. Dumb luck. A queer coincidence."

Rowen nodded. "I'm afraid I'm gonna have to agree with him. When you think about it, pretty much anyone could've taken a stab in the dark and guessed that there might be a lady here giving birth to a five-year-old."

"Lastly and most important," Francesco said. "You've just done yourself a huge disservice."

Sera's eyes popped out of her head. "Huh?!"

"It's kinda sad actually. The fact that you lucked out on this one means the odds of you ever lucking out again just got astronomically worse. It's a numbers game, darling. So I highly recommend you get out of the prophecy business lest you become a laughingstock."

"But all you guys do is laugh at me."

At this, Francesco and Rowen gave each other a look and once again burst out laughing.

"You guys are such jerks."

When they finally settled down, they replied in unison. "And you're too cute!"

Without realizing it, the group had come upon Abaton's main hall, which was noteworthy for three reasons.

First, it was packed with cots on which a number of patients were resting.

"This is where you'll be spending the night," the medical

priest informed them. "Pick any open cot you like."

Second, dotting the walls and decorating the corners were ornate sculptures of Asclepius—God of Healing, Resurrection, and Phallic Symbol-Entwined Phallic Symbols Like Serpent-Entwined Rods.

"All of our medical knowledge has come from the wisdom and compassion of Asclepius and His ever-regenerating serpent, who is often depicted coiled around His staff."

Third, there were a shitload of live snakes. Slithering on the floor, the cots, and the sculptures were throngs upon throngs of snakes. There were so many that it appeared as if the floor and walls themselves were wiggling.

"Don't worry," the medical priest said. "They're not venomous. They're part of the healing process."

The trio frowned.

"Another part of the healing process is getting a good night's sleep, so after dinner, please pick a cot and get some rest. Tomorrow morning, we will begin with a dream interpretation session, so pay close attention to what you see tonight."

***

"I was walking in the woods with my family," Sera said to the medical priest first thing the next morning. Getting to sleep had not been easy, but somehow everyone made it through the night. "And suddenly, the forest in front of us burst into flames."

"Oh my," Rowen gasped, listening in on the session.

"'Fire,' I screamed. But everyone just kept on walking. It was as if they didn't hear me. 'Fire,' I screamed again, frozen in place, watching my family continue toward the conflagration.

"'It's not fire!' one of them shouted, turning back to me. 'It's poison!'

189

"Suddenly, for some strange dream reason, my family had turned into strangers. Wild-eyed men were screaming at me. 'It's poison!' they screamed. And the fire was gone but now there was this eerie, nebulous gas hovering all around me. And the men were fanning it toward me while at the same time warning me about it. It filled my lungs and I coughed and coughed, all the while they were shouting at me. And then, when I was suffocating and about to die, I woke up."

"Very interesting," the medical priest said. "Do you have any idea what it could signify?"

"I think it's about the fumes that I had to breathe when I was working as the Oracle at Delphi."

"Oh, you were Pythia?"

"Yes. Until these gentlemen kidnapped … uhhh, rescued me."

"Well, I can say with great confidence that they did the right thing. It was only a matter of time before those fumes killed you."

"Really? You can say that for sure just based on my dream?"

"Yes. That and the fact that all Pythias up until now have died of either lung cancer or brain damage. Usually, while still relatively young."

"Well, that's wonderful then." Sera turned to Rowen and Francesco. "Thank you very much!"

"Did you experience any other intense dreams?" the medical priest asked.

"I did," Sera replied, groaning. "It was horrible. At first, I was in a lovely garden on a beautiful day enjoying a wonderful picnic with some people I've never met before but for some strange dream reason were my best friends.

"The next thing I knew, they were all snakes. I was surrounded by them. They were slithering through the grass, winding around tree branches, and even invading my picnic basket. I was so frightened I could hardly breathe.

And then suddenly, one of them was wrapped around my neck, but my arms were paralyzed so I couldn't get it off. It was squeezing the life out of me.

"I must have woke up at that point cause I can't recall anything else."

"Very interesting," the medical priest replied. "What do you think it could signify?"

"That this place is crawling with snakes who were slithering all over me when I was trying to sleep, and scaring the crap out of me and everyone else."

"I think you've once again hit the nail on the head. It's quite a common dream here, actually. You will find that once you are no longer sleeping in snake-infested quarters, the nightmare will gradually subside. Gradually."

"Your moaning woke me up," Francesco butt in. "And not only did I catch a glimpse of that snake around your neck, but I saw your knight in shining armor as well."

Now that the dream interpretation session seemed finished, Francesco took the opportunity to embarrass his good friend. "It was your stalker," he said, shifting his eyes from Sera to Rowen.

"What do you mean?" Sera asked.

"I mean there actually was a snake around your neck, and you were actually moaning and groaning about it in your sleep. Fortunately, your stalker in shining armor noticed as well and fought the beast off before you were actually harmed."

"Really?!" Sera exclaimed.

Rowen's face flushed crimson.

"I think he spent the rest of the night watching over you to make sure it didn't happen again," Francesco continued. "Just look at him; he looks as tired as a two dollar tramp."

Sera looked at Rowen and felt a warm tingling flow through her entire being. Her heart melted. Here was a man who truly cared for her. She wasn't exactly sure why, perhaps it was his nature, or fate, or magic, but here was a man who would put her before all others and would love her with all of his heart.

Suddenly, Rowen's absurdly large nose, flanked by bags beneath his eyes from the lack of sleep, inspired feelings of security, and that bushy unibrow scrunched into an expression of concern inspired feelings of tenderness. "You are such a sweetheart, Rowen."

Clearly not one to learn from experience, Rowen broke into huge smile.

Sera instantly clutched her chest as that violent urge to vomit … failed to come.

This time, rather than eliciting nausea, Sera found Rowen's uber-gummy smile to be just off-putting. Not attractive or anything even close, but not vomit-inducing.

Sera smiled warmly at Rowen giving him a I'm-finally-able-to-endure-your-hideous-angry-chimp-smile-but-keep-it-under-lock-and-key-if-you-want-me-to-stick-around look.

Catching her drift, Rowen instantly buttoned his lips, turning his uber-gummy smile into an endearing shit-eating grin.

From that moment on, the two were attached at the hip. Lovebirds who couldn't get enough of each other.

***

On the semi-long, semi-arduous journey back to Pompeii, Rowen and Sera's love blossomed. By the time they reached home, they were engaged to be wed.

Within a couple-few fortnights, the wedding was arranged and on the eve of the big day, Francesco hosted a rehearsal feast with all of Pompeii invited.

Which is to say all of Pompeii's patricians. Plebeians, slaves, and other such gutter-trash were not welcome. Except, of course, for Francesco's slaves who were necessary to prepare the feast, serve it, and clean up afterward.

NEGOTIATIONS WITH GOD

As Gilgamesh refilled Francesco's chalice with wine, Francesco signaled with his fore and middle fingers to keep it coming until the chalice was on the verge of overflowing at which time he forcefully gave the stop sign. Gilgamesh swiftly and dutifully obeyed, avoiding any spillage.

Francesco flashed a satisfied smile and turned to Rowen. "I sure hope you can pour a cup of wine like that, my friend. Because otherwise, I'm afraid I will have to beat you black and blue."

The two were seated at the head of the main table with Sera to Rowen's right and his parents next to her. Francesco's wife and family were on his left, and stationed directly behind him in case he was running low on wine was Gilgamesh.

"What're you talking about?" Rowen replied.

"But pouring wine at parties is the easy part," Francesco continued. "The rough part will be working the mines. I do hope you'll be able to hold up all day in hot, cramped conditions."

"You're not making any sense."

"Of course I am. I'm talking about what it will be like for you when you become my slave."

"Why would I become your slave?"

"Oh, don't play dumb with me. It's the agreed compensation."

"Compensation for this feast?"

"Quit being foolish." Francesco raised his left hand limply in front of Rowen's face, displaying the little crimson scar. "Compensation for this."

"Oh, you mean compensation for the assault. From what Sera said."

"No, not from what Sera said, from what Apollo said."

"Oh, right. But He didn't say that I'd be your slave."

"Yes, He did. He made it clear and simple. He said that you were to provide compensation to me by giving me your most prized possession," Francesco said, triumphantly.

193

"And?"

"*And*?! And that prized possession is your freedom. You are to give me your freedom; i.e., you become my slave."

"That's preposterous," Rowen replied, defiantly. "Apollo didn't mean some kind of metaphorical possession. He meant a physical possession. And as much as it pains me, I fully intend to give you my most prized possession: My bell cow, Juno."

"*Juno*?! Don't be ridiculous! I don't need another cow. Especially one of your boneless-ham cows. No, that won't do at all."

"Well, what else is there for my favorite possession? My gladius sword? My leather toga? My home?!"

A sinister smile emerged on Francesco's face as the optimal solution occurred to him. "Nope. None of those even come close to your favorite possession."

"Well, what is it then?"

Francesco shifted his gaze to the seat next to Rowen. "Sera."

"What?! Sera isn't my favorite possession. I mean, tomorrow she'll become my wife and I will cherish her more than anything else in this world, but she's not my possession. She's a human being."

Francesco laughed, condescendingly. "Of course she's your possession. Or will be from tomorrow, anyway."

"Now *you're* being foolish."

Francesco flicked his hand in the air and at once Gilgamesh was at his shoulder. "Gilgamesh, as of tomorrow, will Sera be Rowen's possession?"

Without hesitation, Gilgamesh weighed in, beginning with a vigorous nod of his head. "I'm sorry to say it, Mr. Rowen, but women are indeed possessions. I traded my second wife for a goat."

Rowen shook his head in disbelief as Gilgamesh took a step back to his station. "I just ... there's no way ... how on ... just no ..."

"Okay, okay," Francesco replied, conciliatorily. "I'm sure we can find a compromise."

Rowen's unibrow raised in hope.

"How about a share?" Francesco proposed. "Thursday evenings through Saturday mornings she's with you, Saturday evenings to Thursday mornings she's mine. Fair enough, yes?"

While Francesco and Rowen were debating the compensation, Sera had stood up and made her way to the platform next to the main table.

Rowen's mother slid over to the seat next to him. "It looks like your lovely bride is about to address everyone."

"We'll continue this discussion later," Francesco said.

"Ladies and gentleman," Sera began. "Thank you all so much for joining us on this joyful occasion. I'm thrilled and honored to have you all here."

There was a round of applause as everyone expressed their appreciation. Sera surveyed the room, smiling at all the guests and then at Rowen and his family.

"The kind welcome that everyone has afforded me, particularly Rowen's beautiful mother and gracious father, has been overwhelming. I could not be happier or more grateful."

Rowen's mother leaned over to him. "She's such a sweet girl."

"I am so happy that tomorrow I will be the wife of such a wonderful, thoughtful, caring man. And I wish I could continue to gush on and on, but at the same time I'm extremely sad."

A collective gasp rippled through the party.

"The reason for this is that Apollo's wrath is nigh. Tomorrow, there will be a volcanic eruption so disastrous that this city and everyone in it will be wiped out of existence. Instead of celebrating, we should be fleeing. I urge everyone here to evacuate immediately if you cherish your loved ones and want to live."

195

A hush fell over the crowd.

"Thank you," Sera finished.

As she walked back toward her seat, Francesco erupted in laughter and in flash all those in attendance were chuckling and clinking glasses.

"To doomsday!" they said playfully before downing their drinks.

Rowen's mother once again leaned into him. "She really is priceless, isn't she?"

Rowen blushed. "Yup," he replied, bursting with pride. "She's quite a catch."

***

"Are you sure I should be doing this?" Rowen asked Francesco on their way to the Classy Cat after the rehearsal feast had ended.

"Of course," Francesco replied, emphatically. "It's your last night of freedom. Your last night as a bachelor."

"So that means that this is my last visit?"

"Of course not, fool. We can go anytime. But tonight is special."

"Welcome, gentleman!" the charismatic hostess said as they entered the reception area. "How are you doing this evening?"

"Fantastic," Francesco replied. "Tomorrow, my good friend here will be making an honest man of himself, so tonight we are in the mood to rejoice."

"Then you have come to the right place."

"I don't suppose that the 'Wolf Girl' is on duty tonight, is she?"

The hostess' eyes lit up. "As luck, or perhaps destiny, would have it, she is. Clearly, the Gods favor you on the eve of such an auspicious day. Lyciska has been here all day and is in just the right mood to help mark the occasion. Right this way, gentlemen."

Francesco and Rowen could barely contain their excitement as they followed the hostess down the long corridor to the special suite at the very end.

The mural above the door depicted the she-wolf on top of one man, underneath another, and engaged with still others in the head, hands, and feet areas.

A fiery growl echoed down the hall as the gentlemen entered the room, and the noises did not let up for a solid hour. It was as if a drunken bull had been let loose in a china shop until Rowen and Francesco finally emerged utterly satisfied and utterly exhausted.

"Come again, boys," the sultry voice of Lyciska purred as they made their way back down the hall toward reception.

As they exited the establishment upon settling their bill, they caught a glimpse of a piercingly bright light flashing at the entrance to Lyciska's chamber.

***

"Empress," Apollo said, genuflecting before Lyciska and clutching her hand with his. "Your wish is my command. Just tell me what I can do for you and it shall be done!"

Lyciska jumped back, startled by the sudden appearance.

"What is it, my dove?" Apollo asked in confused concern.

Lyciska looked the luminous being up and down. She had never seen him before, but clearly, she was face to face with a God. One with an exceedingly handsome face and a chiseled body to boot.

But there was something off-putting about him. Something downright repulsive.

She wasn't sure whether it was his eyes bulging with a kind of desperate intensity, or the tone of his voice, grating and strident, or the words oozing from his mouth, but she was thoroughly disgusted. "What do you want?!"

"Do not be silly, my love. I want you. I burn for you. You are the most beautiful creature I have ever seen. What can I do to have you? Just this one night?"

"Sorry, business hours are over. Why don't you come back tomorrow and someone else can help you?"

"What do you mean?" Apollo pleaded. "I want you. Only you. I'll do anything."

"Well, I'm sorry, pal. You can't have me."

Apollo was dumbfounded. "What do you mean? What about this establishment? This is a … any paying customer can have you, no?"

"I'm not sure where you're getting your information, but I'm afraid that's not correct."

"But … but I watched you all day today. You screwed half the adult males in this city."

Lyciska gave a satisfied yet humble all-in-a-day's-work shrug of her shoulders.

Apollo shook his head in disbelief. "And not just the patricians, you were giving it up to plebeians. I even noticed a few slaves go through who you didn't even charge."

"Those who offer added value don't necessarily have to pay in coinage. You could learn a thing or two from them."

"And you just allowed those two schmucks to spit-roast you!"

"Hey! Rowen is getting married tomorrow. It was a special night!"

Apollo took a deep breath before looking up at Lyciska, his eyes moistening and lips quivering. "But I don't even care about that. I just … you're so lovely. Please. Please just let me have you just once. Just missionary, that's all!"

Lyciska kicked him in the groin. Hard. "Beat it, creep!" she said, standing over him as he writhed in pain on the floor, clutching his family jewels. "I already told you, no, and that's that."

Lyciska gathered her belongings as Apollo struggled to his feet, his teeth clenched and face now trembling with anger. "You're gonna pay for this!" he said. "You and everyone else in this filthy, wretched, utterly immoral town!"

"Don't you ever show your face around here again, you sick creep!" she said, making her way out the door.

"Tomorrow!" Apollo screamed. "You and everyone else in this sinful town will die a slow, painful, torturous death. If you don't come back here and give yourself to me right now, that is your fate."

Lyciska stopped dead in her tracks as the gravity of Apollo's words sunk in.

Very carefully, she weighed the two options.

Surrender her body to this repulsive, needling try-hard of a God or condemn the 15,000 people of Pompeii to their deaths.

With great certainty in her decision, she strode the fuck out of there.

***

At a little past noon the next day, the city of Pompeii shook violently as Mt. Vesuvius erupted.

A column of molten rock spewed high into the sky as torrents of lava began flowing down the mountain, devouring everything in the way.

The sky quickly filled with ash, blotting out the sun. Day had become night.

The people of Pompeii flew into a panic as a slow and steady shower of ash began falling on them.

The darkness grew thicker and darker than any night they had ever experienced. Night had become nightmare.

It was mass hysteria as everyone gathered their families and tried to get as far away from Mt. Vesuvius as possible.

"Come on, my love," Rowen said to Sera. "We have to run if we are to survive."

"High tail it, woman," Francesco added. "I'll not go to

my grave because you're too dainty to run!"

Sera was clearly annoyed. "Okay, so now you wanna flee?!"

"Yes, honey," Rowen said, desperately. "We must run for it if we are to have a chance."

"It's way too late. Unless you're just looking to get some exercise in before we die."

Despite Sera's absolute certainty that they were doomed, she gave in and ran alongside Rowen and Francesco, and their families and slaves.

"We should be having a goodbye feast," Sera announced as they fled. "One last meal with good drink where we can all say our peace before meeting our makers."

"Pipe down and keep moving," Francesco replied. "This is all your fault. If you really knew this was gonna happen, you should've told us in a more straightforward manner. Everyone thought you were joking, trying to add a little spice to the wedding. That kinda thing."

Sera rolled her eyes. "You've gotta be kidding me!"

"Now now, let's not go pointing fingers," Rowen replied. "If anything, it's that wicked Empress Valeria's fault. The chickens have come home to roost. All of the rumors about her sexual promiscuity must certainly be true." Rowen winked at Francesco. "And now the Gods are punishing us all."

As Sera had predicted, fleeing was futile. The shower of ash had become an unyielding downpour and the darkness grew thicker and thicker.

As they trudged through the ash, they came across a man standing in the middle of the road laughing manically. The man was practically buried with only the whites of his eyes being visible.

"I told you the end was nigh!" he shouted. "But did anyone listen?! Nay! …"

"Zeus' taint!" Francesco screamed. "It's the 'the End is Nigh' guy. I can't stand that filthy vagrant. If we're gonna go out, let's at least spend our last moments on Earth doing something enjoyable. Gilgamesh, get this party started with a kick to his back!"

And so it was that Francesco, Gilgamesh, and a handful of other male slaves met their demise. Covered in ash while mercilessly beating a crazy, or perhaps not so crazy, homeless man as Rowen looked on pondering the morality of it.

VERIXION VI

"Is the light of the world finally flicking back on again?" Delemor said sarcastically as Rowen slowly came to opposite the luminous crocodile-faced God.

As Rowen blinked his eyes groggily, out of the corner of his eye, he saw what appeared to be an elephant sitting cross-legged about an arm's length away from him.

"Well?" Delemor boomed. "Are you up yet or not?!"

"I'm up, I'm up," Rowen replied in haste as the image of a snake sinking its fangs deep into his leg flittered through his mind.

"Well? What do you think?" Delemor asked, beginning the usual post-life review. "How did you do?"

Rowen wracked his brain for memories of the life he had just lived. "I don't know. I think I tried my best to be a good person, but ... I don't know. I tried to really give thought to every ethical issue that presented itself but ... I don't know."

"Quit saying you don't know, you mouth-breather. If there's one thing everyone in Verixion knows, it's that you don't know shit."

"I'm sorry. I just ... I feel like I really tried to think about and debate the difficult moral questions of the day, but I feel like that's all I did. I don't think I was able to conclude one way or the other, and even when I did, I don't think I was able to do anything about it."

Delemor chuckled. "Yup. All talk and no action. And mildly entertaining at best. I'll tell you what I did like: I liked that questioning of the Gods bit that you and your boyfriend pulled."

The memory slowly came back to Rowen. "Oh, you mean when we were traveling to Delphi and Francesco brought up the topic of whether Gods exist or not?"

"That's the one," Delemor said, laughing. "That's a great

202

way to get yourself pulverized by lightning."

"Really?"

"Oh yeah," Delemor replied, leaning toward Rowen, a glint in his reptilian eye. "If someone up here had been in a bad mood or was just waiting for a reason to smite you, that was more than enough."

"Well, I guess we lucked out then."

"Not only you, but your friends and family, your community, your entire civilization," Delemor continued excitedly. "Questioning the existence of superior beings is tantamount to requesting a famine, flood, and genital wart pandemic all rolled into one."

"Wow, I had no idea."

Rowen heard the hiss of Delemor's serpent tail beneath the table.

"I'm sorry," he cried. "I know that you know that I know nothing. I'm just surprised that such calamity could come from questioning something. I was under the impression that questioning everything was a good idea. Really investigating everything, putting conscious thought into everything, to make sure that what one was doing was the right thing."

Delemor glared at Rowen. "It all depends. Questioning whether you should insert your penis into a glory hole is probably a good thing for you personally. But questioning whether divine beings – who can crush you like a bug without even batting an eyelash – exist is probably not a good thing for you or anyone inhabiting the same continent as you."

"Oh my God! Was that what caused the eruption? Was it that conversation between Francesco and I?"

"No, but as I say, it could have been. And frankly, your attitude is getting on my nerves."

Rowen's eyes widened in fear and confusion. He had no idea what attitude of his was irritating Delemor. "I don't mean to be rude, I'm just trying to learn if our free thinking was the cause of the catastrophe."

"Your *free thinking*?" Delemor clenched his jagged, razor-sharp teeth and leaned in close to Rowen. Rowen's heart pounded rapidly as he felt Delemor's hot breath on his cheek and neck.

"You think questioning the Gods makes you a free thinker?!" Delemor said in a low, measured tone.

"No. I'm sorry."

"I'll tell you what it makes you. It makes you an arrogant, ignorant, wretched little abomination."

As Delemor breathed the word 'abomination,' Rowen felt the familiar sting of the serpent sinking its fangs deep into his thigh. Rowen practically leapt out of his body as he screamed in pain.

When Delemor finally sat back into his throne, the serpent retracted its fangs and slithered underneath the table. "You don't ever question Us."

As the pain subsided, Rowen realized that he was more clueless on the topic now than before it had even come up. "I'm very sorry."

"That's right. That's the tune you wanna be singing. If I have to put up with any more of your disrespect, I will sentence you to the 7th Circle of Hell without even thinking twice. Do you have any idea what the 7th Circle is like?"

Rowen recalled his last visit to Verixion when Aphrodite had showed him some footage of Hell. "I think I saw a clip of the 4th Circle last time. It was horrible."

"Well the 7th Circle makes the 4th look like a kindergarten playground."

"I'm very sorry. I won't do it again."

"Damn right you won't."

"But may I ask what did cause the eruption?"

"No."

Rowen looked down, unsure of how to proceed. Suddenly, the feeling of being watched was overwhelming and he jerked his head to the side where he indeed saw an enormous elephant sitting cross-legged, quietly observing the back-and-forth.

The luminous pinkish-purple being had six arms, a radiant pearl fixed in the center of its forehead, and a few wisps of white hair on the crown of its head.

Curiously enough, perched on the elephant's pot belly was a pug.

Without warning, Delemor burst out laughing. "I'm just kidding," he said. "You may ask me the question. That's just a bit I do where when someone asks me if they can ask me something, I reject them, unilaterally. I just say 'no.' Flat out 'no.' Conversation over. Isn't that hilarious?!"

Once again unsure of how to proceed, Rowen smiled politely as Delemor's laughter trailed off.

"Go ahead already!" Delemor roared.

"I'm sorry. What was the cause of the eruption?"

"What do you think it was?"

"Well, perhaps it was the hypocrisy? I feel like the culture was egalitarian, yet in practice, bondage and persecution ran rampant. Perhaps that upset the Gods to the point that they wiped us out of existence?"

"Perhaps," Delemor replied. "Anything else you think may have been the cause?" he asked, giving Rowen a knowing glance.

Rowen's head slumped down as he let out a dejected sigh. "There was also the culture of … promiscuity."

Delemor raised an eyebrow. "Go on."

"Was it me? Was it my fault? Was it the double whammy of visiting a brothel on the eve of my wedding?"

"Let me put it this way. Double-teaming Lyciska that night certainly did not help."

Rowen let out a long sigh.

"Don't beat yourself up about it, kiddo. There may have been some other factors."

As Rowen stared blankly at the floor, he was once again struck by the feeling of being watched and his eyes darted to the elephant, who was staring back at him.

Summoning all the courage he could muster, Rowen looked up at Delemor. "Is it okay to address the 800-pound elephant in the room?"

"No." After a few beats of silence, Delemor once again cracked up. "Oh man, I got you again! This is too funny. You'll never learn, will you?! Go ahead. Go ahead. Address the 800-pound elephant. I don't know why you feel the need to guess his weight, but go on. Address your ass off."

Rowen slowly turned his head toward the elephant. "Ummm ... are you who I think you are?"

The elephant smiled graciously. "Ganesha, at your service."

"You hear that, kid?" Delemor chimed in, smirking. "You've got a God at your service. You're free to treat him like your bitch."

Ganesha glared at Delemor. "Pipe down, baby arms," he said in a surprisingly low, gruff voice. Despite being roughly 800 pounds, he had a light, ethereal aura which led Rowen to anticipate a more gentle tone and manner. "I'm just being polite. Rowen was a faithful worshiper his entire life."

"Relax, big guy," Delemor replied, placatingly. "You know I'm just playing around."

"You're quite the joker today, aren't you?"

Delemor flashed a toothy grin. "Everyday. It's kind of my thing."

As the two divinities squabbled, Rowen couldn't help but stare at Ganesha—God of Reason, Intellect, and Outlandishly Phallic Noses.

A peculiar item was perched on each of Ganesha's six palms. There was a balancing scale, a rotating cog, a tiny pagoda, a miniature model of the Washington Monument, a peacock, and a cylindrical glass jar containing a shimmering viscous liquid.

"That one's for you," Ganesha said, noticing that Rowen was staring at the curious gel.

Rowen felt a flutter in his chest. "Really?"

Ganesha's voice softened. "Yes. You have no idea how rare you are. Most people don't even know that I exist, and those that do seem to willingly forget when convenient. Your dedication was admirable."

"I can't take any credit. I was only following what was already there. In my mind and my heart."

"Well I thank you for your devotion."

"And I humbly thank you. I felt a thirst for knowledge and understanding and you never failed to quench it. I only wish I could have been a better follower, preaching your Word for the betterment of society."

As Rowen was speaking, he heard the familiar sound of Delemor's diamond teardrop landing on the table and slowly rolling off.

He glanced at Delemor whose facial expression appeared to change in the blink of an eye from touched to taunting. "Do you two need to get a room?"

Ganesha once again shot daggers at Delemor. "I'm just trying to give the kid a present, so back off, would you?!"

"I'm honored," Rowen said, taking the glass jar from Ganesha's extended arm. "It's beautiful."

As Rowen twirled it in his hand, bits and pieces mixed into the viscous liquid sparkled, reflecting the glorious light all around them.

"It's shampoo for you to wash with. It contains fragments of my ivory tusks, so you can say goodbye to that unsightly frizz."

"Thank you so much!" Rowen was 99% thrilled to receive the kind gift, but 1% disappointed. He turned to Delemor. "So does this mean I'm to bathe now? Instead of progressing to Empyrean?"

"You bet your sweet ass it does. No chance of advancing after that abortion, I can guarantee you that. You're lucky you're getting another chance at all. Frankly, you have Ganesha to thank for that."

Rowen turned back to Ganesha and bowed his head respectfully. "I don't know what to say. You are so kind. So benevolent. So wise. I hope that I can continue to learn from you, and to pray to you."

"Alright, enough already," Delemor barked. "Get out of here and wash that stink off so we can discuss what's next."

Rowen had always felt a deep respect toward Delemor, but the respect he felt for Ganesha was on another level. He jumped to his feet, scurried to the side of the door, and bowed deferentially, waiting for Ganesha to exit the chamber first.

Ganesha smiled graciously and pointed outside with his trunk. "After you."

Rowen bowed again, swiftly made his way through the door, and stepped off the path, allowing Ganesha to amble up alongside him.

"Those who will not reason, are bigots," Ganesha said, his gravelly voice grave and full of weight. "Those who cannot, are fools. And those who dare not, are slaves."

Rowen nodded as the words sunk in and his mind was filled with a great sense of satiation, as if he had absorbed the equivalent of a 5-star, 3-course meal. "Your wisdom knows no bounds."

"I'd like to take credit for that quote, so I will."

Rowen peered up at Ganesha who was smiling sheepishly.

"After all, it was I who put the thought into Lord Byron's head."

For once, Rowen hadn't the faintest idea what Ganesha was talking about. "I'm sorry?"

"Never mind that," Ganesha answered as they reached the bathing facility. "I am off now, but I don't think this is the end of our relationship. I have a feeling our connection will only grow stronger. Enjoy the shampoo."

"Oh, I hope so," Rowen replied, starry-eyed. "Thank you again for everything!"

As Rowen watched Ganesha wade into the water, he heard the pitter-patter of the pug in tow.

"Better to remain silent and be thought a fool than to speak out and remove all doubt," the pug said as he passed by.

Rowen was struck by the odd slapping sound the pug made while trotting down the stone path and looked down to find that instead of paws, it had what appeared to be human hands, and instead of a tail, it had what appeared to be a pair of antennae, like those of a praying mantis, but with a hairy stub at each end.

"Seriously," the pug called just before launching itself into the water. "Don't talk so much. People will realize!"

Rowen watched in awe as Ganesha slowly disappeared into the mist, the pug doggy-paddling after him.

***

As Rowen rubbed the special shampoo into his scalp, he felt a coolness envelop his body and a conflagration ignite in his mind. It was as if all 100 billion neurons in his brain were Fourth of July firecrackers exploding non-stop.

In a word, it was numbing. Rowen's jaw went slack and his eyes fell back into his head. His consciousness soared through space and he felt a wonderful connection with everything in the universe.

Before long, the euphoria trickled down to every cell in his body and he found himself swaying back and forth rhythmically in absolute ecstasy.

He smiled, licked his lips, and through the slits in his eyes, passively took in his surroundings.

On the second highest pine cluster of the miniature evergreen tree, he noticed a curious creature who seemed to be dancing along with him.

It had a human-like body but a fiery sun for a head, with its only facial features being cartoonish eyes and a gaping mouth. Its legs grooved to some beat, bending up and down, while its hands, each holding an ear of corn, fist pumped into the air with reckless abandon.

Rowen leaned in toward the creature, nodding his head and giving it a yeah-this-mutherfucker-knows-what's-up smile.

"Oh, was Ganesha here?" a perturbed voice called from behind him.

Rowen turned to find Aphrodite holding the jar of special shampoo.

"Yeah," Rowen gushed. "That Dude is awesome!"

"Really?!" Aphrodite replied, clearly annoyed. "I think he's kind of a creep. All he cares about is forming conclusions based on logical arguments. It's like everything he says is designed to get under my skin."

"No, no, no. He's a real chill guy. I mean, he's really smart, like mind-blowingly smart, but he's also really chill. And speaking of really chill guys, check out this little dude!"

Rowen spun on his seat and pointed to the dancing sun who proceeded to stop in its tracks. "Me so hungry!" it shouted, before jumping off of its pine cluster, landing on the ground with a thud, and sprinting along the water until it was out of sight.

Rowen turned to Aphrodite expectantly. "Neat," she replied, flatly. "Anyway, care for a drink?"

"Yes, please!"

The divine beverage tasted even more delicious than usual as it served to bring Rowen down softly from his euphoria into a peaceful state of relaxation.

After rinsing off and finishing the drink, he followed Aphrodite into the soothing, tropical water. The current swept them off to a small hill of an island where above the red sand beach was a grove of fig trees.

Rowen enjoyed the feel of the warm, pebbly sand on the soles of his feet as he clambered up the beach. Underneath the first tree that he came to was a solemn-looking figure sitting cross-legged, his head bowed slightly and eyes closed in what appeared to be deep thought.

"Who's that?" Rowen asked Aphrodite.

"That's Buddha—God of Being Unhappy Despite Having Everything, Deserting One's Wife & Child, and Rationalizing Seven Years Of Time Spent Doing Absolutely Nothing."

"Really?" Rowen replied in shock.

"No, I'm just kidding. He's just a run-of-the-mill mortal, same as you. His name is Sid."

Sid woke with a start. "Huh?"

"Sleeping on the job again, are you?" Aphrodite said.

"No, I was meditating," Sid replied, rubbing his eyes. "Pondering the mysterious nature of the universe. I'm actually pretty close to discovering an even higher level of enlightenment."

"I wish I could say I was doubtful, or even disappointed, but we're way past that."

"Hey, since you're here," Sid said, his face lighting up. "Could you do me a huge favor and let me play some Super Mario Bros.? Please? Please? Pleeeeeeeease?"

"Yeah, whatever."

In the blink of an eye, Sid scampered over to a big screen TV and Nintendo game console that was set up under an adjacent fig tree and went to work. His thumbs pounded the controller like a jackhammer as Mario stomped on Koopa Troopas and headbutt floating cubes that spat out shiny gold coins as well as the occasional mushroom which doubled Mario's size when he rammed into it.

"I'm not sure when it's gonna happen," Sid called out, "but I guarantee that someday I'm gonna beat this game on one man; no warping."

Aphrodite laughed dismissively. "Good luck with that! I'd say there's a much greater chance of you traveling back to Earth where your wife and child are and actually becoming a father."

As Aphrodite finished her rebuke, poor Mario was bitten by a Piranha Plant and the electronic tune signifying his demise blared from the TV. "*Do doot, do do doot, do do doot do doot.*"

While it played, Sid released a hand from the controller, lifted it high above his head, and flipped an enlightened, non-violent fuck you to Aphrodite.

"Rowen," Delemor's voice rang out. "Quit slacking off with that deadbeat dad and get back here so we can get down to business."

***

Delemor leaned back in his throne, crossed his legs, and pressed his fingertips together. "So what can I do for you?"

Rowen sighed. "Well, I think that living an examined life didn't have the results I had hoped for."

"How so?"

"I thought that if we questioned and debated everything, we would identify problems in our culture that needed to be rectified, and then we would rectify those problems. But that didn't seem to happen."

"And it was pretty boring, too."

Rowen ignored the slight and continued. "So this time, I'd just like to be a good person."

Delemor raised an eyebrow. "A *good* person?"

"Yeah, I don't want to be evil."

"These are pretty subjective terms you're using. Care to expand?"

"Well, I don't want to commit any crimes or anything. I don't want to do anything bad or bring any harm to my community. I just want to live my entire life as an upstanding citizen so I can be proud of myself when my life is over and we look back on it."

"That sounds pretty boring too, but we may be able to

work with this."

"I don't mind if it's boring, I just don't want to do anything bad. One thing I'm learning is that no matter how good your intentions are, or how good you are for the rest of your life, if you mess up just once, you can go down in infamy for that one incident and be crucified here in Verixion.

"For instance, no matter what you've done with the rest of your life, if in a moment of weakness and desperation, you snatch a fistful of cash from a church collection plate, you'll forever be known as a thief. Or if in a moment of poor judgment and hubris, you get behind the wheel of a car while drunk and cause an accident which kills someone, you'll forever be known as a murderer. Or if, God forbid, in a moment of unbridled hijinks and tomfoolery, you take a selfie where you pretend-molest a hot girl who's sleeping, you'll forever be known as a sexual predator."

Delemor nodded. "You're only as good as your worst sin."

"Yeah, that's exactly what I mean. All it takes is one slip-up and you're doomed. And what's worse, if you've angered or offended the Gods, they might destroy your whole community or even your whole civilization."

"Yeah, that's one of the parts I like."

"Well, I don't. And I'd really like to avoid anything even close to it. I'd just like to be a good person who contributes to my community and doesn't commit any sins."

Delemor thought it over for a split second. "Okay, done."

"Really?" As the question left Rowen's lips, there was a rustle beneath the table. "I'm sorry. I didn't mean 'really' as if I were questioning you, I just meant to say 'thank you.'"

"Go ahead."

"Thank you!"

"You're welcome. You're just lucky you caught me in a generous mood. But of course, I'll need a little sumpin'

213

sumpin' in return."

"Of course."

"For starters, you're gonna have a stick up your ass."

"A stick up my ass? Like literally a stick up there?"

"Yes, literally."

"Like all the time? How would that even work?"

Delemor let out an OMG-I'm-on-fire-today laugh. "No, I'm just kidding. The stick up your ass will be metaphorical. So you'll be able to sleep and poop and have gay sex just fine. You'll just be relatively humorless, relatively rigid, and relatively receptive to religious authority."

Rowen mulled it over. "Actually, it seems like that may help me in my cause."

"Well then you're welcome. In addition, you will have an average sex drive."

"Ummm … Okay."

"But your penis will be smaller than the average."

"Ouch. Can I at least have big muscles?"

"You wanna be strong, do ya? Okay, I can grant you that. But you're gonna be half as tall as everyone else."

"I was thinking it would be nice to be a little tall this time."

"Gettin' greedy, don't you think? Next, you're gonna be telling me that you wanna be tall, dark, and handsome?"

"That wouldn't be the worst thing in the world. But it may actually be dangerous for my cause, so I don't think I need to go that far."

"Showing some restraint, huh? Well, how's about this: I'll grant you tall and dark, but your face is gonna be covered in pock marks from the time you learn to walk."

Rowen grimaced. "That sounds pretty harsh."

"Yup."

"How about instead of pock marks, we go with bad acne that lets up when I'm an adult?"

"You're driving a hard bargain today, but since I'm in such a charitable mood, I'm gonna let you have it."

"Fantastic. Thank you so much!"

"Meng Po!" Delemor called out, suddenly. "Bring in the drink. Nice doing business with you, sucker."

The adorable old lady emerged with the bubbly concoction. "Here you go, sweetheart."

"Thank you, ma'am." Rowen said, receiving the pungent beverage.

"There's no shame in wearing adult diapers," Meng Po said lovingly as Rowen gulped down the drink.

"I'm sorry?" he replied as she helped him to his feet.

"There's no shame in it. Look," she said, pulling her dress up to her chin. "I've got a pair on right now."

Rowen was at a loss. "What the …?" he said staggering, partially in response to the tea, but more partially in response to the stained yellow diapers that Meng Po was proudly displaying.

As his vision went haywire and everything faded to black, he once again heard the high-pitched cackling of the sweet old deity.

PALENQUE, MEXICO

EARLY 7TH CENTURY AD

In the days following the sudden death of their king, the Mayan state of Palenque spiraled into a state of chaos. The pressing issue before the vaunted Council of Priests was that there was no clear heir apparent.

Fortunately, the highly-esteemed High Priest Franco was able to find a solution with the help of his spiritual confidant, Lady Sak Kuk, who lived on the outskirts of Palenque.

Reading the stars that burned so brightly above them, they were able to determine that not only was it her 12-year-old son, Pakal, who was fated to lead them, but that he would usher in a period of great prosperity.

Upon taking the throne, another thorny issue cropped up. Only Gods could be kings, and since Pakal was not a direct descendant of his divine predecessor, how could they be certain of his divinity?

Fortunately, High Priest Franco and Lady Sak Kuk were once again able to find a solution, this time with the aid of ancient mystical texts.

From atop the awe-inspiring stone pyramid that served as the base of the Temple of the Sun, young King Pakal made a public declaration informing his subjects that his mother, Lady Sak Kuk, was the human form of the Goddess of Fertility.

Since Pakal was the son of a Goddess, Pakal too must therefore be a God.

Problem solved.

Mazuma—God of the Harvest, Nature, & Spoken Word...Not To Be Confused With Spoken Word Poetry,

216

Which Is An Abomination And Those Doing It Will Get Their Just Desserts, And Not Like Ice Cream Desserts, But More Like Listening To One Of Their Own Shitty Spoken Word Performances Over And Over For Eternity—was amused.

Even Akna—Goddess of Fertility, Stone Temples, and Wheels To Be Used Only For Toys, Definitely Not For Construction Or Any Other Utilitarian Purpose—got a kick out of it.

***

On the night of his wedding, almost a decade after Pakal's coronation, Rowen paused in the doorway of his bedroom to muster up the confidence to consecrate his marriage to his vibrant, young bride.

There was a certain ambivalence that he needed to overcome before making the first big step in his adult life.

Rowen was born an only child to a pair of honest, hard-working farmers. Both of them had been born into farming families before him and while no one ever believed that his strikingly beautiful mother was working class when she was young, no one ever thought that his brawny, reticent father could be anything else.

Nonetheless, once their marriage had been arranged, they pledged themselves to one another and lived in harmony as they dutifully worked the land, growing corn and sunflower seeds.

While his mother was for the most part kind and caring, she could also be overbearing. She did her damndest to be a good, God-fearing woman, and would have nothing less for her son.

The only time she ever hit him was when she caught him masterbating, his head full of sinful, lustful thoughts. She slapped him so hard that from that day on, just the thought of masterbating gave him a migraine.

217

The night of the incident, she visited Father Franco and set up a meeting for Rowen for the very next morning. Father Franco, whom she had known closely since she was a little girl, was happy to help.

While Rowen would grow to love and respect Father Franco and cherish his time as an altar boy, he had never been so nervous and afraid as he was that morning. To him, Father Franco was the intimidating figure ferociously preaching virtue to his assembly at temple each week. Rowen had been caught sinning. Surely, his comeuppance would be hellfire and brimstone.

Rowen had never seen his mother so agitated as she was when waiting for him to finish breakfast that morning.

Desperate to stave off the meeting for as long as possible, Rowen ate in slow motion, his insides turning. But the longer it took, the more anxious and upset his mother became.

He would never forget the sound of her fingernails tapping impatiently on the table that morning. It was rhythmic and violent. Her pinky striking first followed in quick succession by her ring, middle, and index fingers.

Ta-ta-ta-tap!

Ta-ta-ta-TAP!

TA-TA-TA-TAP!

The sound grew louder and more fierce with each passing moment as she glared at her son, grinding her teeth.

"Let's go already!" she finally screamed.

Rowen gulped apprehensively and reluctantly followed his mother. It was time to take his medicine.

Fortunately for Rowen, the meeting was not nearly as bad as he had feared. It was simply decided that he would become one of Father Franco's assistants. The revered priest would take Rowen under his wing and show him the way.

While Rowen's mother would occasionally nag him about going to temple, there really was no need. Rowen actually found comfort in his religious service.

He found peace and purpose.

He felt a certain satisfaction in sacrifice, a serenity in the routine, and a harmony in the communal spirit. There was not much else he needed from life.

Above all, he loved listening to and learning from Father Franco, who in turn took a liking to young Rowen.

"When we are born," Father Franco said. "We incur a debt to the Gods for the gift of life."

Rowen nodded.

"How is it that we can pay this debt back? Not only for life at birth, but for the sun shining, for the crops growing, and for all the other blessings that sustain our life?"

"Through sacrifice," Rowen replied. For as long as he could remember, his hard-working parents had extolled the virtues of sacrifice.

"That's right. But what can we mere mortals give that has any value at all?"

Rowen tilted his head, at a loss for a suitable answer.

"The most sacred thing we have to offer is our own blood. There is nothing more precious than human blood and nothing more sacred than spilling it. That's why it hurts so much, and why it should never be done in vain, but only with holy intention. By spilling our own blood – by sacrificing it – we repay the debt incurred at creation and in turn the Gods bestow upon us sun, and rain, and crops."

Rowen savored each lesson and quickly learned to love the weekly ritual of bloodletting.

He enjoyed the sting of the prick, the sight of the crimson liquid dripping from the wound, and the sense of satisfaction born from contribution.

Further, the fact that it was performed by every member of the community, regardless of their status, gave Rowen an enormous sense of belonging and pride. Just as a lowly farmer like himself engaged in sacrifice for the long life of his beloved rulers, so too did the king and queen slice their tongues and prick their genitals for their subjects.

***

In contrast to his occasionally overbearing mother, Rowen's father was relatively laid back. He was generally quiet and kept to himself, working the field for as long as the sun was in the sky, and only reprimanding Rowen when he neglected his chores.

Even his avocation entailed great exertion. It took a lot of hard work to maintain a farm of bees from which to make a sweet honey wine.

And even when he partook in the intoxicating beverage, he made sure never to do so in excess.

"It is okay to consume wine," he often said. "But we must never be consumed by it."

"What does that mean?" Rowen once asked.

"It means that drinking honey wine is like playing with fire."

"How so?"

"Because if you drink too much, you will black out, lose your mind, and wake up next to a coyote who will chew your arm off."

Rowen never quite understood the warning but it nevertheless left a great impression. Not only did he make sure to drink only in moderation, he seemed to follow in his father's footsteps in just about every way.

***

As was customary, Rowen's parents arranged his wedding. Which is to say, his mother arranged his wedding.

Capitalizing on her good reputation, she managed to land Rowen a bride from the upper echelon of the working class, who not unlike herself was renowned for her beauty and strength.

On the morning that Rowen first met his bride-to-be, just a week before the wedding, he felt almost as nervous as the day he met with Father Franco.

But upon catching his first glimpse of Serita, and hearing her voice for the first time, he felt as if his heart had been pierced. It was like magic.

Rowen's mother too instantly adored the young beauty.

However, there was one small setback.

Serita's reputation for strength was not for the kind used to husk corn, as Rowen's mother had anticipated, but rather for expressing her own opinion.

"That guy skeezes me out," Serita said when the topic of the High Priest Franco came up.

Rowen's mother could not hide the shock from her face. "Come again?"

"He's so sketchy."

"How so?"

"He handpicked some random kid to be king so that he could pull the strings from behind the scene."

"King Pakal is not just some random kid, he's a God."

"Really?! And how is it that we know he's a God?"

Rowen's mother was again taken aback. "What do you mean?! His mother is a Goddess. He was born a God."

"Yeah, but how do we know that she's a Goddess?"

"Because King Pakal declared it."

"And why should we listen to him?"

"Because he's the king."

"But if he wasn't a God, he wouldn't be king."

"But he is a God because his mother is a Goddess."

"But she wouldn't be a Goddess if he hadn't declared so as king."

Rowen's father butt in to ease the rising tension. "I think we're all getting a little confused here. How about we just leave politics out of our first meeting, enjoy a little honey wine, and get to know young Serita's thoughts on raising corn and children."

The minor disagreement between Rowen's mother and Serita hardly registered with him as he sat in silence, spellbound by his beautiful bride-to-be, lustful thoughts of their first night running guiltily through his head.

***

Looking now into his bedroom at his enchanting newlywed wife, Rowen shook his head as if to clear away all ambivalence and fear, and crossed through the doorway to consummate his marriage.

***

With a ruthless glint in his eye, High Priest Franco lifted a jagged obsidian knife high in the air and in a flash plunged it into the chest of a crying 5-year-old whose horrific screams came to a shocking halt.

***

For the first two decades after King Pakal took the throne, Palenque had prospered as predicted. The state's coffers filled with gold and with crops, while its citizens enjoyed an unprecedented age of abundance and stability.

Likewise, Rowen and his family delighted in overflowing hauls of corn, sunflower seeds, and honey wine.

While Rowen's mother and Serita had bickered about when to have children and how to raise them, for the most part, the whole family lived in bliss as Rowen and Serita were blessed with two adorable children.

This was before a great drought set in.

There wasn't too much concern after the first poor harvest, but as the reserves dwindled due to consecutive years of little to no crops, a sense of panic settled in.

Upon heated deliberation by the Council of Priests, it

was determined that a more sacred sacrifice was necessary to end the drought.

"Something must be done to halt this devastating disaster," Father Franco said to Rowen one day.

Even though Rowen was a head-of-household with a family of his own to take care of, because of his religious devotion, he had maintained his role as one of Father Franco's altar boys.

"I wholeheartedly agree," Rowen replied.

"In order to end such a deadly drought, an equally drastic sacrifice must be made."

Rowen nodded.

Father Franco sighed as he struggled to utter his next sentence. "The time has come to offer up one of our children."

The news came as a shock to Rowen, but nonetheless he replied without hesitation. "It would be an honor. Which one would you like, the girl or the boy?"

Father Franco was surprised at Rowen's eagerness and responded reflexively. "The girl is still a virgin, right?"

"She's five."

"…"

"Yes, she's still a virgin."

Father Franco shook his head, dismissing the idea. "You are a great man."

Rowen was delighted by the praise. Up until that moment, the kindest compliment he had ever received was that he wasn't as stupid as he looked. "Thank you, High Priest," he replied, bowing his head.

"But even more than that, you are a farmer. Which is to say, you are working-class scum. Only a physically perfect child from one of the very finest families in our community would do for such an important sacrifice. I am hesitant to say it, but one of your children would only be an insult to the Gods."

Rowen nodded in agreement.

***

"I don't understand what you're so angry about," Rowen said to Serita. "I was only trying to help."

"I'm angry because you suggested that one of our children be killed."

"Not killed, sacrificed."

"Are you trying to say there's a difference?"

"What he means," Rowen's mother chimed in. "Is that for the good of mankind, he offered to make the greatest sacrifice imaginable. An extremely noble notion, if I may say so myself."

For the most part, Rowen and Serita were simpatico, hardly ever quarrelling. But every once in a while, Rowen did something that was absolutely unthinkable to Serita.

In those cases, matters were always made worse when his mother was around.

Further, whenever his mother and Serita got into it, since his mother had made the correct decision in having him become an altar boy and in choosing him the perfect mate, despite some deep-seated animosity toward her, Rowen somewhat ironically tended to side with his mother.

So whenever there was an argument, it was generally two against one.

"Even if we were fortunate enough to be in the aristocracy," Rowen's mother said. "Your children are not attractive enough to be chosen. Their heads are too round. If they had taken more after our side of the family, why I'm certain they would have perfectly oblong heads to help our cause."

"Our cause?!" Serita repeated, incredulously. "Our cause is not to have our children murdered, it's to give them an opportunity to live a long and happy life."

"How can they possibly have a happy life if they've got nothing to eat?!"

Rowen clutched Serita by the shoulders and repeated

what he had learned from Father Franco. "We are the chosen people. It is us who are destined to maintain this world. We must do everything in our power to ensure that the sun is able to make its way across the sky, and to ensure that the earth has enough nourishment to bear crops, and to ensure that our women have enough sustenance to bear children. The only way we can do this is by blood offerings. And times of great need call for great sacrifice. The only way we can survive is by offering up a human heart. The sun literally feeds off of it."

Serita was once again incredulous. "*Literally*? You're saying that that's how the sun continues to exist? By drinking human blood and eating human hearts that have been tossed into a fire on top of a stone temple on Earth?"

"Yes," Rowen's mother said, nodding. "Literally."

"Really?! The sun eats human hearts?! Despite being way up in the sky all day? And despite not having hands to scoop it, or a mouth to put it in, or a stomach to digest it?"

"You don't know that. It might just be that it's too far away for us to see its face and gullet."

"Regardless of whether the sun *literally* eats hearts or not, in the end, we're still throwing someone's heart in a fire. Offering up blood is one thing, but is it really necessary to take a life?"

Rowen made an expression of tremendous gravity. "With great power, comes great responsibility."

Serita countered with an expression of do-you-even-think-before-you-shit-words-out-of-your-mouth? "Do you seriously not see the irony, here? You are literally killing people – extinguishing their lives – so that we may create more people. It's insane."

"Is it?! Is it so insane to sacrifice one child, albeit an extremely good-looking one, for the benefit of the entire civilization?"

"Even if it weren't completely nuts, why kids?" Serita glanced at Rowen's mother. "Why can't we sacrifice one of our beloved elders?"

"Because there is nothing more sacred than one of our young. And because Rain, one of Mazuma's beloved children, is still a child. Just like we would sacrifice an adult for an adult God, we must sacrifice a child for a child God. It's what pleases them."

"And I suppose that because child God's cry, we must also make the poor sacrificial children cry?!"

"Now *you're* being ridiculous," Rowen replied, sighing and shaking his head. "It's because the tears of children bring down the tears of the sky. Rain."

"It's crazy," Serita replied, clutching her head. "It makes no sense. There's no way that life works this way."

"It's part of our culture because it works," Rowen's mother said, sharply. "Besides, do you have a better idea for how to make the sun rise, how to make rain fall from the sky, and how to make food grow?"

"..."

"I didn't think so. So keep your condescending, smart-ass comments to yourself!"

***

As throngs of Palenquins looked on from the stone steps of the Temple of the Sun and the field below, King Pakal blessed the child who would serve as a sacrifice to the Gods.

"*Oh man,*" Rowen thought to himself as he witnessed the sight from behind the altar. "*That could have been my daughter getting her forehead touched by our divine King Pakal.*"

"Please!" the gorgeous mother of the gorgeously egg-headed child cried from the upper steps of the pyramid. "Don't take our child! If a sacrifice must be done, why not take it from a family willing to give it up?"

A silence hung over the crowd.

The woman looked at Rowen. "Like one of his children.

We've all heard that he would be more than happy to make the sacrifice."

"That's part of the problem," High Priest Franco said, taking his place in front of the altar. "It ain't much of a sacrifice."

"Well, I guess he's got us there, hon," the husband of the hysterical woman said. "Maybe we should just head home and get dinner going."

"No Matter What," the mother cried, staring into her child's eyes. "Do Not Cry! If You Don't Cry, They Can't Sacrifice You!"

High Priest Franco smiled bitterly. "Okay, thank you very much, ma'am. Guards, please escort her away."

As the mother was led down the steep stairs, High Priest Franco looked the 5-year-old girl in the eye with what appeared to be great sympathy. "My child," he said. "Our time is near."

The child eyed him back defiantly, determined not to cry.

"Gentlemen," High Priest Franco called out. "Positions, please."

Rowen's heart fluttered. He'd been an altar boy since he was a teen, but this was the first time he'd be able to live up to the true sense of the title. He was thrilled.

He did his best, though, to look composed and to maintain a straight face as he jumped into action, skillfully pinning the child's left knee to the altar. He could not have been more proud to put his strength to use for something so meaningful.

Rowen looked at the other three altar boys and sensed that the same emotions were surging through them.

Franco dangled the hallowed obsidian dagger before the child's eyes. "I'm afraid that I must plunge this into your heart."

Tears welled up in the child's eyes, but despite the terrifying knife and an intimidating glare from High Priest

Franco, not a single tear dropped.

Recognizing that a sneak attack may be necessary to jar the tears, High Priest Franco suddenly pinched the young girl on the arm.

As this too provided no results, High Priest Franco looked the child in the eye and sighed a deep sigh of regret. "Since we can't get any tears from you, I guess we'll have to let you live."

A gleam of hope appeared in the child's eyes.

High Priest Franco put a hand on Rowen's shoulder. "But you won't be going back to your family. You'll be spending the rest of your life as the daughter of our faithful servant Rowen here."

Before High Priest Franco had even finished his sentence, tears streamed down the poor child's cheeks.

***

While Rowen and three other altar boys held the 5-year-old down, High Priest Franco, covered from head to toe in ceremonial black paint, plunged the sacrificial obsidian knife into the screaming child's chest.

Blood spurted everywhere.

While looking the dying child dead in the eye, High Priest Franco allowed her blood to squirt all over his face. When she ceased to move, he mopped up her blood with his flowing black locks.

As the crowd in witness held its collective breath, he split open the child's rib cage and tore out her steaming, limp heart.

"Mazuma!" High Priest Franco cried, holding the heart above his head while looking skyward. "An offering for You!"

He then dropped the heart into the ever-burning fire by the side of the altar as everyone in attendance fell to their knees and pressed their foreheads to the ground.

***

Mazuma, watching through an orb in Verixion with a cup of crimson ambrosia in hand, was pleased.

***

By the time Rowen reached his home after the ceremony, it was raining.

The harvest that year was good.

After another sacrifice the following year, the harvest was even better.

And the year after that, the Palenquen state coffers began filling up at an unprecedented pace.

"I don't understand why you're still praying to Him," Father Franco said to Rowen one day while Rowen was praying at the Temple of the Sun after finishing up his duties.

Rowen turned toward Father Franco in utter confusion.

"It was I who invoked Mazuma for rain and bountiful harvests, right?" Father Franco said.

Rowen nodded.

"Mazuma then followed through, right?"

"Right."

"In other words, I tell the Gods what to do and they do it.

"I say, 'Make it rain,' and it rains.

"I say, 'Grant us a bountiful harvest,' and we receive a bountiful harvest.

"I say, 'Give me a wife without wrinkles and saggy boobs,' and I get a wife without wrinkles and saggy boobs, right?"

Rowen nodded.

"I control the Gods," Father Franco said, looking off into space. "I'm like a God of the Gods. The Gods' God.

229

"I'm the most powerful being in the universe."

***

Mazuma, who happened to catch the conversation from Verixion, was displeased.

Without the need to see anything further, He created the storm of all storms to punish Franco, Palenque, and anyone impudent enough to live in the region from that day on. Much later, people would call it, El Niño.

***

Rowen woke with a start, his head pounding like never before.

His hands were sticky.

He looked down at them and was horrified to see smatterings of dried blood.

Instinctively, he rose from bed, exited his room and his home, and began walking toward the Temple of the Sun.

He felt an overwhelming sense of panic as the events of the prior day slowly came back.

The horrible day had begun with the funeral of his beloved wife.

He remembered standing quietly in the front row as her body was laid to rest.

He remembered insisting on being alone afterward. And hurrying to The Soggy Cactus.

He remembered ordering a row of seven shots of mezcal to shoot in between beers.

He shuttered as he recalled almost puking during the first few shots, but they had gone down much easier after that.

He remembered a girl sitting next to him when there were only a couple shots left standing.

"She must have been quite a woman," the girl had said

230

as he stared bleakly into his mug of beer.

"She was," Rowen had replied, somehow managing to hold himself together. "She was hard-working and feisty. She darn near raised our children by herself."

"Sounds like she was amazing," the girl had said.

"She was. And not one complaint from her even when our fortunes turned."

"Times have been tough."

"You don't know the half. When we got married and King Pakal was in his prime, everything came easy. But once the Gods deserted us, we barely had enough to live. Every day for the last *three* decades has been a struggle."

"I know it's been difficult," the girl had said, sympathetically.

"But at least we had each other. Times were bad, but as long as we were together, it was all good. And then all of a sudden … she's gone. Not moving. Not breathing. Dead. Gone forever."

"I'm really sorry to hear that."

He recalled being on the verge of tears. "She's the only woman I've ever known. She's my heart and soul. I don't know what I'm going to do without her."

"You really loved her, didn't you?" the girl had said, compassionately placing a hand on top of his.

"I've not once thought of anyone else but her."

"You're such a good man," she had said, smiling at him. "I wish I was lucky enough to have a husband like you."

"Oh, I'm not so good. Father Franco, that's who's good. His sacrifices were what brought our entire civilization prosperity."

"I've heard of him."

"But he grew arrogant. I tried not to grow arrogant. All I've ever tried to be is faithful and humble, and to be respectful of the Gods."

"Just from our conversation, I can tell that you were. And I can tell that you are a good soul."

231

"I have certainly tried to be. But I don't care nothing about myself. All I care about is Serita. It didn't matter whether we lived in a time of everything or a time of nothing, I was just happy to be with her. There's not one thing in this world I wouldn't sacrifice just to be with her."

Rowen recalled that around this time he began hearing a customer somewhere behind him drumming their fingers on a table. Rowen was trying to have a serious conversation with the lovely young girl, but the tapping was breaking his concentration.

Ta-ta-ta-tap.

"I don't know what I'm going to do," he had said. "How do you continue on without your reason for being?! How do you breathe when the air has been sucked out of your world?! How do you keep on living when your heart's missing?!"

"You are such a sweetheart," the girl had said, clutching his hand with both of hers. "I love you."

Rowen remembered looking up at the girl and in addition to the frustration he was feeling from the person tapping behind him – Ta-ta-ta-Tap – suddenly his head was aching.

He downed his second to last shot of mezcal.

"Take it easy, honey," the girl had said, light-heartedly.

Ta-Ta-Ta-TAP.

Rowen slugged down the remainder of his beer, slammed his last shot and, … and that's when things got blurry.

"Can we get out of here?" he had asked.

"Sure," she had said, before polishing off her own drink. "Best to get you home."

Somehow, they had determined that her home was on the way to his, so they headed there first.

He remembered parts of the walk. His drunkenness surging. Her delicate hand holding his. His headache swelling.

232

When they arrived at her home, he remembered eyeing her lips. Cherry red. Moist. Puckered up, beckoning him.

While deep down, he knew it wasn't right, he decided to surrender to the young girl's desire. He planted a kiss on her lush lips.

She had pulled away instantly. "What are you doing?!"

He was confused.

She had looked confused, too. But that look had quickly turned into disgust.

Then there was a feeling welling up inside of him. He had never felt anything so strong before. But what was it?

Was it rejection?

Was it rage?

Was it shame?

Even now he couldn't quite place it, but it had been overwhelming.

He had kissed her again.

She had slapped him. "Stop it, you filthy old man!"

That feeling inside him burned hotter and hotter. He was seething.

He had slapped her back. No. It was a closed fist. He had punched her.

"How dare you?!" he had snarled, standing over her body, now slumped on the ground. "Youuuu!!!!!!!!"

He remembered pulling her dress up and ripping off her underpants.

He remembered the feeling of being inside her. Warm. Pleasurable. But not like Serita.

He remembered growing more and more angry when he was done.

What did you make me do?!!!!!!!

He remembered picking up a large rock.

And he remembered the feeling as it crushed her skull.

It had shattered so easily.

***

The whole harrowing episode had come into focus as Rowen reached the top of the stone steps to the Temple of the Sun.

In the back of his mind, he heard Father Franco's words.

"There is nothing more sacred than spilling blood ... it must never be done in vain."

Rowen looked at the smatterings of blood on his hands and on his pants. He felt the burning sensation of rape in his crotch.

Knowing what must be done, he nodded solemnly to himself, bent his knees, and leapt off the top of the steep stone steps.

He died when his neck snapped the first time his head collided with the stone steps, but his lifeless, old body continued to tumble, the majority of his bones snapping, until he came to a bloody stop on the grass below.

VERIXION VII

Rowen awoke in Delemor's chamber with an intense feeling of déjà vu.

In a daze, he looked around the room and was struck by the light reflecting brilliantly off the gold walls, silver sculptures, and diamond chandeliers, as well as the way it illuminated the mist flowing over the floor.

He began to feel a sense of serenity as the breathtaking magnificence of the scene washed over him.

But it all came to a screeching halt when the radiant divinity across the table came into view, staring at him with his slit pupil eyes and his jagged teeth jutting randomly out of his long, leathery snout.

Delemor!

Rowen was flooded with memories of his last life.

"You fuck! You lied to me!"

Delemor hardly reacted at all, merely raising his eyebrows. "Why Rowen, whatever do you mean?"

"We had a deal," Rowen snarled. "You said that I could be a good person."

"And you were. I mean, you had one of them religious sticks up your ass, but I allowed you to be exactly how you wanted to be."

"I raped and murdered someone."

"Oh. You mean that," Delemor replied, sheepishly. "My bad. The thing is, you could *not* have been more boring so Dionysus and I decided to add a little spice to your life. A little kick to release all that pent-up emotion you let build in the name of being a good person. Honestly, I didn't realize you'd rape and kill someone. That's kinda on you."

Rowen was livid. "No way! I'm not taking responsibility for that. We made a deal that I would be a good person. In no way, shape, or form did I sign on for anything even close to that. That's on you guys. You owe me."

"Alright, alright, Jeez. Settle down, would ya? Or are you intending to rape and kill me, too?"

Rowen glared at Delemor, who smiled guiltily back at him.

"Just kidding," Delemor said, leaning back in his throne and crossing his arms over his hairy, muscular chest. "I tell you what. I'll throw you a bone in the next negotiations. That'll square us up, no?"

Rowen couldn't believe what he had just heard. "I have to go back?! I lived that last life perfectly. I was a good, honest, God-fearing man. What more could I do?"

Delemor scrunched his face into an I-hate-to-be-the-bearer-of-bad-news look. "Ummmm ... you did kinda rape and kill a lovely young woman."

"That was because of you!"

"Come on now, Rowen. Let's not start pointing fingers about who caused who to rape and ..."

Rowen couldn't stop himself from butting in. "*You* caused *me* to rape and kill that girl. It's cut and dry."

"Let's be civil about this, shall we? And let's not forget, you chose to kill yourself. Weren't you taught something about spilling blood? And something about taking your own life?"

Rowen cringed. He felt as if the ground beneath his feet had been ripped out from underneath him.

"There now," Delemor said, patronizingly. "You see how you scum."

Rowen glared at him indignantly. After all that he had done, how could Delemor call him scum? If anyone here was scum, it was Delemor.

As he scowled at the resplendent deity, he felt that Delemor looked a little different than before. Perhaps Delemor had always looked this way and he had never noticed, but one of Delemor's sapphire eyes had no life to it, as if it were made of glass. And the skin on Delemor's muscular human-like body looked blotchy and cracked.

Further, Delemor seemed to be omitting some kind of noxious vapor from every pore in his body.

"Quit staring at me, you abomination!" Delemor barked.

Rowen heard the hissing of Delemor's serpent tail.

"Avert your eyes or suffer the fangs of righteous indignation!"

Rowen immediately averted his eyes to the floor.

"That's better," Delemor said as the hissing ceased. "Now, since I'm still in a generous mood and am happy to make that last little bit of buffoonery up to you, how about you scurry down to the bathing facility and wash that repulsive stink off so we can discuss your next life."

Rowen nodded slowly, stood up quietly, and without a word made his way out of the chamber.

As he lathered his body with crimson suds, he was once again befuddled by his situation.

It seemed that the harder he tried to be good, the worse he got burned.

While he contemplated his next move, he once again came face to face with a bizarre scene.

On the highest pine cluster of the miniature evergreen tree, he saw a cartoon version of himself with long, wavy blonde hair wearing a stars-and-stripes headband and aviator sunglasses. He was slurping down a pint of dark beer while surrounded by scantily-clad Asian beauties vying for his attention with fistfuls of cash.

"Iziza preegu oma," the cartoon called to him, slurring its speech.

"Huh?" Rowen replied.

The cartoon version of himself furrowed its eyebrows in anger. "I zaid, thiz iza pree gu omen!"

"Ooooooh, a pretty good omen."

"Zwhat I zaid. A pree gu omen."

"Yeah … Right … I guess so."

As Rowen eyed the very drunk, very curious, somewhat adorable version of himself in wonder, he heard the familiar voice of Aphrodite. "Care for a drink?"

"Yes, thank you," Rowen replied somewhat meekly, spinning slowly around.

"You seem a little off," the gorgeous deity said.

"There's just no way to win," Rowen said as he accepted the rejuvenating beverage.

"That may be so."

"What should I do?"

"Do whatever it is that you wanna do."

"I'm not even sure what that is."

"You'll figure it out," Aphrodite said, encouragingly. "Just give yourself a chance."

Rowen nodded, then polished off the remainder of the divine drink.

"Come on," Aphrodite said. "Let's take a dip."

Rowen finished rinsing off and followed Aphrodite into the soothing water.

Before long, they drifted to an elliptical island with an expansive grass field enclosed by a ring of white sand.

They apparently arrived in the middle of a polo match where a team of fearsome warriors in fur hats was doing battle with a team of formidable combatants in feathered headdresses.

Watching from the sideline beach were four figures sitting atop white, red, black, and pale horses, respectively.

"Behold," Aphrodite said. "A pale horse and its rider's name is Death."

At first glance, Rowen was startled by the four figures, particularly alarmed by the one on the pale horse who was a ghoulish skeleton with glowing red eyes.

But upon closer inspection, Rowen realized that there wasn't really much to fear precisely because the rider of the pale horse was a skeleton. It had no muscle whatsoever and its bones were so weak and frail that it was struggling to keep hold of its polo stick. Further, the red glow from its eyes was so faded and sickly that rather than being fiery embers, its eyes were more like charred pieces of coal stricken with conjunctivitis.

As Rowen monitored the curious being with distaste, the captain of the fearsome warriors in fur hats came galloping by.

Rowen found this warrior to be much more impressive with his brawny physique, forbidding eyes, and burly black beard covering his tan skin. He looked virile enough to spawn half of the Earth's population.

"Can I get in the game, now?" the meek figure called Death whined.

"I told you," the intimidating captain replied, harshly. "When there's less than a minute left, if we're up by a dozen goals or more, I'll let you play."

"Aw, fiddlesticks," Death lamented, snapping his fingers in disappointment, literally snapping the distal phalange of his middle finger. "Ouuuuch!" he cried.

As Rowen looked on in surprise and disgust, he heard the familiar boom of Delemor's voice. "Rowen, you little skid mark! Who do you think you are?! You think you're better than Death?!"

"I'm sorry?" Rowen replied in confusion.

"You heard me, you little shit! You think you're better than Death, do ya?! Huh?! You ain't shit, you little shit. Get back here before I let Death have his way with you in the 7th Circle of Hell."

***

"So what can I do you for?" Delemor said, crossing his legs and leaning back in his throne.

Rowen studied Delemor for a beat, then opened. "I wanna be popular."

Delemor shuddered as if that was the only sentence in the universe that he didn't want to hear. "… Okay. I'll grant you that. But now we're even."

Rowen continued to stare at the incandescent being. He was extremely intimidated by the look in Delemor's sapphire eyes, real or fake, yet somehow he felt inspired to press on. "I want stumbling blue eyes," he demanded.

Delemor snort-laughed. "What do you mean, 'stumbling?'"

Rowen maintained his business face. "You know, like my eyes will be so blue that when people see them, they'll stumble."

"I think you misheard some song lyrics along the way and mean 'unbelievable' blue eyes, but either way, since I'm in a generous mood, I'll hook you up. But you're gonna need glasses."

"What's the point in having eyes as blue as the Mediterranean sky if you have to hide them behind glasses?' Rowen asked, defiantly.

Delemor clicked his tongue in frustration. "I said you'd be popular."

"I need you to pinky swear," Rowen replied, reaching his pinky finger across the table.

"Fine," Delemor grunted, stretching a pinky finger toward Rowen.

Rowen had to lean fully forward to reach the outstretched pinky of the short-armed deity, but once they interlocked digits, despite Delemor putting a little too much strength into the pinky-shake, Rowen was satisfied.

"I want a baby face."

"Done."

"But not like literally the face of a baby the whole time I'm alive, but like I look young even when I'm old."

Delemor once again clicked his tongue. "Fine. But you're gonna be a late bloomer."

"What do you mean?"

"You're gonna hit puberty well after your peers. I.e., you're gonna encounter some good-natured ribbing in the high school locker room. Like once the captain of the football team notices in the shower that you're yet to mature, he's gonna announce it to everyone. 'Rowen ain't got no pubes!'"

"I wanna be the captain of the football team."

"You got it, stud. But you're still gonna face that ridicule as you make your way up."

"Okay, then I want wavy gold locks."

"You wanna be a male, right?"

"…"

"Fine, I'll grant you that. But you're gonna be a pussy."

"Like a coward?"

"Yup."

"Then can I at least have nice biceps."

"It won't help you to not be a pussy, but sure, nice biceps it is."

"Since you brought up sports, I wanna be athletic."

"Sure, I can do that. So … black dude in America, right?"

"Pro basketball player?"

"Nope. At best, you'll be an average working man."

Rowen winced. "Okay, scratch the athletic talk. I'll take white male in America. But I'd like a full set of lips."

"You literally just said 'white male' and yet you want lips?! How about I smack you in the face right now and send you to the 7th Circle of Hell?!"

"Fine, no lips," Rowen conceded.

After thinking on it for a second, Rowen pressed his luck. "How about you at least grant me a lower lip?"

"Dele-damn, you're driving a hard bargain today. Fine. I'll grant you a lower lip, but you're still gonna be pasty white. Like, dead body white. And on top of that, you're gonna be one of them dudes that pisses the bed."

Rowen clicked his tongue. "Well, if I'm gonna be a bed-wetter, can I at least be a rock star?"

"Nope."

Rowen clicked his tongue again. "Fine. But I wanna be a

Jack of all trades."

"Sure. But you'll be a master of none."

"Fair enough."

"Also, by 'all,' I'm assuming you mean a few."

"A baker's dozen?"

"A few."

"Fine, but I want a big penis."

"I thought you said you didn't wanna be black."

"Shit," Rowen groaned. "Big penis for a white guy?"

"Alright."

Rowen smiled, satisfied that this was his best negotiation yet. At the same time, he wracked his brain for more attributes that might come in handy.

Delemor smiled too, seemingly happy that Rowen had finally offered a challenge. But apparently not wanting to concede too much, he took advantage of the silence to end negotiations. "Meng Po!" he cried. "Bring out that intoxicating concoction of yours."

"I uh …" Rowen mumbled.

Delemor mimicked Rowen's stumbling facial expression. "I uh … How's about you stop fuckin' this up and start grabbing life by the pigtails?!"

Rowen felt like he was punched in the gut. Was Delemor actually encouraging him?!

While Rowen tried to interpret the situation, the adorable hunchback emerged with her fizzy beverage.

"Here you go, sweetheart. Today's brew is guaranteed to put some ass on you. Even if you're fated to be a white boy."

"Thank you very much," Rowen replied, receiving the cup with both hands and doing his best not to gag while drinking it down.

Meng Po once again helped him up. "Go to Japan," she screamed in his ear. "You'll be *huuuge* there!"

Rowen conked out as Meng Po giggled.

Delemor couldn't help but chuckle as well. "Why do you

always do that?"

"Do what?" Meng Po replied.

"Say something to him while he's right on the verge of having his memory erased."

"Do I need to tell you?" Meng Po replied, raising an eyebrow.

"…"

"Just fucking with him."

TOKYO, JAPAN

EARLY 21ST CENTURY AD

A week before coming to Tokyo, Rowen Boozewell, at 33 years old, informed his parents that he was moving out of the basement of their suburban New York home to live out his dream of getting paid by Japanese girls to party and sleep with them.

Rowen's parents did their best to hide their shock and mortification behind supportive smiles.

"Son, that's great," Rowen's dad replied half-heartedly as he gave Rowen a pat on the back. "Perhaps you'll be able to pick up some of the language this time."

Rowen had spent about a year 'teaching English' in the beautiful countryside of Japan a few years earlier, but all he had to show for it was a self-published novel that was the literary equivalent of the MTV show, Jersey Shore.

"Yeah," Rowen's mom said smiling through her teeth. "Perhaps you'll meet a wonderful Japanese girl who you can settle down with."

"I'm gonna need a loan," Rowen declared.

"Sure, bud," Rowen's dad replied, encouragingly. "Whatever it takes. Unfortunately, with the way the economy's been, we don't have much cash on hand, but we can move a few things around on our credit cards to get you a plane ticket, and I'm sure we can scrounge up enough cash to get you through a few months while you look for work."

Rowen nodded. "Cool."

Rowen's mom gave his dad a furtive are-you-sure-we-want-to-help-our-son-become-a-male-hooker? glance.

As Rowen turned to head back to the basement,

Rowen's dad called to him. "Hey, son. You know, I could help you get a job."

Rowen turned back around. "What on God's green earth are you talking about, old man?"

"I mean, I know parents are supposed to allow their kids to find their own way, and I know you'd hate to be thought of as someone who got their job via nepotism, but all you have to do is say the word and I'll find you something at the accounting firm. It's not glamorous and it doesn't pay much, but once you learn the trade, you'll have a stable job for life."

Rowen's eyes lit up with sarcasm. "You mean, I can have a job that's *not* glamorous *and* pays shit?! And all I have to do is study a bunch of boring crap for years and years and then I can count beans … for life?!!!"

"…"

Rowen turned on his heels. "Get lost."

As the basement door slammed shut, Rowen's mom looked at his dad. "Who would have thought that offering unconditional love and support would yield such monumentally shitty results?"

***

"Thank you for coming," the cheerful receptionist said as Rowen entered one of Red Cross' 11 blood donation centers in Tokyo.

"Oh, nothing for me, thanks," Rowen replied, bowing his head politely while rushing toward the donator lounge. "I'm just here to meet a friend."

The receptionist watched in disbelief as Rowen strode up to the only other white guy in the facility.

Trevor was holding a styrofoam cup of hot chocolate and munching on a sugar cookie while taking in the view of Shibuya Crossing below.

"T-Rex! Long time no see!" Rowen called out to his best

245

friend from the English school they had taught at.

"Nobody calls me, T-Rex, bro. But it's good to see you."

"It's good to see you, too."

"Congratulations on Memoirs of a Douchebag. I didn't think you had it in you to write a blog post about school girl undies in vending machines, let alone an entire 'book.'"

The fact that Trevor made air quotes when saying 'book' didn't mitigate Rowen's elation at the congratulations. "Thanks, man!"

"I have a strict policy against reading word diarrhea, but I made an exception in your case and skimmed a good deal of it."

Rowen's eyes lit up again. "Thanks, brother! What'd you think?"

"I was surprised by how many of my stories you usurped … and butchered."

Rowen smiled sheepishly. "Yeah, sorry about that. For the life of me, I cannot tell stories nearly as good as you."

"You probably shouldn't write them then."

Rowen optimistically interpreted this as a playful jab. "Aw, c'mon, man. It's gonna hit big someday and I'll buy you a drink."

"I won't hold my breathe. Why did you use a pen name, anyway?"

"Oh, you know. I didn't want people to read all those crazy tales and vulgar thoughts and get the idea that I'm some kinda twisted deviant."

"You are a twisted deviant."

"I know, but I don't want other people to know."

"You and everyone else on Earth. Pussy."

"Cut me some slack, bro."

"Speaking of pussy, why'd you go with the pen name, John Box? Is that 'Box' as in 'vagina?'"

Rowen smiled with pride. "Yeah."

"So you're admitting to the world that you are a walking vagina? I guess that's kind of refreshing for a pussy."

"No, no, no. That's not what I'm going for. I've got a bunch of different names. Like a rock star name … and a porn star name … and … okay, I've got three names. Rock star, porn star, and my literary name."

"John Box is literary-sounding to you?!"

Rowen winced. "Well, it makes more sense when you hear the other ones."

Trevor eyed him, blankly. "Go ahead."

Rowen entered salesman mode. "Okay, so my rock star name is Johnny Box."

"Fuck yeah!" Trevor said, sarcastically. I totally see it now. Awwwwwwwwesome."

Rowen pushed through the sarcasm. "And my porn star name is Jack in the Box."

"That sucks."

"Come on, at least the porn star name is decent."

"Sucks."

"Well, what would you go with?"

"I don't know, I haven't put any thought into it."

"Well, how about we try to come up with something?"

Trevor thought about it for a split-second. "T-Bone."

Rowen's lips slowly curled into a smile as images of T-Bone steaks and car wrecks overlapped with Trevor's first initial and a rock-solid boner. "Oh yeah," he replied, laughing. "That's way better than mine. You mind if I use it?"

"Doesn't really make sense for you, but go ahead, bro."

As Trevor and Rowen were talking, another *gaijin* sidled up. He had slicked back hair, dark eyes, and a shady smile. "Hey, guys."

"Francesco!" Rowen exclaimed, spreading his arms to welcome him with a hug. "It's great to see you."

"Long time no see," Francesco said.

Rowen turned to Trevor. "This is the guy I was telling you about. We met at our old watering hole, the Beer Haus. He was studying at a Japanese language school while getting his medical degree."

"Nice to meet you," Francesco said to Trevor, extending a hand.

Trevor eyed him suspiciously, but shook his hand nonetheless.

"So, we ready to hit that party now?" Francesco asked.

"Yeah," Rowen replied, turning to Trevor. "Why'd you wanna meet up at a Red Cross, anyway?"

"If I'm gonna drink at your pace and still get a buzz, I need to thin out the ole blood a bit."

Rowen and Francesco laughed.

As the trio began walking toward the exit, Trevor grabbed Rowen by the elbow and in a hushed tone offered a warning. "This dude strikes me as a complete scumbag, bro. I'd watch your step with him."

***

Underneath massive billboards featuring the hottest actors and enormous jumbotrons streaming the latest J-pop music videos is the five-corner intersection famous for being the world's busiest pedestrian crossing.

After fighting their way through the dense crowd, the guys headed down a narrow side street and descended to the basement level of a surprisingly non-descript building.

They opened the door to the "international party" to find themselves in what looked to be a decaying conference room devoid of any furniture or decorations save for a makeshift bar near the entrance.

Shitty music blared over shitty speakers while a multitude of chinless dorks with bulging eyes interacted with a handful of eager-to-speak-English Japanese girls.

Unbeknownst to everyone in attendance, a spirited Dionysus cheered on an inebriated Aphrodite as she haphazardly sprayed the crowd with her mischievous arrows.

A few of them plunged deep into the hearts of the unsuspecting victims. Some were mere flesh wounds. But for the most part, they seemed to hit the sexual organs of greasy *gaijins* finally getting a taste of popularity.

While Rowen had promised himself that he wouldn't get involved with anyone romantically – because it wouldn't be fair to them while he researched the host world and engaged in debauched affairs – at the precise moment that he locked eyes with a vivacious cutie, he was struck by one of Aphrodite's fateful arrows, making him feel as if a hydrogen bomb had gone off in his chest.

Despite a severe case of the butterflies, he approached the apple of his eye and blurted out the first thing that came to mind. "What has two thumbs and wants to hump the crap outta you?"

"I'm sorry?" she replied in utter confusion.

"I mean, what has two thumbs and yellow fever?" he said, as if this line was somehow less inappropriate.

The wide-eyed girl mulled over the bizarre question. "A person with malaria?"

Rowen excitedly pointed both thumbs at his chest. "This guy!"

Surprisingly, the girl laughed. "You are a unique one, aren't you?"

"I sure am. And you have a unique taste in clothes." Rowen pointed at her sheer scarf which featured images of pink hearts mixed with a plethora of sushi dishes. "Do you have some kind of *hentai* food fetish?"

"You don't think it's cute?" she replied, feeling self-conscious and for some reason hoping for his approval.

"No, no. It's cute. It's absolutely adorable. Just like your dimples."

She smiled not only at the compliment, but also at the sincerity in Rowen's eyes when he said it. "Thank you. You seem different than most guys."

"I've been called 'special' since I was a little tyke."

"All the other guys just ask to buy me a drink. Then I'm stuck chugging it as fast as possible to get out of monotonous small talk and awkward silence."

"Well you'll get no awkward silence from me, I can guarantee you that. Even if we've run out of conversation topics, you can count on me to sing little ditties like Turning Japanese by The Vapors."

She giggled.

"I'm Rowen."

"I'm Sera."

"Well, it's very nice to meet you, Sera. Can I offer you a drink?"

"Only if you promise not to sing."

***

"Dudes, I'm in a bit of a pickle," Rowen said upon returning to Trevor and Francesco.

"Yeah, talking to a hot girl sucks," Trevor replied, sarcastically.

"I don't think I've ever been this attracted to a girl in my whole life … except maybe Jessica Alba who refuses to respond to any of my telepathic love letters, warnings, or threats."

"But she rejected you?" Francesco asked.

"No. She gave me her digits. That's the problem. I'm here to research my masterpiece, which means getting paid to party and sleep with tons of Japanese cuties, you know, for the sake of literature, and it just wouldn't be fair to that poor girl."

"That's too bad," Francesco said, leaving the two and heading for the bar.

Rowen looked at Trevor in desperation. "What am I gonna do?!"

"Well for starters, you can stop being a douchebag."

"You know that's not possible."

"Then you could quit chasing waterfalls."

"I wish I could, but I can't cause I don't even know what that means. Sure, the water itself is always moving, but the waterfall is always in the same place. How the fuck do you chase a stationary object?!"

Trevor's tone suddenly turned serious. "Well, there's at least one thing that you definitely should not do, and that's trust that Francesco scumbag."

"Why not?"

Trevor simply pointed across the room where Francesco was approaching Sera with a couple drinks.

"Oh, he's not doing anything. Just saying hello is all. Besides, I just told him that I can't have a relationship with her so technically…"

"The dude's a scumbag."

"Yeah, but so are you. You say so all the time, to anyone who'll listen."

Trevor raised his eyebrows and looked Rowen square in the eye. "I'd never nail your girl."

Rowen countered with an I'm-calling-bullshit look.

"Okay, yeah, I guess I shouldn't say 'never.' But if I did nail your girl, I'd tell you about it like 30 seconds after nuttin' on her, cause I care about you!"

***

"Are you seriously here to write a book about the host world?" Trevor asked Rowen as he handed him a freshly poured pint of Guinness and took a healthy gulp of his own.

The duo had fled the 'international party' and trudged back through Shibuya Crossing to one of Trevor's favorite drinking haunts.

"Yup," Rowen replied.

"Didn't you get that shit out of your system with that diary business?"

251

"Nope."

"That's not good man, cause I hate writers."

"What?! How can you hate writers?! They bring us nothing but reading and viewing pleasure. Except all the crappy ones out there, which granted is the vast majority."

"All writers are either liars or simpletons. Or they treat their readers as simpletons."

"How so?"

"Almost every character is so one-dimensional it's sickening. Human beings are nuanced, bro. Every single one of us experiences every single emotion and trait there is. Yet writers pigeonhole characters as either good or evil. Even the 'critically acclaimed' writers do this. Sure, they might show a character as good at first, then later reveal that that character is actually evil, but that's still portraying the character as one-dimensional. Like good people can't do bad things. Like bad people can't do good things. Like everyone can't do everything. It makes me sick."

"I guess you may have a point there."

"And they're so obvious and trite in their audience manipulations. Like, do you know one of the most common ways they get you to hate a character on screen? To show us that he's a villain?"

"..."

"They just have the cocksucker chew with his mouth open."

"I hate that."

"Me too. Everyone does. It's low hanging fruit."

"Well, you clearly have a point there. And seriously, I wholeheartedly believe that anyone who chews with their mouth open should kill themselves."

"That's the first thing you've ever said that was cool."

"Thanks, man!"

Trevor took another pull off his Guinness while stewing in his disgust for writers. Rowen did likewise while basking in the glow of what might have been the first ever compliment he had received from his mentor.

"Hey," Rowen said, abruptly. "I don't think you've told me yet. What is it that you're up to now? Still teaching English?"

Trevor's eyes darted left and right. Then, out of the corner of his mouth, he made a series of electronic beeping sounds and picked up his cell phone. "Oh shit, I gotta take this."

Rowen nodded as Trevor turned his head to the side.

"What's that you say? There's a thing that I've got to get to right now? Is it that important? … A life or death thing? … Okay, I'll just polish off the rest of my beer without any time for further conversation and get out to the thing right away."

Trevor put his phone into his pocket and downed the remainder of his Guinness. "Sorry, dude. There's a … thing."

***

Rowen blissfully made his way down a winding path in Kabukicho, a green apple chu-high, his favorite Japanese alcoholic beverage, in one hand and a menthol cigarette in the other.

The path was nothing but a walkway to those who traversed it each day, but to Rowen, it was a cultural heritage hub.

He couldn't help but marvel at the ragged, dilapidated low-rise buildings to his right, oddly known as Golden Town, which housed hundreds of tiny bars in an area roughly the size of a basketball court.

At the end of the trail was the infamous red-light district that was home to the most prestigious host clubs in Japan.

But Rowen was most grateful for the public toilet at the head of the trail. While on reconnaissance missions, no less than a quarter of his time was spent going back and forth to this lifeline. The rest of the time, he wandered the streets admiring club facades and billboards, as well as the hosts and patrons themselves who were constantly spilling out into the street in merriment.

"Do you mind if we hit a convenience store, first?" Francesco asked upon meeting up with Rowen at the end of the path.

"Sure, no problem," Rowen replied, cheerfully. "The chu-highs are on me since I appreciate you helping me with my research."

After purchasing a bagful of strong chu-highs, the duo had a seat on a concrete parking bumper at the edge of the host club area.

Smiling down upon them was Angel, the No. 1 host of Tokyo's premier host club, Club Cirrus.

On the top of a seven-story building was a billboard so massive that Rowen assumed it was visible from Osaka. Framed by neon pink lights, Angel was surrounded by a bright blue sky with streaks of heavenly clouds. His long hair was dyed blond and teased, his eyebrows were tweezed, and the fingertip resting on his lower lip managed to convey to potential customers that not only was he considerate and intelligent, but he was also a total fucking party animal.

Rowen stared at the billboard in awe. "That dude is the spitting image of Bret Michaels from his Look What the Cat Dragged In days."

Francesco cocked his head. "If Bret Michaels were Asian."

"Yeah, of course. If Bret Michaels were Asian. The important thing is, those dudes from Poison uncovered the secret to getting hot chicks: Dressing up and styling their hair exactly like the hot chicks they're trying to get."

"Not to mention the same makeup."

"Yeah. Exactly. It was genius. It completely paved the way for the host club industry in Japan 20 years later and now all these guys here get to reap the rewards without all the bother of having to learn to play instruments and perform songs and whatnot. These guys are even more genius."

"Yup. It's the American dream," Francesco replied.

Rowen couldn't tell whether he was being sarcastic or not, but after a long pull off his chu-high, he continued. "That's my dream, man."

"Yeah, you keep telling me. You wanna be a host and write a book about it."

"No," Rowen said, turning to Francesco, passion burning in his eyes. "I wanna be up there. I wanna be the No. 1 host in Tokyo. I don't just wanna be paid by a few girls to party and make earth-shattering love to them, I wanna earn the respect of my fellow hosts and work my way to the top."

"That's really cool, man," Francesco replied. "I respect that you have a dream that you're doing your best to live out."

"Thanks, bro." Rowen pulled out a couple cigarettes and a couple fresh chu-highs and handed one of each to Francesco. "And I respect that you're doing the same thing. Especially since a lot of people would say that becoming a doctor is even more commendable than becoming a host."

"Thanks man, that means a lot."

The two puffed their cigarettes and had a few swigs of booze in silence as Rowen contemplated his dream of becoming the world's greatest host and compared it to Francesco's dream of becoming a doctor, which he was already living out. To Rowen, it wasn't much of a comparison, but he still found a few aspects of being a doctor that might be enjoyable. "It must be cool to have patients come up to you after you save their life and be like, 'Thank you so much for saving my life.'"

"I don't deal with patients. I'm a research physician."

"Research? Really? I didn't know that. What are you researching?"

Francesco paused for a moment. "We're searching for a cure for cancer."

"Cancer?! Wow. Yeah, a cure would definitely be useful. Keep on keepin' on, good sir."

Francesco nodded.

"So what made you decide to do that?"

Francesco paused yet again, deciding how much information he wanted to share. Then he took a deep breath and turned to look Rowen in the eye. "My baby brother."

"I didn't know you had a little brother."

"Well, apparently, there's a lot about me you don't know. But let's just say I don't talk about him to too many people."

"Oh, I getcha," Rowen replied, winking to emphasize that he was fully picking up what Francesco was laying down. "He's the black sheep of the family, is he?"

"*Was*, Rowen," Francesco replied, biting his lip. "He's gone now. Leukemia."

"Oh shit, man. That's really sad. I'm very very sorry to hear that."

"Yeah, thanks. And he wasn't the black sheep. I was."

"Oh, c'mon. Black sheep don't become doctors, they become promoters of bum fights."

"Yeah, well this black sheep did. Not that it will ever make a difference. Fen – that's my little brother's name – he was the golden boy. Everybody loved him. He was always happy, always active, always fun to be around."

"Ew. Sounds a little too upbeat, huh?"

"No, he was great. Even though I've always been a little less happy, a little less active, and hardly ever fun to be around, I always loved him. He had a spark in his eye that would just lift you out of whatever funk you were in. Just one look from him would cheer anyone up. He was so adorable, with his big eyes and pointy ears like Fox McCloud." Francesco smiled, wistfully. "He actually wanted to be a pilot like McCloud, too."

"Sounds like a great kid."

"He was. And he was tough, too. He actually beat cancer."

"He did? … But I thought …"

"The first time." Francesco sighed as his head sank. "But the fucking cancer came back."

"Fucking remission."

"You mean recurrence, Rowen."

"Yeah, sorry. Fucking recurrence!"

"But the kid stayed strong, bro. He was a fighter. He was so positive, so upbeat, so optimistic. But it was too much." A single tear streamed down Francesco's cheek which he wiped away with a sniffle.

"That really sucks, man. I'm really sorry."

"But that's why I'm here. That's what's made me. I'm gonna destroy the disease that destroyed my baby brother."

"That's wonderful, man. I didn't know there was a cancer research place around here."

"There is. One of the best in the world."

Rowen and Francesco fell silent as they had a few more swigs of chu-high and finished off their cigarettes.

"Wait a second," Rowen exclaimed. "What the hell are you doing smoking?!"

Francesco smiled sheepishly. "Yeah, I know, I know. It's ridiculous. But it's the only thing that calms my anxiety."

The guys continued to drink and smoke, and gradually, the conversation lightened, turned back to the host world, and as Rowen finished his last chu-high, he felt sufficiently drunk to take the next step.

"Okay, I'm going for it," he said, spiritedly. "I'm fucking going to Club Cirrus and I am gonna explode their heads. They're gonna get down on their hands and knees and beg me to work for them. Without even saying a word, they're gonna recognize that I've got it. I'm talking about *It*, bro! They're gonna call me the Great White Host!"

Francesco smiled. "You go, girl!"

"C'mon."

Rowen staggered to his feet and led Francesco into the heart of the host district. A den of dreams and debauchery. Neon signs, lit-up billboard ads, and intoxicated merrymakers everywhere.

He stopped in front of the glitzy semi-circular building that housed Club Cirrus on the second floor. The building itself was constructed of shimmering, gold-plated bricks while pink neon letters floated on a cloud above the sleek marble steps leading up to Paradise.

Just before taking the first step, Rowen turned back to Francesco. "Wait here for me, bro. Time to make this dream a reality." He slowly lifted a leg above the first step. "One small step for man ... one giant leap for male prostitutes."

At the precise moment that Rowen planted his foot on the first step, a wave of hosts cascaded down the steps in an inebriated frenzy.

Rowen's jaw dropped as he gazed upon the group of charismatic hosts. With their perfectly coifed glam metal hair, custom-tailored suits, and fashionable accessories like silver necklaces with diamond-studded skull-and-cross pendants, they were full of confidence, charm, and revelry.

What's more, each host had at least one gorgeous, equally stylish woman hanging all over him.

Rowen watched in awe as the group swept by. So full of audacity, amusement, and alcohol. Clearly, they were way out of Rowen's league.

Speechless and dejected, he turned on a heel and headed back to Francesco who was watching in astonishment as Rowen's soul was crushed.

"Maybe tonight's not the night," Rowen whimpered.

"Holy shit," Francesco exclaimed. "I have never seen someone pussy out so hard in my life. You could actually see the confidence you started with deflate like a punctured tire and be replaced by pure, unadulterated pussiness. My God, bro. What the fuck?!"

Rowen just stared at the ground and sighed. It was bad enough to chicken out, but to have it thrown right back in his face by a friend made it all the more painful. He felt as if he had been stabbed in the gut.

"Hey, man," Francesco said, softening his tone. "Don't worry about it. Maybe it's just not your thing. The hosting or the writing. I mean, seriously, who's gonna pay $7 for a book written by you?!"

The knife was now twisting.

Francesco tried to backpedal. "You know what I mean, man."

Rowen's despondence quickly morphed into indignation. "Fuck you, man! It's not that easy for me, okay? But I still fuckin' believe in myself. Maybe not tonight and maybe not tomorrow, but one of these nights, I'm gonna walk up those stairs and start living out my dream. And I'm gonna write a kick-ass book about it. I don't give a shit what you say, or what society says, or what my stupid parents say, it's gonna be awesome. And you're gonna feel like an asshole for not recognizing it earlier."

"Okay, man. I'm sorry. I didn't mean it, alright?"

"And fuck your fucking $7. That's less than a fucking pint at a bar, which lasts for like 15 fuckin' minutes. I'm talking about a book, bro. That's like two months of unbridled entertainment. A Goddamn bargain, bro!"

"Okay, calm down. I honestly didn't mean it. I'd definitely buy your book for $7. Hell, I'd pay 7.50. I was only trying to help."

"Well, you're fuckin' horrible at it."

"I just meant that if you were to give up, here's a rationalization for you to do so. I was just trying to give you an out."

"Well, that out sucks."

"I got another one."

"No thanks."

"No, man, hear me out. Translation. You could use your Japanese skills to translate kick-ass Japanese books into English. That way, you can leave all the hard work up to someone else and just take a proven commodity and bring it to a wider audience."

"You're still not helping. I can write my own damn books."

"Yeah, of course you can. But maybe as a way to break into the industry…"

"Plus, my Japanese probably isn't as good as you think it is. It takes me around an hour to read a short paragraph."

Francesco was shocked yet again. "Oh shit, dude. That's horrible. How are you gonna hold a conversation at a host club if your Japanese is such garbage?!"

Rowen glared at Francesco who quickly returned to damage control mode. "I'm sorry," he said. "But it sounds like you're in a bit of a pinch. Maybe you should ask your friend Trevor for some help."

"Huh?"

"Your friend Trevor. I heard it through the *gaijin* grapevine that he's a big deal here."

"Here?"

"Yeah, here. In Kabukicho. He's like the most successful *gaijin* host ever or something."

"My Trevor?"

"Yeah, your Trevor. He didn't mention it to you?"

"Come to think of it, he still hasn't told me what he's been up to in Tokyo."

"I think he's been hosting, bro."

For some reason, Rowen was having a hard time wrapping his head around the idea. "Trevor's cool and all, and I fuckin' love the guy, but I don't think the ladies do."

"Well, like I said, I heard he's been doing pretty well."

"I guess maybe he could be like a server or something … Yeah, that sounds like a good idea. I'll ask him. Maybe

260

he knows someone who could plug me in. Or maybe he's heard some pretty cool stories that he could relay to me so that I can dress 'em up. Knead 'em into something entertaining."

"Yeah, man. That's the way to go. Just write down stories that no one else would ever put to paper. Lord knows those hosts can't read or write to save their lives."

"And if the stories he gets me aren't up to snuff, I can just come back here and crush it myself."

"That's the spirit."

***

Trevor handed Rowen a fresh pint of Guinness and had a quick pull off of his. "Okay, so what'd you wanna talk about? I don't have much time, I have a ... thing."

"A thing?" Rowen replied. "Like what *thing* exactly?"

"Business, bro. Get to the point."

"Well, I think that is the point. What exactly is it you're doing in Tokyo?"

"Working, bro. Keepin' it real."

"And by 'keepin' it real,' you mean ...?"

Trevor had another swig of beer. "Look, dude. I'm kinda busy today, so get to the point or I'll leave you to play 20 questions with your Guinness."

"I heard you're a host."

"Oh, shit."

"So it's true."

"Yeah," Trevor replied, reluctantly.

"You know that's what I'm here to do, so why didn't you tell me?"

"Because of this. Because you're a pain in the ass and telling you would only result in more pain in the assness."

"Bro, I'm like a little brother to you. How could you leave me hanging?"

"I literally just answered that question. You see how

261

you're a pain in the ass?!"

Rowen hung his head. "…"

"Alright, so what do you want?"

"Your help, bro. If you really are working at a club, how about hooking a little brother up with an in? With a gig?"

Trevor snort-laughed. "Rowen, I know you wanna write a book about the host world, but I'm afraid you ain't got what it takes."

"How dare you!"

"Rowen, your Japanese sucks, you know nothing about Japanese pop-culture, and you don't have anything interesting to talk about whatsoever."

"That hurts, bro."

"It's true though."

"It's not true."

"So your Japanese is good?"

Rowen's head slumped down once again. "No."

"You're up to date on Japanese pop references?"

"Is that song, Turning Japanese, still popular here?"

"It never was."

"Well, I at least have plenty of interesting things to talk about."

"Okay, give me one."

"What, you mean like now?" Rowen replied, caught off guard.

"Yeah, give me one interesting story."

"Okay. Well, for starters, there's that … ummm … and the …"

"You see? You got nothing."

"No, hold on. I just need a second is all." Rowen took a long pull off his beer. "Got it. What has two thumbs and wants to hump the crap outta you?"

"You see what I mean, bro? I can't recommend you at Club Cirrus."

Rowen just about jumped out of his skin. "You work at Club Cirrus?!"

"Yeah."

"Doing what? Bussing tables?"

"I'm No. 2 there."

"Are you fuckin' shitting me?! But girls despise you."

Trevor rolled his eyes. "Bro, I know what a woman wants, and I give it to her."

"You're sleeping with them?"

"Maybe. But that's not how you get 'em. You gotta understand their needs first."

"I understand a woman's needs."

Trevor raised an eyebrow as he looked down his nose at Rowen. "What has two thumbs and thinks women love cocky assholes with obnoxious come-on lines?"

As Trevor's point sunk in, Rowen grimaced before slowly raising his thumbs to his chest. "This guy?"

"Yeah, that guy. I tell you what. I'll check around for you. See if I can't find a place that's more up your alley."

Rowen's eyes lit up. "Seriously?! You'll do that for me?!"

"Don't get your hopes up, but yeah, I'll do what I can."

"Thanks, T-Bone. You're the man! And if things don't go all that well, maybe you can just share some of your experiences with me and I can put a literary touch on 'em."

Trevor again looked down his nose at Rowen. "Right. A literary touch. If I do share any stories with you, you better not fuck 'em up like you did with that fake diary you self-published."

"No need to worry, sir. It will be some National Lampoon level shit."

As Trevor rolled his eyes, his cell phone buzzed. He polished off his Guinness while reading the text message. "I may have a little sumpin' sumpin' for you after tonight. Looks like some nuru-nuru action is in the cards."

***

"Oh, look," Sera said to Rowen. "There's an open

263

bench."

"Move it or lose it!" Rowen shouted as he beelined it through the crowd, leaving Sera in the dust. "I don't care if you *are* elderly or disabled, that bench is mine!"

Since meeting at the 'international party,' Rowen and Sera had met up a few times and had further hit it off playing tennis, watching sumo wrestling, and dining together.

Today, they met up at a picturesque park across town from Kabukicho for a plum blossom festival. In the corner of the park, on a gently sloping grass hill, was a grove of plum trees. Weaving in and out of the porcelain white, taffy pink, and ruby red blossoms were stone paths dotted with benches.

After visiting the adjacent food stall area and loading up on skewers of grilled chicken, balls of fried octopus, and cups of piping hot *sake*, Rowen and Sera had meandered along the paths in search of a place to sit. The weather was unseasonably warm and sunny so the park was packed.

Rowen popped a ball of fried octopus into his mouth and beamed at Sera as she strolled over. Everything about her made him googly eyed. Her walk, her style, her carefree attitude.

But Rowen remained steadfast in his pledge. No matter how much it killed him, he refused to make a move. While he had made zero progress in finding work as a host, he still had hope. And once he was a host, he could potentially be researching the role for months or even years. Which almost certainly meant sleeping with a girl or two for the sake of his craft.

He couldn't do that to Sera. He felt too strongly for her to do anything that might hurt her. So for her own good, he had to keep things platonic.

Plus, he had no idea whether she was into him romantically.

She had responded favorably to all of his text messages

and invites, and every moment they spent together was pure joy, but either he hadn't picked up on a signal that she was interested in taking their relationship to the next level, or she hadn't sent one.

Regardless, even if she threw herself at him, he told himself that he had to remain strong. For her.

"I found us a good one," Rowen said, as Sera took a seat next to him.

"You're such a clever boy," she replied, flashing her adorable smile.

Rowen held the basket of octopus out toward her. "Care for one of my balls?"

Sera shook her head. "And all that cleverness is flushed down the toilet. But yes, gimme some of them balls."

They savored the delicious snacks and the warm burn of *sake* as they took in the view. Gorgeous plum blossoms in full bloom everywhere. A beautiful blue sky above. Throngs of families and friends doing the same.

"My God, what a lovely day," Rowen said.

"Um-hum," Sera agreed.

"The only thing that could make it even better would be a little karaoke. Care for a tune, my lady?"

Sera glanced at Rowen, then looked at the mobs of people within earshot. "How about a haiku instead?"

Rowen jumped in his seat. "Oh! Even better. An opportunity to display my improv skills and sensitivity. I just need to consult with my Muse."

Rowen slowly slurped down half a glass of *sake* as he mulled it over.

"A palette of pink;
Mirthful laugher, flowing drink;
Hot octopus balls."

Rowen grinned as Sera afforded him a few mock claps. "You really nailed the Japanese spirit. We're the perfect mix of wistful poetry and toilet bowl humor."

"How 'bout you?" Rowen challenged. "Can you do any better?"

Sera thought on it a moment and chuckled to herself.

> "Plum trees in full bloom;
> Sitting with a booze vacuum;
> He's huge in Japan."

Rowen's face lit up like it was Christmas morning. "Holy shit, you fucking nailed it!"

***

"This is the place," Rowen said to Francesco, beaming in front a glitzy sign displaying the club's name, The Lily Pad.

"A *kyaba-kura*?" Francesco replied, puzzled.

"Yeah, let's head in."

The guys walked down a flight of stairs to the entrance of the *kyaba-kura*, which is like a host club with the roles reversed. Girls dressed up in evening gowns entertaining guys via conversation, drink making, and cigarette lighting.

Rowen was awed by the floor-to-ceiling mirrors on every wall and pillar, the abundance of mirror balls twirling above, and the velvet curtains partitioning the establishment into private booths.

They were seated at a plush, four-seater sofa encircling a sleek glass table stocked with booze, an ice bucket, and glasses.

"So what are we doing here, man?" Francesco asked as they waited for a couple hostesses to arrive.

"What are you talking about?" Rowen replied, as if that was the dumbest question he had ever heard. "Research."

"These places can be pretty expensive. Especially for the inebriated."

266

Rowen waved him off. "Don't worry about it. I got you covered."

"How do you figure this is research, anyway?"

"What do you mean? Not only do I get a firsthand look at how customer service is done in the industry, but maybe I can pick up a few conversational tricks. Plus," Rowen added, leering at the pair of girls coming down the aisle to their table. "Check out the eye candy."

"Okay, you're the boss."

Rowen continued to ogle the hostess who approached his side of the sofa. She was wearing a silky beige dress with thin straps revealing a delicate collarbone and elegant shoulders.

"I'm Yuma," she said, holding out a name card.

"What has two thumbs and wants to hump the crap outta you?" Rowen blurted out, before he had even received the card.

Yuma tilted her head in confusion.

"This guy!"

Yuma broke into gratuitously loud laughter.

Pleased with himself, Rowen accepted the card and put it face up on the table as is customary. "I'm Rowen."

"It's a pleasure to meet you. May I have a seat?"

"Of course."

"May I pour you a drink?"

"Of course."

"Is *shochu* okay?" she asked, referring to the Japanese liquor that's typically 50 proof and is comparable to vodka.

"Of course. On the rocks, please."

"Where are you from?" she asked as she gracefully picked up a glass, used a pair of steel tongs to carefully drop three ice cubes in, and skillfully filled the glass from the carafe of *shochu*.

"America," Rowen replied with pride.

Yuma's eyes lit up. "Oh, America. How wonderful!"

"Yeah, I'm pretty proud of being born there. It was

267

quite an accomplishment."

"Yes, it's very cool. You must be very rich."

Rowen shrugged his shoulders and smiled as if embarrassed by his wealth.

"What are you doing in Japan?"

"I'm writing a book," he replied, smugly. He then took a large gulp of *shochu* which burned his throat and chest, transforming his look of self-satisfaction into an unsightly wince.

Yuma was nonetheless very impressed. "Oh my God! An author," she said, placing a hand on his forearm. "You must have so much money."

Rowen blushed. "Well, I do have a smash-hit novel under my belt and I'm here to write another one."

"About Japan?"

"Yeah. Well, about host clubs anyway."

"Host clubs? Why?"

"Because I find them fascinating."

"Fascinating? Why?"

"Well, you might not believe it, but we don't have host clubs in America."

"Really?!"

"Yeah, for some reason it's not part of our culture for girls to pay guys to party with them."

"Yeah, I guess I can see that. But they're very popular here. A lot of Japanese girls are boy crazy."

"Just as God intended. Anyhoo, I plan on getting a job at a host club and then writing a book based on the experience."

"Oh, there are lots of those in Japan."

"Is that right?"

"Yup. Tons."

"Well, there aren't any in the States. I don't think there are, anyway."

"Well, I think you're gonna do great."

"Really?"

"Oh, yeah. With those blue eyes of yours, you'll do very well."

Rowen blushed. "Oh, these old things?"

"I bet you've always been very popular with the ladies."

"Well, now that you mention it, I guess I have. Especially since the Lasik surgery. I mean, I had conjunctivitis for like two years after the surgery, like I was cursed or something, but after that, the old Mediterranean blues have been reeling 'em in like fish in a bucket."

"I'll bet. And they'll be even more useful here since they're so rare."

"Well, thank you very much."

"You know what?" Yuma said, as she pulled out a pen and flipped her name card over. "Here's my cell phone number. Text me any time and maybe I can help. I bet your book will be even bigger than the first."

As Yuma finished writing her number down, she noticed Francesco's hostess rising from the sofa.

"It's time to switch," Yuma said to Rowen.

"I'm so glad I met you."

"Me too," she replied, dollar signs in her eyes.

***

"It's good to see you again," Rowen said to Francesco before taking a big fat bite out of his Double Quarter Pounder.

"Yeah, it's been awhile," Francesco replied. "Since the *kyaba-kura*, right? How'd the rest of the night go after I left?"

"It was great," Rowen said, thinking back fondly on the parade of hostesses that visited his table, a steady stream even after Francesco had gone home.

"That first girl, Yuma, she seemed pretty into you. Any extracurricular activity there?"

Rowen smiled sheepishly. "I kinda drilled her that

269

night."

Francesco leaned forward. "No kidding?! Did you have to pay?"

"What?! No."

"Really?!" Francesco replied, raising both eyebrows with great interest.

Rowen found Francesco's reaction to be a little odd. "Yeah, really. Why? Is something up or something?"

"No," Francesco replied with a shake of the head. "So, what's been going on since then?"

Rowen let out a long sigh. "Well, it's been really good and really bad. She texts me every day and has invited me out a bunch of times. She's really a great girl, but you know, I can't get into a serious relationship because of the host research, so I'm kind of in a pickle."

"Right. The 'research.' What's up with that, anyway? Other than staring at billboards and paying money to chase tail at *kyaba-kuras*, are you ever gonna start?"

"I've been researching, bro. Everything I do here is research."

"Like what?"

"Like being here in Tokyo …"

"And?"

"…and listening to Trevor's host club stories. That certainly hasn't hurt."

"You should really consider translation."

"I told you, my Japanese reading ability isn't that good."

"Yeah, but still."

***

"Holy crap, that was incredible," Francesco said, taking a post-coital puff off his cigarette while staring at the ceiling in complete satisfaction.

"Yeah, baby. You were wonderful," Yuma replied, snatching the cigarette out of his hand, taking a drag, and slowly blowing a cloud of smoke in his face.

"You're so bad."

"I know."

"It makes you even sexier."

"I know."

"We should do this again."

"Sure. But before you go, I've got another little present for you." Yuma put out the cigarette, rolled Francesco onto his stomach, and began giving him a full body massage.

"Holy crap, this feels so good!"

***

"Cheers!" Rowen said as he tapped his Cheesy Gordita Crunch into Francesco's Double Chalupa before taking a big-ass bite out of it.

Francesco dug in as well.

"So, how's the cancer research going?" Rowen asked.

"Not bad."

"You got a cure yet?"

Francesco smiled wryly. "Not yet."

"Well, you keep at it," Rowen said in that quintessential high-pitched tone that the speaker thinks is encouraging but everyone else finds unbearably patronizing.

"How 'bout you? How's the host research coming?"

"Fantastic. I have a feeling that I'm on the cusp of hearing of a potential lead from Trevor soon."

"Wonderful," Francesco said, flatly. "How about on the lady front. Any updates there?"

"Yes and no. I've still been hanging out with Yuma and not only is she a great girl, she also really enjoys giving massages and head."

"She's great at both."

"What?!" Rowen exclaimed, unable to believe his ears.

"I mean, I bet she's good at both. You could just tell, you know? From how she looked at the *kyaba-kura* and how

271

she moved. She had a very sensual vibe."

"Right, yeah. So anyhoo, she's a really great girl, but she's a little possessive. I get the sense that she's trying to dig her claws into me. I don't really know why, maybe she thinks I'm gonna take care of her or something, but whenever I pull back a little, things go downhill fast."

"Really?! Like what?"

"Well, again, she's usually really great, but every once in a while we fight and one of them was really bad. She was saying some shit that she must have pulled from a shitty after-school TV special. Like, 'Just push me down the stairs and it's over. But you don't have the guts!' Shit like that."

"Oh dude, sounds like you got a Fatal Attraction psycho on your hands."

"But she really is a sweet girl. And to be honest, the fight was probably my fault. For making her feel insecure. She said 'I love you' to me when I was drunk and then she asked how I felt. I started rambling awkwardly about how I can't seem to fall for anyone since high school and how my heart always grows cold; some weird shit like that."

"What about that chick from the international party? You were completely gaga over her."

"Yeah, I guess I've fallen pretty hard for her, but I don't think bringing that up would have helped the situation. The bottom line is that I should probably break it off with Yuma, but I don't wanna break her heart. Because, for the most part, she really is a good girl."

"You gotta do what you gotta do, man," Francesco said, finishing his Double Chalupa.

Rowen polished off the last bite of his Cheesy Gordita Crunch. "You still hungry?"

"Yeah."

"Me too. But it's insane how much more expensive Taco Bell is here than in the U.S. The prices have gotta be like double."

"Yeah, it's total crap."

***

Utterly satisfied and completely worn out, Francesco blew a huge cloud of smoke at the ceiling. "Damn, that was some seriously acrobatic stuff you threw in there today."

"I've been doing yoga," Yuma replied.

"I don't know what those yogis had in mind when they came up with that shit, but God bless 'em."

Francesco and Yuma puffed their cigarettes as their heart rates slowly returned to normal.

"You won't believe what Rowen said to me the other day," Yuma said, turning toward Francesco and propping herself up on an elbow.

"What's that?"

"He fuckin' said that he hasn't been able to fall in love with someone since his high school sweetheart."

"That's weird. What prompted that?"

"Oh, you know. I told him I loved him and blah blah blah."

"Well, that's a weird reply. Kinda cold, actually."

"Right?! What a dick."

"Was he drunk?"

"Very."

"Well, there you have it. When he's drunk, he thinks he's the king of the world, God's gift to women. So he was probably thinking that he needed some kind of excuse to keep things light between you two."

Yuma's face scrunched up in frustration. "Light, huh? I was kinda hoping he'd start coming around."

"You never know, he may. Just try to give him a little space."

"What does he say about me?"

"About you? Nothing. He keeps his relationship stuff close to his chest. Kinda strange, actually. You'd think he'd talk about it a little more."

***

"Kanpai," Francesco said, holding his draft of Heineken up in the air.

"To Emi," Rowen said, referring to their Hooters server. "What she lacks for in cleavage, she more than makes up for in charisma."

After taking a gulp of beer and devouring a blue cheese-drenched boneless chicken wing, Rowen once again held up his mug. "Kanpai!"

"Didn't we just do this?" Francesco replied.

"This one's to me."

"I'll pass."

"But you're looking at the newest addition to the host club ranks."

"No shit?"

"No shit." Rowen lifted his beer a notch higher. "To the Great White Host!"

"Well, to the Great White Host it is then," Francesco said, clinking Rowen's glass and shaking his head in amazed disbelief. "How'd you make it happen?"

"I don't really remember.`"

"What?!"

"I was really drunk. It's all a big blur, but I basically just showed up at the GPS point that Trevor input into my cell phone and the rest is history."

"Oh, nice. So Trevor hooked you up?"

"Yeah. He got me an in at a club that he said was right up my alley."

"How was the club?"

"Great! I mean, I can't recall it all that well, but I remember being welcomed with open arms. No applications, no interviews, no Japanese language tests, no nothing."

"Sounds perfect for you."

"Yeah, they totally recognized my ability at first glance."

"And the novelty of being a white guy with blue eyes probably didn't hurt."

"No. Not at all. I think that may have actually helped me somewhat. Anyhoo, it was awesome. I remember chugging Budweiser tall boys with everyone, and then people spraying suds all over the place like we had just won the World Series. And I was totally the center of attention."

"Do you mean you were the center of attention like everyone was fascinated by you? Or like everyone was dumping their beer on you."

"You know, I don't really recall all that well. Maybe a little of both. But they were definitely asking me all kinds of questions. And everyone was definitely awesome. The dudes were really cool and fun to drink with and the chicks were totally hot and wild."

"I don't wanna rain on your parade – well, actually, I don't really mind raining on your parade – but you mentioned you were really drunk. Are you sure you can trust your memory that all the chicks were 'totally hot and wild?'"

"Good point. I have to admit that my history in judging the attractiveness of women when completely shit-housed is sketchy at best."

"But you definitely got a job?"

"Yeah, definitely. I 100% recall them saying that I could come back at any time. Mostly because I woke up drenched in one of the bathroom stalls and the guy that was still on duty at the crack of dawn said so."

"That's great, man. Sounds like you should get some good stories for your book."

"I sure hope so. But it definitely means I've got to break it off with Yuma because it's not fair to her."

"Why not?"

"Dude, we've been through this. Because of all the sleeping with girls I'll have to do."

"Yeah, but she's a hostess. She's in the exact same boat as you."

"No, dude. It's different."

"How so?"

"Because she loves me."

"Really?!"

"Yeah, she says it to me all the time. And she's always hugging all over me and saying that she misses me when we're not together. I mean, it's gonna kill her. It's gonna absolutely devastate her, but I've got to do it because it's the right thing to do."

"Sounds rough, bro. But if she's that madly in love with you, you should probably literally kill her because that would be easier on her. It would be the nice thing to do."

As Francesco's possibly sarcastic words sunk in, Rowen's facial expression went from Do-you-have-to-serve-prison-time-for-mercy-a-killing? to What's-the-least-painful-way-to-kill-someone-from-the-killer's-perspective? to Dude-get-the-fuck-outta-here-No-way-am-I-killing-someone. "Dude, get the fuck outta here! You know I can't kill her."

"Alright, then you should marry her. No doubt. I mean, it sounds like you got a good thing going. She's a hostess so she'll understand whatever you gotta do as a host, plus she loves giving massages and head. You put a ring on that, Rowen! You put a ring on that shit as fast as you can!"

***

"Well, this is a far cry from Club Cirrus," Rowen said out loud to himself as he looked at the sign above the decaying entrance of the host club to which he now belonged.

While not sober, Rowen was not nearly as drunk for his second visit, so his brain was able to absorb the surroundings.

276

Once again arriving safely thanks to the GPS point that Trevor had plugged into his cell phone, he was surprised to see that the vast majority of the light bulbs on the marquee were either burnt out, missing, or shattered. Nonetheless, he was able to make out the club's name.

Club Cirrhosis

Rowen questioned the owner's judgment in giving the establishment such a pessimistic name, but at the same time, he respected its honesty.

I just hope it has a better ring to it in Japanese and that no one has a clue what it means, he thought to himself.

Despite it being prime business hours, Rowen was surprised to see damp cardboard boxes strewn about the entrance and crumpled beer cans here and there.

When he walked through the entrance, he heard music coming from the main room but there was no one at reception. He slowly took in the sights and smells.

A beaded curtain to the main room looking more like the dreads of a homeless Rastafarian.

Used condoms entwined in the mop, which looked to be the only cleaning implement in the club.

Stale beer.

Vomit.

"Lake Titicaca!"

Rowen turned his head to find a host spreading the curtain dreads open and beaming at him. "Hi. I'm Rowen. Do you remember me?"

"Yeah! You're Lake Titicaca!"

"I'm sorry?"

"You said you wanted to be called Lake or Rake or something, so we went with the host name, Lake Titicaca."

Rowen smiled uncomfortably. "Wonderful."

"How are you? Are you sick? You don't seem very energetic."

"No, I'm fine. I uhhh …"

The host held out a Budweiser tall boy. "You need some more fuel?"

Rowen's mouth instinctively made a sucking motion like a newborn lusting after his mother's nipple. "Yes, please!"

The host flung the can at Rowen, who managed to catch the lukewarm beer at his feet.

"C'mon in," the host said, waving. "Time for work."

Rowen followed him into the main room where the smell emitting from the bathrooms mixed with the toxic cloud of stale beer and vomit.

Faux leather sofas with rips and tears were scattered about at random. A single spotlight flickered in the corner, illuminating the cloud of cigarette smoke hovering over the room. Budweiser cans, empty, full, and everywhere in between, were strewn all over the place.

A handful of hosts sat lethargically on sofas while a few misfit customers did likewise.

"So, what was your name again?" Rowen asked the host who had just greeted him.

"Maxima."

"Okay, cool. Nice to meet you, Maxima … again."

Maxima smiled and offered Rowen a seat against the wall, then sat down next to him. Across from them was a thickset girl with pigtails, thick eyebrows, and a prominent snaggletooth.

"This is my customer, Ms. Welltree."

Rowen smiled politely. "I'm Lake Titicaca. It's nice to meet you."

Ms. Welltree perked up a bit. "Nice to meet you, too."

"May we have a couple drinks?" Maxima asked.

"Sure," Ms. Welltree replied, leaning down to pluck a couple tallboys out of her 12-pack.

Rowen popped open the one from earlier but made sure to accept the 'fresh' one from her and set it on the table in front of him. "Boy, this place is very unique."

278

"In Japan," Maxima explained. "Unique is not really a good thing."

"Roger that," Rowen replied with a nod. "So I'm not seeing any *shochu* on the table. Do you guys not serve that here?"

"That's right. Just Budweiser."

"I see. And I suppose you save the good stuff for the champagne calls?"

"Nope, not here. Everything is just Budweiser."

"But I thought that was how the customers paid. They pay a fuckton of money for a cheap bottle of champagne and the host and club split the profit."

"Nope, not here. Everything is Bud. Our customers bring cases of tallboy cans and we drink it."

"Oh no," Rowen said, burying his head into his hands.

"What's wrong?"

Rowen looked at Maxima in great distress. "I came here to live out my dream. The dream of being paid to party and sleep with Japanese girls."

"I'll pay you to sleep with me," Ms. Welltree chimed in.

"Really?" Rowen replied, encouraged by the development. "At like a love hotel?"

Ms. Welltree shook her head. "Nah, a bathroom stall here would work just fine."

Rowen felt a little disappointed but was not wholeheartedly against the idea. "Are you gonna pay me in Budweiser tallboys?"

"I can switch it up if you like. Leave a little bill on the toilet seat if the job is done well."

Rowen mulled it over a second. "Okay, deal. Just lemme polish off a few beers first."

"Sure, take your time."

As the alcohol worked its magic, Rowen felt a surge of adrenaline and euphoria. "This is gonna be the most epic book ever!"

279

***

"There's something different about you," Trevor said to Rowen as he handed him a fresh pint of Guinness at one of his favorite drinking haunts in Shibuya.

Rowen did indeed have an air about him that was much different than when he had arrived in Tokyo reeking of desperation. Today, he was full of pomp, pretension, and arrogance. Mainly due to the fact that he was wearing a scarf and sunglasses indoors.

"I'm just about done with the book," Rowen boasted.

"That's great, bro. Kanpai!"

They clinked glasses and Rowen slugged down about half of his beer. "Coupling your experience with mine, I've had more than enough material to write a literary masterpiece."

Trevor attempted to hold back a derisive laugh, but failed.

"What are you laughing about, man? I'm serious."

"I'm sorry," Trevor replied, doing his best to put on a straight face. "I'm sure it'll be great if you're able to just write down what I've told you word for word."

A smug smile materialized on Rowen's face. "If I'm gonna win a Pulitzer, I've got to add some panache."

"Okay, whatever."

"But seriously, man. Thanks. I couldn't have done it without you. You helped me live out the dream of being a successful host and the dream of writing a smash-hit novel about it. Now there's just one thing left."

Rowen paused, waiting for Trevor to bite. Trevor, on the other hand, had a sip of beer while scrolling through text messages on his cell phone.

"The dream of all dreams," Rowen continued. "The most honorable and virtuous dream known to man."

Rowen paused again.

Trevor looked up in irritation. "Okay, already. What is

it?!"

"It's Sera, man. She's my *dream*. The destiny I was put on Earth to fulfill is being with her so we can both have true happiness."

"Sounds great," Trevor replied, glancing back down at his cell phone.

"But I'm afraid of hurting Yuma by breaking up with her. I mean, she'll probably throw herself in front of a train, but I've gotta do it."

"Who's Yuma again?"

Rowen clicked his tongue. "That hostess I've been seeing. It'll tear me up inside to shatter her poor heart, but it has to be done. To get to Heaven, you gotta go through Hell."

"I'm not sure you do."

"Yes, you do. And my only chance at true happiness is to confess my feelings to Sera with a clear conscience. To put myself out there. Then the rest is up to Fate."

"Sera probably has a say in it, too."

"Alright, that's enough, smart guy," Rowen said, raising his Guinness high in the air. "Let's just drink to the pursuit of eternal love!"

***

After finishing his book and emailing it to the preeminent boutique publisher that is 6.8 Books, the fateful day had arrived.

Be brave, big man, Rowen said to himself. *It's all part of the plan.*

Rowen took a deep breath. "There's been an illness in the family and I'm afraid I have to return to America. I'm very sorry, but I guess this means we can't be together anymore. You are a great person and I hope you find happiness with someone else …

… and send!"

Rowen let out a sigh of relief as he turned his cell phone off and stuffed it in his pocket. *Man, that took a lot of guts, but they don't call you Kid Courage for nothin'! Great job, Row Dog!!!*

With his head held high, he popped open a strong peach chu-high and headed to the park bench where he and Sera had shared that special plum blossom day. It seemed like ages ago.

Fortunately, he arrived first and had some time to polish off a couple more chu-highs.

When Sera finally appeared, they engaged in small talk about the weather, how they'd been since the last time they hung out, and the burgeoning threat of North Korea.

Partly feeling that the moment of destiny had arrived, but more partly because he really had to go pee, Rowen bit his lower lip while turning to look Sera in the eye and plunged into the matter at hand.

"Sera," he said, trembling like a leaf. "I love you."

He had done it. He had put himself out there.

Sera's face lit up with a smile like the sunrise. "I'm so happy," she said.

"Oh, thank God!" Rowen gasped.

"But I wish you had told me a month ago."

Rowen's heart fell through his chest. "Huh?"

"I'm really sorry, but I'm engaged to be married. My parents set up a formal marriage interview, and while the guy's not as exciting as you – he's just a boring Japanese accountant – he's very serious about marriage and family. So when he asked, I said okay. And I can't break that promise to him now."

"Ohhhhhhh farts."

VERIXION VIII

Rowen awoke in Delemor's chamber confused and angry. "What the fuck?!" he blurted out instinctively while trying to process exactly what had just happened.

"Is the Great White Abomination finally back with us?" Delemor boomed.

"What the fuck?!" Rowen repeated. He was filled with frustration, but still unsure of the source.

"Shall I show you what the fuck?!" Delemor asked, condescendingly.

"Yes, please," Rowen replied.

"Scooch over here," Delemor instructed, standing next to an orb as big as a refrigerator.

Rowen eyed him in wonder. As his memories of past lives on Earth and experiences in Verixion came rushing back, it occurred to him that this may be the first time he was seeing Delemor standing up.

The contrast of his fearsome crocodile head with his hairy human chest was at once awe-inspiring and absurd.

Nonetheless, he followed Delemor's directive and positioned himself in front of the orb.

Delemor tapped the top of the mysterious device and in a flash Rowen had an unobstructed bird's eye view of his previous self staggering into a shady Tokyo bar. "Do you remember walking into this delightful hole in the wall?"

Rowen nodded as he felt a strange, out-of-body sensation.

"It was your third Roppongi bar of the night." Delemor pressed his forefinger on the top of the orb and Rowen's earthly endeavor began moving in fast-forward until Delemor let up. "How about this text message from Yuma, replying to the one you sent earlier in the day?"

The screen split and one of the angles rotated and zoomed in such a way that Rowen could see both the message on his cell phone on one side and his reaction to it on the other.

The message read, "Don't care. I've been fucking Francesco since I met you."

Rowen watched as he slammed his phone down in rage, "Fucking Francesco!" He then ordered three shots of vodka and knocked them back as soon as they arrived. "God Damn Fucking Francesco!!!"

"How about this little shithole in the wall, your fifth of the night?" Delemor asked after fast-forwarding through a few more drinks and a whole lot of staggering through seedy back alley streets.

Rowen was swaying on a barstool while talking to a bar top gaming machine that he had mistaken for a friendly ear.

"Nope," Rowen replied, oddly defiant.

"And how about when you got into a heated argument with the video poker dealer for being 'a whore of biblical proportion?'"

"Nope."

Delemor chuckled as he fast-forwarded to the good parts. "How about when you were thrown out of the bar onto the fire escape?"

"Nope." Rowen's defiance was slowly transforming into shame while Delemor's amusement level continued to escalate.

"And how about when you slumped down comatose on said fire escape?"

"..."

"And peed yourself?"

"..."

"And vomited on yourself?"

"..."

"And choked on your own vomit."

"..."

"And died."

Rowen remained silent as he contemplated the last day

of his life. It had started out with such hope and ended in such disgrace.

Without warning, the ground shook and he turned to see one of Delemor's diamond teardrops wobbling on the floor next to him.

"What the hell is that?" Rowen cried.

Delemor laughed. "You know what really killed me? You finally put yourself out there – which I must admit I respect – and you confessed your love to Sera, and what did it get you? … Nothing."

Rowen hung his head. "And I suppose you're gonna give me shit for breaking up with Yuma via text message, right?"

Delemor was visibly perplexed. "Huh? Why would I give you shit for that?"

"You know, cause you're supposed to do that type of thing in person."

"Why the hell would you do that?"

"Beats me. To be a real man or something."

"Well, it would certainly make it more interesting for Me, but I can't fathom how it would help either of you."

"I don't know. I think someone once told me that it was the right thing to do so that you could be there to comfort them."

"Who would want to be comforted by the person who just rejected them? By the person who just said, 'You know what, I think I've had about as much of you in my life as I can stand. Please leave.'"

"I don't know, I'm just saying." For once, Rowen was more than happy to hear Delemor's point of view and he suddenly felt a lot less depressed. Almost upbeat.

But the feeling faded fast when he recalled his book. "Oh man, worst of all, I put all that research and blood and sweat into American Gigolo in Japan and I suppose that turned to shit, too?"

"I don't know. What do you think?" Delemor replied,

mysteriously.

As the gears inside Rowen's head slowly turned, a ray of hope sprouted. "Well … maybe after I died … somehow someone put it out there. And maybe it actually did turn into a smash hit like that Swedish dude who wrote those three books about girls with tattoos. Or maybe it was more like A Confederacy of Dunces by that guy John Tool who all of a sudden was recognized as a genius?!"

"How's about we have a look-see?" Delemor said, placing his index finger on top of the orb. The screen instantly lapsed into black and white fuzz, but somehow Delemor was able to decipher the outcome.

"Your death did in fact make the news."

Rowen held his breath in anticipation.

"Apparently, the *gaijin* community picked up the story because of the problem of foreigners being drugged in Roppongi."

"Maybe I was drugged, too."

"You weren't drugged."

"Okay, back to the book please."

"While the investigation revealed that you were just a pathetic loser who choked to death on his own vomit, the fact that you were in the news, and dead, led to a financial decision by 6.8 Books to publish MaleWhore posthumously."

"Oh, I like that!"

"And let's see how it did … Sales peaked on the three-month anniversary of your death, which was the launch date. They went all the way up to 17. And three weeks later, you got your best review."

"Well, the sales aren't spectacular, but let's hear that review."

"Okay, here it goes. Rating: 3 stars. Review: 'I don't have the same sense of humor that Rowen Boozewell did, but I can see how he might have found some of his stuff funny. Particularly since he seemed to drink a lot of alcohol.'"

"…"

"Not too shabby."

"…"

"For an abomination, anyway."

Rowen was clearly upset and whether that was the cause of Delemor's vexation or not, Delemor had had enough. "Go clean that stink off so we can discuss your next life."

Rowen slogged down to the bathing facility, but as soon as he applied a handful of Ganesha's shampoo to his head, he felt rejuvenated. And not only was he eager to negotiate his next life, but he was also looking forward to defending his last life, despite his disgraceful demise.

To his surprise, before he had even finished washing his hair, Delemor's voice rang out. "C'mon girly boy, this isn't a day spa! Hurry up and get in here so we get down to business. I've got a … thing!"

Rowen quickly rinsed the soap out of his hair, but before hustling up to Delemor's chamber, he gave his face and body a once over as well.

"So what can I do for you today?" Delemor asked once Rowen was sitting on his heals respectfully across from the reptilian God.

"Well, I don't care too much when I meet the love of my life, provided I'm not too gray, but I would like to marry her and enjoy at least a portion of adulthood together."

Delemor grinned. "I get it. You wanna have sex with the love of your life. Fair enough. Anything else?"

"I'd like to have a job that I like."

"Do you understand what the word 'job' means?"

"Okay, fine. I'd like a job that's not too laborious or too boring or too low paying and that's something that most people would find interesting."

"Okay, I can do that. But you're gonna cheat on your wife."

287

"No deal. That doesn't even make sense. I'm discussing work and all of sudden you're making me an immoral villain."

"Morality is relative, Rowen. Do you need a little reminder to help jog your memory?"

Rowen heard the familiar rattle beneath the table. "Okay, fine. But we're talking about work now, so if you need to offset something, can it at least be work-related?"

Delemor made a mock sobby face. "Can't we do both?!"

Rowen held firm.

"Fine. I'll grant your work terms, but you're gonna be sexually harassed by your boss."

"I'm a dude?"

"Yup?"

"And my boss is a dude?"

"Nope."

"I'm not sure which is better, but okay. I'll learn to live with that."

"How about physically?"

"I'd like to be tall."

"Nope, you're gonna be short your whole life, picked on for it your whole life, and you're gonna have freckles."

"Fine. But I want eyes as green as the Emerald Isle."

"Okay, I'm in a generous mood. But you're gonna be a hunchback."

"No deal. If I'm a hunchback, there's a good chance that my kids will be hunchbacks or at least grow up with some kinda complex because their dad is a hunchback."

"We haven't mentioned kids yet."

"I want kids. And I want them to be proud of their father."

"Alright, I can grant you that. But they're gonna die in a fiery car wreck as soon as they're old enough to drive."

"No deal. My kids get happy lives."

"Are you trying to upset me?!"

Rowen once again heard the intimidating rattle of

Delemor's tail. The sound was much closer this time.

"No," he replied, determinedly. "I'm not trying to upset you. But I won't have my kids dying early because of some clause in our negotiations. If nothing else, their happiness should be in their hands. In their negotiations."

"I can't imagine any loser who would negotiate to be the son or daughter of an epic abomination such as yourself."

"Let's leave it up to them then."

"Fine. But you're starting to get on my nerves."

"I apologize for that, but there's one more thing I need."

"What's that?"

"Forgiveness."

"…"

"Forgiveness on two levels. First, forgiveness from the Gods. There are a lot of factors down there and I'm sure I'll make my fair share of mistakes. As long as I don't commit any egregious crimes, I'm gonna need your forgiveness. I'd like your word that I won't be punished for wearing a pink shirt or praising the wrong God or even wearing a god-damned fedora hat. Because I need to keep going; to keep grinding; to find my way. More importantly, I need your word that my friends and family won't suffer for some kind of error in my judgment or decision-making. I can't have Sera or anyone else suffer because I've unwittingly offended a God that I probably don't even know exists. You've got to promise me your forgiveness."

Delemor glared silently at Rowen who continued with conviction.

"Second, I need forgiveness from Sera. I haven't lived a single life where I haven't screwed her over and I feel horrible about it. I need her like nothing else in this universe. I feel it in every fiber of my being. Every cell in my body longs to be with her. So when I inevitably fuck up, I'm gonna need that forgiveness. I'm gonna need her to look past my mistakes and my faults and to know that what

I'm trying to do is to earn her love. I just want her to love me and to be proud of me. And I want her to know that I will do whatever the fuck it takes to make her happy. No matter what you Gods may bring."

Delemor paused a moment before pounding the table with his fist. "You've really become a huge pain in the ass," he roared. "Meng Po! Get in here!"

The sweet old lady hobbled into the room.

"Give him the wine."

"Huh?" Rowen exclaimed, utterly perplexed. "What about the tea?"

"Just shut up and drink the fuckin' wine."

With an amiable smile, Meng Po handed him an antique chalice filled with dark red wine. "The blood of crocs, the drink of prelation."

"Enjoy your life in Empyrean," Delemor said, benevolently, as Rowen downed the harsh libation.

POSTLUDE

"By the way," Delemor said as Rowen took his last gulp. "I would have passed you after Russia."

"Huh?"

"After Russia. If you hadn't turned back into a pumpkin when you got back here – check that, if you hadn't turned back into a pussy when you got back here – you'd have been in Empyrean long ago."

Before Rowen could even recall what had happened after his life in Russia, he exploded into a thousand million shards of light.

CLIFFHANGER

Rowen is probably gonna fuck up in Empyrean and hijinks are probably gonna ensue.

DOMO ARIGATO

Thanks for reading, you God among mortals. After enjoying the following Reader's Guide, please leave a glowing 5-star review on Amazon (it doesn't even need to be honest).

Also, please check out the blurbs at the end for more R.W. Sowrider-related books and info.

READER'S GUIDE

Questions for Discussion:

- Discuss the ways that Rowen grew as a human being from his first life on Earth to his last. If you didn't notice any growth, read the book again. If you still don't notice any growth, go fuck yourself.

- Discuss the broader question of morality as it resonates throughout the book. During that absorbing, soul-enriching discussion, touch on the topic of Gods making sex with humans.

- During Rowen's life in Pompeii, he and Francesco gush on and on about the positive aspects of a public, open-air toilet and how those not using them are not living their lives right. Discuss possible motives behind this conversation. Is it simply a typical conversation that people would have had at the time? Is it mocking historians who sneer at modernity and romanticize antiquity? Or do you think it's that Mr. Sowrider just really really wants to shit outside while talking to strangers.

- The first miracle that Rowen performs as Rasputin is curing a woman who is on the verge of death. Right before Rowen cures her, the woman snaps back to life and looks at Rowen in horror. Discuss the motivation behind this reaction. How do you think you would react if you suddenly came to and a rapey-looking stranger was in your bed with one hand on your forehead and the other on one of your boobs?

- How is the character of Sera a metaphor for Mr. Sowrider's uncompromising love and respect for autocracies?

- Discuss what delicious foods you would eat if you visited Tokyo. Would you opt for a Cheesy Gordita Crunch from Taco Bell? Or a flame-broiled Whopper with Cheese from Burger King?

- Under various pen names, John Box has written *Memoirs of a Douchebag, American Gigolo in Japan, The Stars' Fault,* and now *Negotiations with God.* In which of these works do you think Box' style, use of language, and artistic innovations are most finely tuned, most expertly crafted, most powerfully worked out? Basically, what I'm trying to get at it is which book do you think is gonna get him the most pussy?

- What is Rowen's most admirable quality? More importantly, what is Mr. Sowrider's most admirable quality? Keep in mind that Mr. Sowrider created Rowen's most admirable quality so that in turn makes him like 10 times as admirable. Maybe even more. When the gravity of his admirability hits you, yield to your emotions and pleasure yourself without regard to your surroundings. For that is true communion with God.

- While in Verixion, Rowen glimpses the 4th Circle of Hell and views a young Bill Walton being tortured there for eternity. What makes Bill Walton so repugnant to the Gods? Does Mr. Sowrider appear to share the Gods' antagonism? Does he ever seem to criticize it? How about you? Do you share the

Gods' antagonism for that cumstain, Bill Walton? Discuss all the ways he makes you so sick to your stomach that all you want to do is kick the bellies of pregnant ladies who might possibly be carrying a red head who grows up to be so tall that he thinks he's a God.

- After Rowen beds Aphrodite in the form of Svetlana, there is an extraordinary scene, at once rhapsodic, repulsive, and hilarious, in which Rowen pushes her out of bed with his foot. What is the social impact of this deed? Have you ever pushed someone out of bed post-coitusly with your foot? Did that person get all hysterical on you and call the cops, too? Fuckin' A, right?!

- What is the meaning behind Mr. Sowrider's Cliffhanger at the end of the book? Is this simply to inform the reader that the protagonist may encounter problems in Empyrean? Or is there a deeper, more insidious intention? Like Mr. Sowrider plans on shitting out a sequel that he wants you to buy so he has money for Big Macs, Exotic Berry wine coolers, and strippers?

Multiple Choice Test:

- Why does the miniature tiger in Verixion bite Rowen's testicle?
  A) Reproductive organs are great sources of protein.
  B) Foreshadowing.
  C) Nature vs. nurture.
  D) Tasty balls.

- Three times in this book, Mr. Sowrider chooses to use the word "snicker" over the equally acceptable "snigger." Why?
  A) "Snicker" sounds funnier than "snigger."
  B) Symbolism.
  C) Not only is Mr. Sowrider terrified of using the n-word himself, he's scared to death of being responsible for one of his readers inadvertently saying it. Even just in their head.
  D) In deference to the popular candy bar Snickers which contains the light of the world: Nougat.

- What are multiple choice tests most effective at measuring?
  A) One's knowledge.
  B) One's ability to barely recall the answer to a question when it's one of four possible answers.
  C) Metaphor.
  D) One's ability to do well on multiple choice quizzes.

Suggested Essay Topics:

- How did Mr. Sowrider imply that Rowen is a Christ-like figure? And don't just write, "He didn't." Even if you don't think he did, fuck, even if it's the case that he in fact did not, I want at least a page on this shit. And no double-spacing or super wide margins either. Honestly, stop embarrassing your parents and write a fucking thoughtful-sounding essay, no matter how much bullshit is entailed. How the fuck do you think they got into college?!

- Overall, does *Negotiations with God* put forth a positive and uplifting view of humanity, or one of darkness and pessimism? Those are your only two options. It is absolutely forbidden to go with, "A little bit of Column A and a little bit of Column B."

- Write an essay on how unsightly booger moles are and how easily they can be removed by even a moderately talented doctor. I guess that's really all that needs to be said so you can just go ahead and copy-paste that first sentence.

- Research the life of Mr. Sowrider, then write an essay explaining how his experiences as a hunter, bare-knuckle boxer, bootlegger, lover, cardiologist, oil tycoon, chess grandmaster, and cold-blooded assassin influenced him when he wrote *Negotiations with God*.

- List some of the literary techniques used by Mr. Sowrider to evoke and maintain the novel's awesomeness. Email them to Mr. Sowrider so that he understands what the fuck Ms. Michiko Kakutani is talking about when she interviews him for the New York Times.

- Write an informative essay that identifies and analyzes Rowen's internal and external conflicts. Keep in mind that we are not fucking around here. It seriously needs to be informative. We're all tired of your bullshit essays with absolutely no illumination whatsoever. Honestly, your essays are the literary equivalent of empty calories. Get your shit together already!

BECOME A LITERARY GROUPIE

Sign up for John Box' mailing list to receive blog posts, comedic novel reviews, info on new stories, and all the dick-pics you can handle. Simply email 6.8books68@gmail.com with the subject heading "Mailing List" or "Dick-Pics Please," or visit John Box' website at www.pearlsbeforeswine68.com.

SPREAD THE GOOD WORD

Please help spread the Good Word by recommending this book to your friends and by visiting the *Negotiations with God* Facebook page to give it a Like and to make use of some one-click shareables.
https://www.facebook.com/NegotiationsWithGod

OTHER BOOKS BY JOHN BOX/ROWEN BOOZEWELL/R.W. SOWRIDER

Memoirs of a Douchebag chronicles the adventures of John Box as he spends a year traveling around Japan, teaching English, and discovering himself—nightly. Through this life-changing journey, John comes to such revelations as: he hates working, and kids, and food that makes liver spots drenched in mucous seem like crème brulee. A hilarious parody of journeys of self-discovery. (Ages 18 & over)

***American Gigolo in Japan* –** A red-blooded American horndog. A sleazy Japanese host club. His new job comes with fantastic benefits. If you like low-brow humor and fun-loving, narcissistic characters, then you'll love this raunchy comedy. (Ages 18 & over)

The Stars' Fault – A 10-year old fighting cancer. A space captain fighting for his species. Can they conquer their enemies before it's too late? This 66-page novella is a heartbreaking and humorous fantasy tale. If you like space battles, gut-wrenching emotion, and surprising twists, then you'll love this madcap story.

ABOUT R.W. SOWRIDER

R.W. Sowrider is the pen of Rowen Boozewell which is the pen name of John Box which is probably the pen name of some dude with a horrible-sounding name and/or without the gonads to associate his actual name with all the filth that he writes. Or she. It totally could be a she. Probably not an 'it' though.